SUCKER PUNCH

SUCKER
PUNCH

MARC STRANGE

A Castle Street Mystery

THE DUNDURN GROUP
TORONTO

Editor: Michael Carroll
Proofreader: Jennifer Gallant
Designer: Erin Mallory
Printer: Webcom

Library and Archives Canada Cataloguing in Publication

Strange, Marc
    Sucker punch : a Joe Grundy mystery / Marc Strange.

ISBN 978-1-55002-702-0

    I. Title.

PS8637.T725S82 2007   C813'.6   C2007-900089-4

1   2   3   4   5   11   10   09   08   07

Conseil des Arts
du Canada

Canada Council
for the Arts

Canadä

ONTARIO ARTS COUNCIL
CONSEIL DES ARTS DE L'ONTARIO
an Ontario Government Agency
un organisme du gouvernement de l'Ontario

We acknowledge the support of the **Canada Council for the Arts** and the **Ontario Arts Council** for our publishing program. We also acknowledge the financial support of the **Government of Canada** through the **Book Publishing Industry Development Program** and **The Association for the Export of Canadian Books**, and the **Government of Ontario** through the **Ontario Book Publishers Tax Credit program**, and the **Ontario Media Development Corporation**.

Care has been taken to trace the ownership of copyright material used in this book. The author and the publisher welcome any information enabling them to rectify any references or credits in subsequent editions.

J. Kirk Howard, President

Printed and bound in Canada.
www.dundurn.com

Dundurn Press	Gazelle Book Services Limited	Dundurn Press
3 Church Street, Suite 500	White Cross Mills	2250 Military Road
Toronto, Ontario, Canada	High Town, Lancaster, England	Tonawanda, NY
M5E 1M2	LA1 4XS	U.S.A. 14150

For Karen

chapter one

Most afternoons I have a nap between three and six so I'm fresh for the evening shift, and then I have some toast and coffee at the Lobby Café next door to the magazine shop. The café closes at six, but Hattie lets me in through the kitchen and gives me an order of toast and a short pot of coffee, better coffee than you can get from room service.

"You want to look at the paper, Joe?"

"Is the crossword done?"

"Not by me," she says.

Hattie brings me a copy of the *Emblem* with my cup.

"How'd you like to be him?" she asks.

The front page has a banner headline that says IT's ALL HIS! and a photograph of a young, bearded guy surrounded by reporters on the courthouse steps.

"What's all his?" I ask.

"Some old geezer left him a boatload of money. They've been fighting the will for two years, but he won. It's all his."

"So it says." I open the paper for the crossword, but

someone's been there before me and made a mess of the job. I turn to the comics and read the ones I like. Hattie brings me toast with extra butter, no jam, and heats up my coffee.

"Half a billion," she says. "What would you do with all that money?"

There's a large man in a wide green jacket peering in from the lobby. He's rapping the window and jiggling the handle of the sliding glass door. The sign in front of his face reads CLOSED, but he chooses to ignore it. Hattie looks sternly over her shoulder, points to the large clock behind her, which reads 6:09, makes a brisk two-palm gesture that in baseball might signal "safe" but otherwise means over, done, finished. The Lobby Café is closed, and Hattie doesn't care to debate the issue.

"Buy some new shoes," I tell her. "Maybe a suit."

The man in the green jacket raps again, but Hattie ignores him. She's run the Lobby Café since before I got here. She's hard to rattle.

"Now there's a guy who needs a new suit," she says. "The jolly green giant. His jacket's about to split at the seams."

A green foothill lumbers across the red carpet towards the front desk. "I miss *Calvin and Hobbes*," I say.

"I miss *Terry and the Pirates*," Hattie says.

It's six-thirty when I take my first walkabout. The pre-evening lull admits echoes from above where seminars are disengaging on the mezzanine level. Most of the lobby traffic is moving from the entrance to the elevators, guests in a hurry to change for dinner or straggling in from excursions, looking forward to a hot bath and a room-service tray. The hotel's shuttle bus is off-loading luggage, and a group tour is checking in, late arrivals from the airport, still complaining about the flight.

I spot Gritch sitting near his favourite palm tree, pretending to read the *Globe and Mail*. The world sees me coming a block away, but Gritch can disappear behind a Boston fern. He is sixty-one years old, short, egg-shaped.

He sees all and is rarely noticed. My eyes and ears. When I took the security job about seven years ago, Leo Alexander told me to hire Wallace Gritchfield. "The Lord Douglas isn't an office building," Leo said. "It's a castle. Secret rooms, hidden staircases, wouldn't be surprised if there was a dungeon somewhere."

If there is a dungeon, Gritch knows about it, how to get there, and how to break out.

"You're off," I say.

"You might want me to stick around."

He's never in a hurry to go home. He keeps trying to move in with me, and his wife can't see that it would make much difference in their lives, but I insist he visit her once in a while if only to pick out a suit that doesn't smell of bad cigars.

"S'up?" I ask.

"Talk to Margo," Gritch says. "She's got a VIP checking in soon and she thinks maybe there'll be a crowd."

"She still here?"

"Yeah, she'll be down in a minute. I think she went up to check the Governor's Suite, make sure housekeeping has the towels folded."

"I'll be back in fifteen," I say.

I leave him sitting in the lobby with his newspaper and continue my tour. The Palm Court is filling up. Rolf Kalman has his reservation book open and has already begun pocketing the discreetly folded bills that ensure the good tables and attentive service to which the guests are already entitled. The Only, the hotel's justly famous seafood house, is dealing oysters, chowder, and planked salmon; the Street Level Sports Bar is filling up. The Street's bouncer, Dougray Crain, a former linebacker with the B.C. Lions, gives me a thumbs-up. My job doesn't involve security for the hotel's bars, but I like to get a feel for how an evening is building.

There's a big wedding reception in the Gabriola Ballroom, and in the hotel's most exclusive function room, Floor Eleven, a retiring city father is being roasted at five hundred dollars a plate. Various conventions of widget manufacturers and consulting dermatologists are dispersing to plumb the city's nightlife. Everything is copacetic. Suits me fine.

I head down to Olive's, one flight of wide marble stairs below the lobby. Olive's used to be the Press Club years ago, back when reporters drank and smoked, but for sixteen years it's been Olive May's place and will remain so until she decides to retire. Like me, Olive has tenure at the Lord Douglas Hotel, at least for as long as Leo Alexander is alive. Maybe longer if it's the same will he wrote seven years ago when I managed to stumble into the path of a few bullets that were meant for him.

Olive's is quiet. The stockbrokers have gone home and the jazz buffs don't start showing up until after nine o'clock when Olive does her first set. This week she's booked a California trio doing Latin-flavoured stuff. Sometimes she sits in with the guest artists. She plays piano like Joe Louis boxed: no fuss, no muss, both hands. She sings, too.

Olive isn't there yet, but Barney Geller is behind the bar. "Hi, champ," he says as I come in. Barney won a thousand dollars on me one night in 1985, one of the good nights, which is why he insists on calling me "champ." He still has a picture of me taped to the long mirror behind the row of Scotch. I have my gloves up like a good boy. I look young and eager. What did I know?

"Those movie people still in the house, champ?"

"Checked out this afternoon, Barney."

"Too bad. Good tippers."

"They'll be back in a week. They're blowing up a boat down in Steveston."

"Too early for your beer."

"Just passing through, Barney. I'll see you later."

I keep moving, down the long bar and up three steps to the street entrance. Outside are four more steps, concrete this time, and then I'm on the sidewalk about halfway down the block from the main entrance. It's a warm evening. Early September. The office building across the street has a fine sunset splashed high across its glass wall, and the Lord Douglas is benefitting from the lighting effect. The old girl looks good.

As I walk up the street towards the main entrance, I spot Maxine, a wiry little woman with a cute monkey face and straight black hair, getting out of her cab. She talks to me across the hood. "You missed it, Grundy. Andrew's eyes nearly fell out of his head."

Andrew, our doorman, wears a uniform that would look good on a Bolivian field marshal. He wears it well, with a straight face. On him it doesn't seem completely ridiculous. Maxine wears a black T-shirt and no bra. She's built like a twelve-year-old boy.

"He was looking like there was a bad smell somewhere and then the guy slipped him a tip and Andrew nearly had a bird."

Andrew has come up behind my left shoulder.

"How much was it, Andrew?" Maxine asks.

"That is none of your affair," Andrew says. "Good evening, Mr. Grundy."

"Hi, Andrew. Nice evening."

"Very pleasant."

"Andrew's being coy."

Andrew turns on his heel with grave dignity and returns to his post in time to open the big brass door for a young couple who don't bother to tip him, an oversight Andrew disdains to notice.

"Don't know what he's being so secretive about. I got the same thing." She's come around to the sidewalk.

"Yeah, well, don't go yelling too loud, okay, Maxine?"

"What ya gonna do, Grundy, punch me out?"

She hits me in the belly. She has a bony fist.

"You've got a bony fist," I tell her.

"Too slow, Joe. That's why you were a bust as a fighter."

"That and my glass jaw," I say.

"This your cab?"

Some guy is opening the passenger door, looks like he's in a hurry.

"Yeah, wanna buy it?" She fakes another shot at my gut, and I reach out with my left hand and tug her right earlobe. She doesn't get it. She climbs into the cab, and I hear the passenger say, "Channel 20, the side door," before they pull away.

Andrew opens the front door for me. "It was a hundred-dollar bill," he says quietly.

"Nice tip," I say.

Andrew fixes my tie for me. He's a bit of a fuss-budget. He likes things to look nice.

"Yes," he says. "None of her business, though."

The lobby of the Lord Douglas Hotel is old style, with a wide, curving staircase leading up to the mezzanine level and a balcony overlooking the half-acre of burgundy carpet below. The reading area has leather couches and a newspaper rack, and the front desk is as long as a Texas bar. The six elevators have polished brass doors, and the floor indicator lights are like rubies set in a sundial. Maurice, the bell captain, is getting off one of the elevators as I cross the floor, and I see him sneak a peek at a folded bill in his hand.

"It's a C-note, Maurice," I tell him.

"That's what I thought it was."

"Is it real?"

"That's what I was trying to find out," he says. "The guy looked like a street person. Could be a rock star, I guess."

Margo Traynor, the assistant manager, is trying to catch my eye. When she gets it, she nods me towards her office, back of the front desk. When I get to the desk, I see that Melanie, the reservations manager, is checking her computer.

"Get your hundred?" I ask her as I walk by.

She looks coy for a second. "Mmm-hmm."

"Must be nice."

"Didn't get one?"

"Not my night, I guess."

Melanie goes back to her customer, a luminous woman with curly dark hair and a face I almost recognize. "Yes, Ms. Gagliardi," Melanie says. "Here it is. Room 1221."

"Is that a non-smoking floor?" Connie Gagliardi asks.

I've identified her now. Channel 20, NewsWatch. Her face is familiar even to a non-viewer, because it's on the side of quite a few buses and at least three billboards downtown. She's shorter than I thought she'd be.

Margo Traynor is occupying Lloyd Gruber's office while our general manager is enjoying his first vacation in ten years, a fact he found it necessary to belabour us with on more than one occasion before he actually pried himself loose. Margo is sitting at Lloyd Gruber's desk, and I think she looks as if she belongs. There's someone else in the room.

"Joe, this is Mr. Axelrode," she says. "Joe Grundy, our head of security."

"Hi, how are you?" I say to the guy. It's Green Jacket. He looks like a linebacker ten years and thirty pounds past training camp. Almost as tall as I am, certainly wider. His jacket button will pop any minute. He's pretty sure he scares people. He doesn't offer to shake my hand.

"How many men have you got?" he asks me.

"On duty tonight? There'll be three."

"That won't be enough," he says, standing to better confront the problem. I worry about his jacket button.

"I'm not having policemen walking up and down the hallways," Margo says.

Axelrode had the solution all along. "I was thinking along the lines of a private security team."

Margo stands, too. Now we're all standing. "No," she says. "And I have that on the authority of Mr. Gruber, the manager, who is unfortunately not with us at this time. I mean, he's away. I'm in charge."

"What do you want me to do, Ms. Traynor?" I ask.

She appreciates that and smiles at me. "Mr. Axelrode thinks we may have a bit of a security problem. A guest has just checked in carrying a considerable sum of money."

"Two hundred and fifty thousand dollars in cash," Axelrode says.

"In hundred-dollar bills," I throw in for something to say.

"Fresh out of the bank," Axelrode adds.

"Who is he?" I still haven't seen the guy in question.

"His name's Jacob Buznardo," Margo says. "He's in the Governor's Suite."

"Should I know him?"

"You will," Axelrode says. "He just inherited more than half a billion dollars."

chapter two

Back out in the lobby, I search for Gritch's newspaper. He's behind it, sitting over by the big ferns like HumptyDumpty with his neat little feet barely touching the floor. I head for the office, and he gets up and follows me down the hall.

"Guest just checked into the Governor's Suite," I say over my shoulder.

"Guy in the paper. Maybe twenty-five, thirty," Gritch says, right behind me, "blond hair down to his butt crack, hippie-dippie type, one beat-up leather bag, one new attaché case, Samsonite. Maurice took him up. Maurice got a nice tip."

I turn on the lights in the office. Already my shirt doesn't feel fresh. "Where's Arnie?"

"Working his way down. Probably mooching leftovers at the wedding reception. He's off at eight."

"Maybe not," I say. I find the phone number I'm looking for. "Maybe Arnie works overtime. Maybe we all work overtime."

"What's up?"

"There's two hundred and fifty thousand cash in that briefcase."

Gritch whistles a soft note. "Is that legal?"

"It's his money." I hand Gritch the card with the number on it. "Make a call, see if Dan Howard can come in."

"Yeah, all right. Which number?"

"Don't be a wise guy. Hey, you spot that bruiser with the ugly green sports coat?"

"What do you pay me for?" he says. "Name's Axelrode."

"We've been introduced."

"Oh, yeah? They call him Axe."

"Really? He was hassling Margo about the security arrangements."

"Yeah, he's a rent-a-cop these days. Used to be on the job. What's his connection?"

"Not sure yet," I say at the door. "When Arnie gets down, hold on to him."

"Yo."

I hear him pick up the phone and then I'm heading for the elevators. I turn when Gritch says my name.

"Joe?"

"What?"

"That guy Axelrode? If you get in a beef with him, don't putz around. The guy's not nice. He got retired from the job for excessive you-know-whats."

I'm heading for the elevators when Margo catches up to me. "You on your way up to fifteen?"

"Yep."

"There's a rock band in the other suite," she says. "We've had a couple of complaints about the noise."

"I'll mention it to them."

"There's a TV crew wants to set up shop on the mezzanine."

"For the rock band?"

She shakes her head. "Mr. Buznardo says he's calling a press conference for 9:00 a.m., but that Gagliardi person is trying to get an interview before then."

"This man, Buznardo, has he got people with him?"

"Just his lawyer."

"I'll try to talk him into putting the money in the safe."

"The way he's handing it out it'll be gone by morning."

She heads back to the front desk. A young woman with a lot of responsibility. Holding up well.

The elevator arrives and a woman gets out. My age, or a bit older. Nicely turned out, raw silk suit, good bag, good shoes, not too much heel, nice legs walking away, heading for the staircase down to Olive's. She gives me a look over her shoulder before the door slides shut. Or maybe she was just glancing back. Ash-blond hair, cool grey eyes. Out of my league.

The Lord Douglas elevators won't be rushed. It takes a couple of minutes to get to the top floor. I press fifteen and stand in the corner watching the lighted numbers climb until they skip from twelve to fourteen. Back when the Lord Douglas was built, people didn't like staying on a thirteenth floor — I don't think they care as much anymore. According to Gritch, there *is* a thirteenth floor; you just can't get there via these elevators. I study my shoes to make a change from watching the numbers, and on the floor I notice a crumpled-up bill. It's a C-note, new, still crisp, but crushed once as if in someone's fist and dropped or thrown away. I smooth it, fold it, and stick it in my pants pocket as the doors open on fifteen. Seems I got one, anyway.

There are two big suites on fifteen, at opposite ends of the building. The Ambassador's Suite is 1529–1531 at the north end. I hear the music halfway down the hall — guitar and a synthesizer and some kind of drums.

A short guy with spiked hair that's too young for his face opens the door and looks at me. He says, "Too loud, right?"

"There's plaster falling on fourteen."

"You the house dick?"

"That's right. Look, there's a rehearsal room down on the mezzanine floor you could book. It's pretty good. Sound system, piano. Dwight Yoakam used it last year."

"Now there's a recommendation," he says. "It's okay. We're gonna knock off, anyway. We sound like shit."

"I wouldn't know," I tell him.

"Trust me."

The Governor's Suite is 1502–1504, on the west side of the building, at the end of a full city block of carpeted hallway wide enough for a compact car. The carpets on fifteen were recently replaced. Brighter than the old roses I used to tread but the distance is the same. It's a long stroll. When I reach the other end, the door to 1502 is open and a man is taking his leave, talking to someone inside.

"No reporters, that's all I'm saying. Anybody gets through you just refer them to me. Can you do that?"

I can't hear the reply, and neither can the man because he bends farther into the suite. His comb-over lifts like a shingle when he leans sideways.

"Buzz, can you do that?"

I guess the answer is affirmative, because the man nods to himself without conviction and comes out into the hall where he spots me approaching and spreads his arms as if to bar the door. It's a wide door. His arms are short. I admire his pluck. "Mr. Buznardo isn't receiving just now."

"That's fine, sir," I tell him. "I just need a minute of his time."

"He's asked not to be disturbed."

"The hotel will certainly honour that, sir. My name's Joe Grundy, hotel security. I just want to ensure our guest is satisfied with arrangements."

The man relaxes a little and sticks out his hand. "Oh. Good. I'm Alvin Neagle, Mr. Buznardo's lawyer. I'm hoping to keep the lid on his whereabouts for a while."

"How do you do, sir?" I shake his damp hand. "I think

the word may have leaked out. We'll try to keep your client from being bothered too much."

"He's had a long day. He needs to relax."

"I won't keep him long."

"All right, okay. I have to take off, but I'd like to talk to you later about arrangements for tomorrow."

"Yes, sir. You just tell Ms. Traynor, the assistant general manager, what you need and we'll make sure you get it."

"It's going to be a madhouse however it's arranged. I know it."

"Excuse me, sir, have you arranged for extra security for your client?"

He throws up his hands. "He won't hear of it. He thinks he's invulnerable."

Neagle takes a deep breath and heads off in the direction of the elevators, shaking his head and muttering. A small round man in a blue polyester suit patting his shingle back into place and facing the fact that he's now in the eye of a hurricane.

"It's open," a voice from inside 1502 says.

The best suite in the hotel. Four big bedrooms, reception room, private lounge, full kitchen, and real antique furniture — some of it, anyway. I hear the shower running in one of the bathrooms and I have a look around. On the desk is a sheaf of hundred-dollar bills fanned out. I call out to the bathroom. "Mr. Buznardo?"

"There's money on the desk, man. Help yourself."

I go to the bedroom door and talk to the bathroom. "My name's Grundy, Mr. Buznardo. Hotel security. Like to talk to you for a minute."

He comes out of the bathroom wearing a towel — a skinny blond Jesus. "Out there on the desk. Take as much as you need."

"Before we get to that, maybe we could talk a bit."

There's another knock.

"Yo," he says.

"Room service."

I recognize the voice. It's Phil Marsden.

"Bring it on in," Buznardo says. "Help yourself to a tip. It's on the desk."

I step back into the sitting room. Phil is holding a silver bucket with a magnum of Veuve Clicquot up to its shoulders in ice. He has two champagne glasses in his other hand. He's staring at the cash on the desk.

"It's okay, Phil. Take one."

He glances at me and blinks. "Yeah?"

"That's what the man says."

Phil puts down the bucket and glasses, then selects one of the bills from the fan as if he's choosing a card. "Would you like me to open this for you, sir?" Phil asks Buznardo.

"I want to talk to him," I say.

"I've got to get that thing signed."

"I think he's good for it."

Phil heads for the door. He still hasn't pocketed the C-note. "Okay. I'll pick it up later." He turns at the door. "He wants anything else, tell him to ask for Phil."

Phil shuts the door as Buznardo comes out of the bedroom. He lifts the champagne bottle out of the ice and peers at the label. "Want a glass?"

"No, thank you, sir."

"It's a celebration."

"I guess it is."

"I wasn't going to get this fancy. Alvin arranged things. I don't usually hang in places like this."

"I guess your life's about to change a bit."

"Sure," he says. "Some of the day-to-day details, for a while, anyway, but in the long run not so much." He puts the champagne back in the bucket. "Not so much."

I hand him the bill. "Room service will want you to sign this."

"You bet." He finds a hotel pen in the desk drawer and bends to scrawl his name. His towel drops to the floor. He doesn't bother to pick it up. "Should I add a gratuity to this?"

"I think you already gave him a generous tip."

Buznardo puts the pen and signed chit on the dresser alongside the fan of fresh hundred-dollar bills. He stares at himself in the mirror, pale and naked, his eyes flatly curious, as if contemplating a drawing. Picking up one of the bills by its corner, he shows it to his mirror image, studying the effect it makes on the composition. "How about you?"

"That's not necessary, sir. I found one of your hundred-dollar bills in the elevator. Someone must have dropped it." I hold it out to him.

He raises his hands as if he doesn't want anything to do with a bill that isn't smooth. "It's gone. That one's left my hands. I'm not responsible for it anymore. You keep it, or find the owner. Whatever." He finally picks up the towel and wraps it around his bony hips. "Hotel security, that's like a detective, right?"

"More like a watchdog. I understand you have a large amount of cash with you."

"Want to see it?" He grabs a new Samsonite attaché case from behind the couch and pops it open. Hundred-dollar bills in hundred-bill packets with tight paper bands. Twenty-four freshly wrapped plus the broken one on the desk makes two hundred and fifty thousand, give or take.

"That's a lot of money. The thing of it is, Mr. Buznardo —"

"Call me Buzz 'cause everybody does." He makes it sound like a nursery rhyme.

"Okay, Buzz, the thing is the hotel's a bit worried about having that much cash lying around. Wouldn't you feel more secure with that case in the hotel safe?"

"No, I need it with me. As soon as the banks get their act together, I'm getting more."

"Mind my asking what you need it for?"

"I'm not here to buy dope or anything." He closes the case and puts it back behind the couch. As good a stash as any, I suppose.

"We're just concerned that someone might try to steal it."

"Aw, man, they'd be welcome, if they want it bad enough to do something like that. I don't think of this money as mine. Not now that it *is* mine, and I can do what I want with it."

"Which is?"

He lets the towel drop again and begins pulling on jeans and a T-shirt, but no underwear. The shirt says CONFOUND THE PREVAILING PARADIGM — whatever that means.

"I'm going to give it away."

"All of it? The whole briefcase?"

"All of it. The whole six hundred and eighty-eight million dollars."

He smiles at me again, but he doesn't look demented or drugged or as if he's kidding. He seems like a skinny blond Jesus with a long wet ponytail and a neatly trimmed beard and a face suffused with holy determination.

chapter three

When I get back to the office, Gritch is odourizing the room with cigar exhaust and Arnie McKellar is squatting at the second desk, filling out his report and bitching about the "special ushers" handling security on Floor Eleven for the civic function.

"They don't ask *me* for ID. I ask *them* for ID. Where do they get off?"

"Why bother with Floor Eleven in the first place?" Gritch says. "Not your responsibility."

"Maybe not, but I'm entitled to check it out without getting hassled by assholes in red jackets. Where do they hire these guys?"

"Leave Floor Eleven alone," I say as I come in. "And leave your report. You're going out again."

Arnie doesn't want to go. "I gotta eat something."

Gritch snorts cigar smoke. Arnie McKellar is obese. A furtive eater, never satisfied, always hard done by, as if somebody stole his lunch pail.

"Just stand in the hall on fifteen where you can see the doors to the Governor's Suite."

"How long?" he asks. "I was going home."

"Just stand in the hall until I can think of a better plan. I'll send you home as soon as I can."

Arnie puts on his jacket and slouches out. Gritch shakes his head. He thinks I should can Arnie. I'd like to. I cut Arnie extra slack as a personal favour to Lloyd Gruber, keeping him on staff long past the point I would have fired someone without an in-house connection.

"While he's mooching around on Floor Eleven looking for free hors d'oeuvres, Maurice has probably ushered three working girls up the back way," Gritch says.

"You get hold of Dan?" I ask him.

"His wife says he's sleeping. I think he's playing cards somewhere or trying to hitch a ride home from the track. She says he'll call as soon as she can wake him up, which means track him down. I should have told her to try his mother's place."

"But you didn't."

"Not me, pal."

I pick up the phone. "Melanie, Joe Grundy. We need a room on fifteen. Can you move somebody? Give 'em a better view or something? I've got Arnie standing in the hall up there, but we don't need that all night. Yeah, I'll be here."

"So?" Gritch isn't satisfied with the way his cigar stump is drawing.

"He's going to give it away."

"Who what?" He's looking for matches.

"The kid upstairs. He's handing it out to anybody who shows up."

"That'll make him popular." He locates a forgotten Bic lighter in the second desk and fires up.

"The whole six hundred and eighty-eight million."

"Is he nuts?" Gritch has it going again.

"I don't think so. He's kind of a sweet guy. That's how

he comes across. But we've got a problem. He's holding a press conference in the morning. Once word gets out…"

"He's going to hand it out *here*?"

"I don't know."

"I'll go watch the lobby."

"Maybe you should get some sleep," I suggest. "Use my bed. I'm good for four hours or so. I'll wake you up."

"I'll go doze in the lobby with one eye open."

"Yeah, okay, but not with that thing."

He takes a last blast off the cigar and leaves it behind to die a natural death in the ashtray.

Melanie calls back as soon as I've flushed the cigar stub down the donniker. "Mel? What did you get?"

"You can have 1507," she says. "I moved the Bryants to the corner suite on nine. It's a better room. They're happy. You want 1507 made up?"

"Leave it messy. It'll be fine. Tell Margo I'll keep somebody in there all the time with the door open a bit. Keep an eye on who goes in and out. I'll come see her as soon as I set it up. You're the best."

When I get back up to fifteen, Arnie is leaning against the wall near the elevators like a guy who wants to sell reefers to kids. I open 1507. Melanie's got us a good base camp. With the door open a foot or so, you can see both of the Governor's Suite's doors, 1502 and 1504. I move a chair over beside the door.

"Keep the lights on, but don't play the television," I tell Arnie. "Just watch until Dan gets here, maybe an hour, then you can go home. But I'll need you back by nine in the morning."

"I'm supposed to get a day off."

"You're going to get double time for the extra hours, Arnie, and all you have to do is sit up straight and pay attention. If that's too tough for you, then you can walk. Permanently. You hear what I'm saying?"

"I'm just saying —"

"You're just complaining, Arnie, which is what you do most of the time when you aren't filling your face. Normally, I don't mind a whole helluva lot, but tonight I'd appreciate it if you'd just do the job."

Arnie doesn't bother to argue anymore. He plunks himself in the chair like a kid who's been cuffed on the back of the head, then fumbles inside his jacket pocket for a bag of M&M's. "What am I looking for?"

"Trouble," I tell him. "We don't want any."

I go back down to the main floor again where I find Margo in Lloyd's office, looking beleaguered. She tilts her head when I walk in. Axelrode is still there, sitting in the corner. Margo's eyes shift to indicate the guy and then back to me with an eyebrow jump that tells me she wants him out of there.

"Mr. Axelrode," I say, "is there anything else we can do for you, sir?"

"I still think you're going to need some professionals," he says. "You're going to have big problems when he starts shooting off his mouth on TV. You're going to have every freeloader on the coast lined up with their hands out."

"Are you associated with Mr. Buznardo, sir?"

"I have an interest in his security and the security of the cash he's carrying."

"You with a bank?"

He looks annoyed. He doesn't like explaining himself. "No, I'm not with a bank."

"Oh," I say. "Because if you don't have any official relationship with Mr. Buznardo, perhaps you could worry about his welfare somewhere else. Ms. Traynor has a big hotel to run."

He stands again. I think he's used to things happening when he stands. "I'm not at all satisfied things are being attended to."

"There's a good jazz club down one flight." I'm crowding him towards the door. "Or you could wait in the lobby. For a while."

Axelrode stops, glares at me, doesn't like people in his face. He stretches his neck to show me how ready he is. "If anything happens to Mr. Buznardo, I'll be asking some serious questions."

"Why don't you go and talk to Mr. Buznardo yourself and tell him how concerned you are? He seems like a nice enough guy. Very welcoming."

He sneers. "He's an idiot, and I wouldn't piss on him if he caught fire. But it's my job to keep an eye on him until they can clean up the mess he's made."

"And who would 'they' be, sir?"

He gives me a scowl he probably saves for lower life forms and stalks out.

"Thanks," Margo says.

"How long has he been here?"

"He went out for a while, said he had to make some calls, then waltzed back in and started telling me what's wrong with our operation. He was pretty thorough."

"You know where he fits into this?"

"He says he works for Prescott Holdings. Up until this afternoon Prescott Holdings controlled more than a half-billion dollars of the late Parker Prescott's money."

"I guess it's hard to let go sometimes."

"How many people have you got, really?"

"It's thin," I tell her. "Black Jack's taking his week. He's fishing the Kispiox. No way to get him. Arthur Blomquist went to work for NightWatch."

"That's too bad."

"Good man. I couldn't match what they were offering him."

"How much were they offering?"

"The company, more or less."

"Maybe we should call the police," Margo says.

"We'll be okay for tonight. There'll be three of us rotating. I'll line up some replacements in the morning."

"Will you talk to Leo? With Mr. Gruber not here I'm feeling a bit exposed."

"You're doing great," I tell her.

"Tonight's an unusual situation."

I'm back in my office when Arnie calls down from 1507.

"He's got a visitor. Some girl showed up. They kissed, hugged, jumped around. Happy to see each other."

"Anything else?"

"That's all. Dan here yet?"

"No. He's not here in half an hour, I'll send Gritch up to take over. That okay? You can hang in that long?"

"I guess."

"That's nice he got a visitor."

"Good-looking, too. Redhead. Hold it, they're coming out. I'll get back to you."

"Coming down the elevator?"

"Wait a sec." There's a pause while he steps out into the hall to check, then he's back. "No, they went right by it. All the way down the hall. Knocked on 1529. Invited inside. Visiting the neighbours."

"Okay, I'll come by in about twenty minutes."

I hang up and check my watch: 9:05. Leo will be watching television. I might have to watch a repeat of *Frasier* or something. Gritch comes in from the lobby and looks around for his cigar stub.

"It's long gone, partner," I say.

"I was getting to the good part."

"Those things don't have a good part. What's happening with Dan?"

"Danny boy's on his way in. His wife says he just woke up. If you believe that, I've got a deal for you on some swampland."

"I'm going up to talk to the old man. When Dan gets here, send him up to relieve Arnie, then you grab some sack time in my room. I'm going to need you when Dan takes off."

"Like what, you figure — 1:00 a.m.?"

"Yeah, like that. One, one-thirty. Dan's got to grab some sleep and get back here as early as he can. We're going to have to pick up a couple of people for tomorrow. Maybe from Moonlight."

"Those guys make me nervous," Gritch says. "They're like Mormons, with their black suits and short haircuts. I keep expecting them to hand me a tract."

"I know. Neat, polite, professional. Helluva way to run an operation."

I get back on the elevator. Up and down. Half my life. I need the special elevator key to rise all the way. Leo lives on top, high above the fifteenth floor. Has for the past seven years. His apartments are in the dome. The view used to be better before all the high-rises and skyscrapers cut off some of his sightlines to the harbour, but it's still an impressive aerie. I think it's the main reason he won't sell the place.

Leo Alexander is seventy-two now. Retired since that night seven years ago. Gave control of most of his business to his two sons, Theo and Lenny, fifty and forty-six respectively, with the proviso they leave the Lord Douglas alone. Neither one lives at the hotel and they don't speak to each other unless they have to. Leo doesn't much care for either one of his offspring, but he's done okay by them. They can't sell the Lord Douglas while Leo is alive.

There's an NFL game on tonight. I'd forgotten about that. The New York Jets are at home to the Oakland Raiders. It's running late. It's past midnight on the East Coast.

"Ever been to Oakland, Joseph?" Leo asks.

"Yes, sir. Twice."

"How did you do?"

"I won."

"Both times?"

"Yes, sir."

"The city has good memories for you."

"I don't remember the city. I remember a short guy who

hit me so hard I wet myself inside my cup."

"Fumble!" Leo says.

Leo wears a track suit to watch sporting events. This evening's garment is navy blue velour with a thin burgundy stripe. It's very handsome. I won't compliment him on it. If I do, he'll buy me one.

"Can't anyone catch a pass? That's twice he's been open."

End of the third quarter. There's a break in the action and the television screen is taken over by new cars, great beers, discounts on long-distance calls, more new cars. Leo lights a cigar. "Want one?"

"No thanks, sir."

He mutes the TV with his remote and turns to look at me. He's still got all his hair, keeps it short, that's how much he has. And he's in good shape for a man his age — skinny but not feeble. His hands don't shake, his eyes are clear, and his voice is strong. Don't know why he doesn't get out more, but I guess that's his business.

"So, Joe, how are things?"

"We have a bit of excitement tonight. Margo's a little concerned."

"Miss Traynor? Always liked that girl. She started what, eight years ago?"

"Something like that, sir."

"Nice girl, brown hair, the same shade as my first wife's, bless her heart. What's she worried about?"

"Security for a guest with a lot of cash."

"You can handle it."

"She was just wondering if there was anything more you wanted her to do."

"Tell Miss Traynor I have the utmost confidence in her."

"Yes, sir, I'll tell her."

"Want to watch the last quarter?"

"I'd better get back, sir. I'm bringing in an extra man for the night."

"Good, you do that."

I head for the door. One of the maids, Raquel, I think, is turning down his bed. Leo probably gets two chocolates.

"Our guest with all the cash?"

"Yes, sir, it's a Mr. Buznardo. He inherited a lot of money."

"He did more than that. He's got a hundred charities scared witless they're going to lose their funding. He's putting at least a thousand people who've been nursing at the Prescott Holdings teat for twenty years out of a job, and he made Wade Hubble look like a grifter in front of the whole country."

"All that?"

"Took him two years in court against some of the highest-priced legal talent in the city."

"He must have had a good lawyer."

"Buznardo? Ha! He had Alvin Neagle handling it." Leo shakes his head. "I remember when Alvin was chasing ambulances. I guess some people rise to the occasion when they know they might win the big one."

"Maybe I'd better get some rent-a-cops. Sounds like Buznardo might have made a few enemies."

"Well," the old man says, reaching for his brandy, "you can't be responsible for a man with a half-billion dollars. People like that have to learn to insulate themselves." He spreads his arms to indicate his own comfy fortress. "Come on up on Sunday. Green Bay's playing the 49ers."

"I'll try to make it, sir, thanks."

"We can have a pizza."

"Sounds good," I say, heading for the door. "Good night, sir."

Raquel, I think it's Raquel, is running his bath now.

chapter four

I stop off on fifteen and Arnie is watching the same thing Leo was watching.

"You're supposed to be watching the door," I say.

"Shit, they're in for the night. Just had four pizzas delivered." He sounds envious.

"They came back from 1529?"

"No, they're still down there. It's a party."

"Did they take an attaché case with them? Samsonite? Black?"

"What? To the party? No. Him and the woman took a couple of bottles of wine."

"Arnie, just watch the door. There's two hundred and fifty thousand dollars in a briefcase, give or take a few hundred-dollar tips, and if somebody decides to steal it, I'd like it if you could give me a description."

"I didn't know about the money." He still wants to see what's going on with the football game.

"Turn off the TV, Arnie."

I go back down the hall to the Ambassador's Suite and knock. Somebody's playing a guitar inside, not too loud, kind of folkie. The same young guy with the old face opens the door.

"This can't be too loud, man. This is a solid old building, thick walls, we're in a *suite*."

I hold up my hands in innocence. "No, sir, no problem. It sounds really nice. I just wondered if I could speak with one of your guests for a moment. Hotel business. Mr. Buznardo."

"Hey, sure, come on in, Detective."

"I don't want to disturb your party, sir. I could talk to Mr. Buznardo in the hall."

He grabs my arm and pulls me through the doorway. "Screw that. Come in. Welcome. This is Bubba, our road manager, Mr. Carno from Yolanda Records..." I'm introduced as "the house dick" and everybody seems cool with that.

There are about a dozen people in the room. Furniture has been rearranged to form a group circle with two tables of pizzas and wine in the middle. A lingering herbal sweetness hangs in the air. As long as it doesn't filter into the hall, we don't comment anymore. This is a smoking suite. A guy with a handlebar moustache is finger-picking a nice old Martin guitar and singing an Appalachian murder song in a sweet tenor voice. "Down by the banks of the Ohio..." His name is John-John. He doesn't stop picking while introductions are made by my host, but he nods in my direction and smiles when he sings, "I held my knife against her breast, while into my arms she pressed. She cried 'O Lord, don't murder me, I'm not prepared for Eternity.'" I smile at the pure relish of his delivery.

It's a celebration. The people in the room have just finished a two-month recording stint and will soon launch a new CD. The group is called Redhorn — three guys and a couple of studio musicians who aren't part of the group but play on the new CD. The disc was produced by the man sitting at the end of the sofa, a guy named Barnett Sharpe, who's supposed to be the best record producer on the West Coast, according to one of the studio musicians, who offers me a slice of pepperoni, double cheese, which I decline with thanks. There are women who could be girlfriends or backup singers. One of them has long silver hair and a haunting soprano voice. She harmonizes with the guitar player when they reach the refrain: "And only say that you'll be mine, and in no other arms entwine…"

There are a couple of older people wearing suits, record people, I'm told. The guy who looks like a biker is as big as me but has more hair. He slaps a can of Coors in my hand and claps me on the shoulder. His name is Bubba, he tells me again. "Welcome, friend."

The young guy with the old face is named Sandy Washburn. He plays keyboards and writes most of their stuff. I wind up staying half an hour. They play a couple more tunes, including one of the new songs that's on the CD. I drink the beer.

Jake Buznardo's face displays unabashed emotions — rapture at the sounds, sadness at the story. When he sees me, he grins with immediate recognition and makes room for me at his end of a couch. I fit myself in between him and his companion. Her name is Molly MacKay, Buznardo tells me, pronounced "Mack-eye," he's careful to enunciate. Molly has a thick tangle of red hair, freckles, and green eyes. She's his sister.

"This is my first trip to the city in four years, Mr. Grundy, and Redhorn's giving us a private concert." Like her brother, she's open in her pleasure. Her eyes are wiser than his, or sadder, which might be the same thing.

"And your brother just won his court case," I offer. On-the-job Grundy.

"Sheesh, am I glad that's over. It took forever."

"Mr. Buznardo?" I lean close so as not to interfere with the music, but I'm thinking it's time I did what I came to do.

"Call me Buzz, please, man. It's my name, really."

"Okay, Buzz. It's just that you left all that money behind in your room and the hotel really can't assume liability if someone should take it."

"Oh, right. That's what you're worried about. I can dig it. But really, I wouldn't hold the hotel responsible. Tell him, Molly."

She shakes her head and smiles like an older sister. "He wouldn't. Not his philosophy of life. Doesn't blame, doesn't judge, doesn't hate, and definitely doesn't give a shit."

Buzz reaches behind me and fluffs her hair. "Couldn't have said it better myself."

"You did say it yourself," she says. "I'm just repeating the Buzz words."

"Well, okay, sir. That's reassuring. Still, I'll have someone keep an eye on your room, if you don't mind. Robbers aren't usually gentle souls like yourself."

"You do what you think is right, man," he tells me. "That's all we can do." He closes his eyes, tilts his head back, smiles his seraphic smile, and lets the music wash over him. His sister with the thick red hair gazes at him with patient love and baffled wonder. I feel old and cramped in my worries and responsibilities.

I stand and salute the gathering, now listening to Redhorn rocking gently on "Long Black Veil." I hand Bubba my empty beer can and take my leave, wishing I could stick around. A warm room of friendly people and good music — I haven't been part of one of those for many years. When Bubba opens the door for me, Connie Gagliardi and a woman aiming a TV camera are standing in the hall.

Bubba says to her, "I don't think he wants to talk to anybody."

Behind him, Washburn gets up. "It's okay, Bubba. She's expected."

Connie Gagliardi lifts her chin and looks up at me as she passes. She has dark eyes. I see Buzz getting off the couch to greet her. When he stands, he winces and reaches for his sister's shoulder. His smile never wavers. Bubba gently closes the door in my face.

Walking down the hall, I spot Dan Howard standing near the elevator. He's talking to a big man in a green jacket.

"Hey, boss," Dan says, "what's up?"

I check my watch. It's 10:05. I was listening to music longer than I thought.

"Mr. Axelrode," I say, "have you taken a room on this floor?"

He measures me. I know the look. He's considering what would happen. I know what would happen. "Checking arrangements," he says.

"Check elsewhere." I press the down button, and we wait in silence until No. 6 arrives. Axelrode steps inside. He nods at me as the door closes.

"You know that guy?" I ask Dan.

"Jeff Axelrode. He's got a security company. I used to work for him a few years back."

"What did he want?"

"Hey, I don't know. I don't even know what's going on. There's some rich dude we're babysitting?"

"You have enough sleep, Dan?"

"What? Yeah, I guess."

Dan doesn't seem well rested. He looks as if he's had a long day.

"You had much to drink?"

He shakes his head. "No. I thought I had the night off. I was going to have a few pops to ease my troubled soul, but I'm here now."

In a good light, and when he smiles, Dan Howard gives a handsome first impression — regular features, blue eyes, a fine head of hair. It takes a moment to note that the corners of his mouth are perpetually soured as if by a bad taste on the back of his tongue. Dan has legendary rotten luck.

"Okay," I say, "you give me four hours, until 2:00 a.m. Can you do that?"

"Sure. What's going on?"

When we get to 1507, Arnie is eating a box of McNuggets and watching detectives sift through garbage. He snaps the television off when we come in. "All quiet, Joe. I had the door wide open. Nobody went down the hall."

"Where'd you get the McDonald's?" I ask him.

Arnie looks guilty. "Maurice sent 'em up for me."

"Anybody come up the fire stairs? Service elevator?"

Arnie glances over at Dan and changes the subject. "What took you so long?"

"Go home, Arnie," I tell him. "Get some sleep. Get back by 9:00 a.m."

"Yeah, okay," he says. He collects his McNuggets and his large Coke and waddles out.

After Arnie goes, I tell Dan what's going on.

"It's just sitting in there?"

"Just sitting in there. I don't want anyone taking it. I don't know if the hotel would be liable or not, but it would sure make the front pages if it went missing, and Leo Alexander wouldn't like that."

"Bet his kids would," Dan says.

"Maybe, but I wouldn't like it, either. I'll carry the cell phone with me. Let me know what's happening whenever it happens. I'll have Gritch relieve you at 2:00 a.m. If you start getting sleepy, tell me. And let me know when Buznardo and his sister get home from the party down the hall."

"Don't worry about it, Joe. Knowing how much money is lying around is going to keep me wide awake."

Standing in front of the elevators, I hear traces of music sifting down the hall from 1529, but I don't want to go back there anymore.

chapter five

"Grab some sleep," I tell Gritch when I get back to the office. "Dan's good for four hours. I'll wake you at one-thirty."

"Arnie didn't fill out his report," he says. "Just hauled ass out of here."

"I don't want to fire him until Lloyd gets back."

Gritch sits down to untie his shoes. "Are they real brothers-in-law? He and Lloyd?"

"I don't know how it works. Arnie's wife is Lloyd's sister-in-law. There's some kind of connection."

"Not enough of one to put up with his crapola," Gritch says.

"I have to eat something. Any of that chicken left in the fridge?"

"See?" Gritch says. "That's what I'm talking about. He goes through the fridge like a cucaracha convention. Never leaves anything for anybody else, never buys anything."

"I'll get something in the kitchen," I say.

Gritch has located an abused cigar stub in his ashtray on the second desk. He rummages in the desk drawer and finds a pack of matches, which seems to cheer him up. "Not to mention Dan Howard, the world's worst gambler," he says. "We've got some serious staff problems around here, slugger."

"I know." I open the window to move some fresh air inside. The street below is beginning to shine. A light rain is falling. Connor's Diner closed hours ago. In the Scientology Reading Room next door, a dozen or more well-groomed young people are discussing something important, something they're all sure about. I wish I knew what it was.

The Palm Court's main kitchen is shutting down. An acre of newly wiped stainless steel. In a cloud of steam at the far end of the room, the last of the day's pots and pans are being scrubbed. The laundry bins are stuffed with sweaty kitchen whites. One of the young line cooks offers me a bowl of the pasta he's fixing for the staff. It looks pretty good, smells even better. Simple Italian fare, sausage and peppers and a solid hit of garlic. I still have people to deal with, so I settle for a slice of leftover roast beef and a cold dinner roll. The young cook tries to talk me into something less spartan, but I'm not really hungry. I just need fuel.

The cell phone in my pocket starts ringing. Hotel property. It plays a song. I never know which button to push to make the music stop. The little lid annoys me.

"Yep? I'm here." Talking with my mouth full.

"Hey, champ, it's Barney. We had a D and D on a bar tab and one of the girls tried to stop the asshole and he pushed her."

The good thing about a cell phone, of course, is that you don't have to hang up before you can start moving. I park the sandwich and head for the kitchen stairs.

"She okay?" I ask.

"She hurt her wrist."

Down one flight, around the corner, I hear the music. "I'm right there, Barney."

Barney spots me coming in and points to the far end of the bar, closer to the street entrance, where one of the servers is sitting at a table with her back to the crowd.

"How bad is it?" I ask her. "It's Laurel, right?"

"Hi. Yes. It's not too bad. I tried to stop myself from falling."

"This just happen?"

"Like two minutes ago. He just went out there. He was chasing somebody."

"What's he look like?"

"Big, moustache, green jacket."

"I'll be right back, Laurel. Sit tight."

On the street there's no sign of Green Jacket in either direction.

"Andrew?" I ask our doorman. "Big man, green jacket, just came out of Olive's?"

"He didn't pass the front, Joe. Maybe he went the other way."

"Hey, Grundy." Maxine has her cab parked third in line in front of the hotel. "You looking for somebody?"

"Big guy, ran out on his bar tab."

"Went thattaway," she says. "Chasing a little dude. All the way down and around the corner."

"Thanks."

All the way down and around the corner is the full length of the hotel plus the adjacent vacant lot where the Warburton Building stood until a year ago. A roofed walkway of plywood and scaffolding surrounds the lot, and the sidewalk superintendent windows look in on a hole in the ground and not much more. No sign of the man I'm searching for, or of the little dude he was after. Two blocks away a car runs a red light and gets away with it. I retrace my steps.

Maxine gets out of her cab, holding a newspaper over her head to keep off the drizzle. "Long gone?"

"Yeah, missed him."

"Hop in. We'll chase him."

"That's okay. I'll find him when I need him." Andrew is waving her forward from the steps. "You're up," I tell her.

Andrew holds an umbrella over the ash-blond hair and grey silk suit of the woman now stepping off the carpet to the sidewalk.

"Excuse me," I say to her.

She turns to look at me. Her eyes are pale, unwavering. "Yes?"

"I work for the hotel. After you left the elevator earlier, I found this on the floor and I was wondering if you dropped it." I take the hundred-dollar bill out of my pocket and show it to her without flashing it around.

"Certainly not."

"My apologies," I say. "One of the other guests must have lost it."

"I wouldn't know," she says as she gets into Maxine's taxi. Andrew closes the door for her. She doesn't acknowledge either of us.

"Do you know that woman, Andrew?"

"No. Nice shoes, though."

Back inside, the trio has finished its set to distracted applause. Laurel is being helped into her coat by Barney, who is careful not to jar her arm.

"I missed him," I say. "Sorry."

"I just called my boyfriend," she says. "He's coming to get me."

"Let me take you in to Emergency. Get an X-ray."

"It's not bad," Laurel says. "I just can't carry a tray."

"How much did he run out on?"

"Wasn't even that much," Barney says. "Two beers, plus a bar Scotch for the little guy, then they started arguing about something and the little guy left in a huff and the big guy says something like, 'I'm not finished with you, asshole,' and chases after him."

Laurel says, "And I'm, like, excuse me, sir, and he pushes me out of the way and I put my hand out to grab the railing and bend it back a little. Ow!"

"I think a doctor should look at it," I say.

"Petey'll be here in a minute. He can take me."

When Petey arrives, I prevail upon him to make sure Laurel gets an X-ray. Petey's a nice guy. He says all the right things about how if he ever sees the guy, and how he wishes he'd been here, and in the end he promises to get Laurel to Emergency to have it looked at.

Barney is back behind the bar taking care of business. The jazz buffs are thinning out after the last set. I find an empty stool at the end nearest the door and wait for Barney to get a free minute.

"Soon as he came in, champ, I spotted him as bad news," Barney says. "Just had that look, you know. Two Buds, out of the bottle, sank the first one in two gulps. Carried the second one with him when he joined a table."

"This the little guy at the table?"

"This was before. He takes his second beer over there, Kyra's station, number thirteen. Nice-looking blonde sitting by herself, white wine. She didn't touch it, though. So, oh, yeah, when he first comes in, he comes to the bar, drains the Bud, checks out your picture, asks what year it was. I told him it was the year you beat Olivera in six and won me a G-note. Then he gets the other Bud and carries it over to the table and stands there talking to the woman. I think for a minute maybe he's hitting on her. She's not smiling. He's giving her static, she's giving him the high hat. I figure she's going to tell him to piss off, but he sits down and they have a conversation with him doing most of the talking. Anyway, he makes his point, I guess, and he gets up. That's when the other guy shows up."

"Here's where I say, what other guy?"

"And I say, short guy, fifties, blue polyester, comb-over starting to unravel."

"Does he join them?"

"No, him and the big guy grab a pair of stools at the bar. The little guy has bar Scotch and soda, the big guy's still nursing the second Bud. They've got their heads together, so I don't hear much with the sax player and the drummer doing their thing. But it's the little guy who's doing most of the talking, and the big guy doesn't like what he's saying. Then the comb-over takes off for the street door. The big guy yells something and takes off after him, and poor Laurel gets in his way."

"What did the woman do?"

"She went out the other way, up to the lobby. She might still be up there."

"No, she got in a cab," I say. "Give me the guy's bar tab."

"Don't worry about it, champ. Small potatoes. The D and D fund can handle it."

"I know, Barney, but it's not just a dine and dash. He assaulted one of the hotel's people. He's going to answer for the assault, and he's going to pay for any medical treatment and lost income." Barney hands me the printout: $16.45. "And he's going to pay his bar tab."

Kyra is the other server working this shift. Often she works the day shift behind the bar, but she makes more money working the floor. Kyra has soft brown hair down to her sacrum. Says it takes her two hours a day to keep her hair that gorgeous. I'm sure it's worth it.

"She wanted to know what white wine we served by the glass," Kyra says. "She went for the imported, but she wasn't impressed. I don't think she wanted a drink. She was waiting for somebody."

"The big guy in the sports coat?"

"Not him. She wasn't happy to see him. He was asking her stuff, and she was shaking her head. I heard her say, 'Only if it comes to that.' He says, 'It's not coming to that,' whatever *that* is, and she says, 'I hope not,' and he goes off to the bar. Ten minutes later she still hasn't tasted the wine, and I ask her if she'd prefer something else. She looks at me like she just woke up. She says no, it's fine, and she has a sip. She says it's fine, that she's just listening to the music. Then that thing happens over by the door, and when I turn around she's gone."

I find Olive May sitting at her little banquette in the dark corner around the far end of the bar. She has her usual rum and Coke, her pack of Winstons, and her gold lighter that says "Warm Valley." She's talking on the phone. "Friday night. *Fri*-day night. Don't keep saying maybe. It's Friday night. Well, what's a booking to you? What does it mean to *you*?" She winks at me. "Same thing it means to me. It means someone's booked. Friday night. He's booked Friday night. I don't care if he *is* unhappy as long as he brings his horn. Friday night. Yes, sir. Goodbye, sir."

She smiles across the table at me and offers me one of her Winstons. I take it. There's no smoking in bars in Vancouver these days, but somehow it doesn't seem to apply to Olive's corner.

"Who's going to be here Friday night?" I ask as she lights me up.

"He won't be here. Been yanking my chain for a year." She has a sip of her drink, mostly Coke and ice. "I keep after him. You've got to try. The fool will probably kill himself before the year's out. Good player, but it costs him too much. How's the kid?"

"She'll be okay," I say, "but that wrist's going to hurt for a while."

"We'll look after her."

"Yes, we will." I have a shallow drag on the Winston. Abstemious Grundy. One smoke a day, one beer a day. You'd think I was still in training. "Did you see it happen?"

"You know me, Joe honey. I keep my back to the room."

"You have a good view of both entrances. You can see the staircase coming down from the lobby, and you can see the street door in that mirror."

"I didn't say I was oblivious, darling, merely exclusive."

"There was a woman here wearing a grey suit."

"A statue. She didn't belong."

"And you saw the man who talked to her."

"What was he, a cop?"

"Used to be."

"Looked like a cop. Cop moustache. Kind of guy likes to push people around with his belly."

"He was working for someone, but I can't figure out who."

"What is he, private eye, hired muscle?"

"Something like that."

"I can't help you, honey. Never saw him before. But I know the type."

"Me, too," I say.

"He was heeled."

"You saw it?"

"His jacket button popped. He had a piece under his belt. Don't know how he expected to get it out of there with his belly hanging over."

chapter six

I check for messages when I'm back in the office, then pass through to the adjacent suite and into my bedroom to wake Gritch up. He comes to slowly, but he doesn't grumble. He washes his face in the bathroom, then gargles with some of my Scope while I give Dan in 1507 a call.

"What's up?" I ask.

"He came back."

"Alone?"

"Just him."

"His sister still at the party?"

"Bunch of them went down half an hour ago. She could've been one of them. What's she look like?"

"Redhead."

"I was watching the guy's door, so I don't know who was in the group."

"Okay," I say. "Gritch is on his way up. You go straight home. I need you back as early as you can make it. Eleven would be good, ten would be better."

"All right, boss," he says. "I'll pack up."

Gritch comes out of the bathroom.

"You okay for a few hours?" I ask.

"Outstanding. I dreamed I had a pocketful of money. All in nickels. Couldn't walk. Quiet night?"

"Mostly. That guy Axelrode got into some kind of dust-up with Buznardo's lawyer down in Olive's. Chased him out of the place."

"You chased him out?"

"No. He chased Neagle out. Bumped one of the servers and hurt her wrist. Ran out on his bar tab."

"I'm telling you," Gritch says, "that guy's a stone shithead."

"Got his bar tab. I'll collect in person."

"I'll sell tickets." Gritch heads out. "Have somebody send up a pot of coffee."

"You got it. I'll see you in about four hours."

I order a pot of coffee sent up to 1507 and a wake-up call for me for 5:00 a.m. I'm not sure I'll be able to sleep, but I'll give it a shot.

My bedroom is connected to the office, but it was once a separate suite. I can get there by passing through what Gritch calls my "private space," or by going one door farther down the hall. My private space is an inner office that rarely gets used. Louis Schurr's old oaken desk takes up most of the room.

On a corkboard above the wooden filing cabinet — also salvaged from Louis's office — is a poster from my last fight. My picture isn't on it. The main event that night was a middleweight championship. I'm at the top of the undercard: "Heavyweights: Joe Grundy vs. Ramón Vanez." Fixed to the bottom of the poster with yellowing Scotch tape is a rough square of paper torn from a magazine. It reads: "By far the best scrap of the night was on the undercard, where dogged old warhorse Joe Grundy prevailed over ungraceful, heavy-punching Ramón Vanez in eight punishing rounds." — *Ring* magazine.

I remember Morley Kline showing the issue to me with some pride. "*Ring*," he said. "We haven't had a mention in *Ring* in three years. You should save this."

I did, but not for the reason he thought. The phrase "dogged old warhorse" landed like a heavy left hand. I was thirty-three. When exactly had I gone from being a "hard-hitting up-and-comer" to a "dogged old warhorse"? I remember holding the magazine and facing a simple truth: I'd gone as far as I was going to. I never put the gloves on again.

I undress and climb into bed. My pillow smells of Gritch's Brylcreem, and I have to get the spare one out of the bottom drawer where I've stashed my Gideon Bible and the .357 I haven't carried in years. Without the pillow hiding them they look forlorn.

The phone beside the bed starts ringing at 3:37, according to my clock radio, and it takes a few seconds before I'm hearing clearly. Something about someone pounding on a door, and then words begin getting through the fog in my head.

"She's yelling or something and pounding."

"What? Who's this?"

"It's Raymond, Joe." Raymond D'Aquino, the night manager.

"What's wrong?"

"Somebody's pounding on 1502. A woman. She's yelling. Woke a bunch of people up."

"Did you call Gritch? He's in 1507."

"No answer, Joe. I let it ring."

"He's probably with her."

"I don't know. I've had two complaints. She's making a big fuss."

"Okay, Ray," I say. "I'll get right up there."

I pull on some pants and a sweatshirt and dial 1507 for myself while I look for my shoes. No answer. No Gritch. Not good.

The quickest way up to fifteen this time of night is via one of the service elevators on the other side of the main kitchen, which is closer than the lobby. I cut down the passageway behind the ballroom and into the kitchen, now dark and quiet for the night. The service elevators are through double swinging doors into the service corridor where the trolleys are parked for the night. One of the trolleys is sticking into the middle of the corridor, and as I barge through the double doors, I bang my shin in the dark, a sharp, stabbing pain that makes me hop on one foot for a second and spin around. And that's when someone hiding in the shadows hits me with something heavy and the world disappears.

I hate coming to. Hate it more than getting knocked out. I was kayoed three times in my boxing career, and I remember well the sick reeling wooziness of regaining consciousness. Blurry moon faces looming over you. People pestering, holding up fingers and demanding you count them. The moon face looming over me this time is the night manager's. Raymond D'Aquino is a worried young man.

"Mr. Grundy? Wake up. Joe? I'll call an ambulance. Should I call an ambulance?"

"What?" I gasp. "Ambulance? What?" Oh, Lord, I'm passing out again. No, I'm going to be sick, need to get on my feet.

"Get me up," I hear my voice say. Part of me is standing in a corner watching me flopping like a fish on the floor of the service corridor. "Get me up."

"Is that a good idea?" Raymond asks. "I don't think you're supposed to move."

"Who the hell told you that? That's a crock. How many fights have you had? Get me up. At least sit me on something."

I hear him scramble around, hear the double doors swing, the lights go on and blind me. I feel as if I'm going to be sick, but instead I manage to roll away from the glare, face down with my forehead on the cool terrazzo floor.

"I got a milk crate."

I hear him coming back from the kitchen and see the red plastic case he sets down beside my head.

"Help me up."

Getting to your feet when you've been knocked out is a matter of pride and vanity and focusing on simple things; palms flat on the floor, right knee, left foot, don't fall sideways. Raymond isn't a big guy, but he's stronger than he looks. A few grunts and one or two curses, and I'm sitting on the overturned milk crate with my back against the wall between two service elevators. I have a hard time focusing, but I see well enough to note the concern on Raymond's face. He's worried about more than my health.

"What happened, Raymond?"

"Oh, shit, Joe. I don't know what's going on. Somebody called the front desk, said you were passed out in the kitchen, then the woman came down from fifteen and started screaming that something's happened to her brother. She's hysterical. Gritch won't answer the phone…"

I get a very bad feeling. Gritch is as reliable as a railway watch. I reach around and ring for a service elevator, and the doors to my left open.

"What should I do about the woman?"

I slide my milk crate backwards into the cab and press fifteen.

"Go back to the front desk. Keep her there. Tell her I'll check things out." I stick out my hand to keep the doors open. "Who called?"

"What?"

"Who told you I was lying in the kitchen?"

"I don't know."

"Man or woman?"

"Man."

"Okay," I say. "Call Margo." The doors close on his

worried face, and I ride up to fifteen sitting on my milk crate with my forehead pressed against a brass panel, grateful for the cold pressure above my eyes, wondering who was worried enough to let Raymond know they had just knocked me out.

The service elevators are on the east side of the building, and it's a long walk around to the central corridor. All the doors are closed, but I hear a few voices from inside a room, guests awakened and unable to get back to sleep. There will be some early checkouts this morning. I'm walking okay. Maybe lurching is a more accurate description. But I'm making progress. I don't know what I look like. I check for blood, but there's nothing sticky around the lump on the back of my head. Merely pain.

Inside 1507 there's no sign of Gritch. Room-service coffee Thermos on the desk, no cup, two newspapers on the floor.

I cross the hall to 1502 and stand for a moment with my head against the wall. I really don't want to go in there. I give one sharp knock for the sake of form and then use my passkey.

And it's as bad as I feared. Jake Buznardo is on his back near the opposite wall. He's wearing the T-shirt he had on earlier; the words *Confound* and *Paradigm* have been obliterated by deep red stains and small dark holes. Five of them. He's dead.

Steadying myself on the back of the couch, I look down to make sure I'm not standing in blood. The Samsonite attaché case is gone, and when I turn my throbbing head, I see that the money on the desk is gone, too.

I back out of the room quietly, close the door, and make sure it's locked. Then I go back inside 1507 and call the police.

"Hello, it's Joe Grundy," I say to the woman who answers, "hotel security at the Lord Douglas. One of our guests has been shot. Dead. Room 1502. Yes, I'll wait right here. Could you tell them not to use their sirens? This all

must have happened an hour ago. Yes, I'm sure he's dead.
Yes. Thank you."

I call the desk and hear Raymond's cautious voice.

"Is that you, Mr. Grundy? What's going on?"

"Where is the woman now, Ray? Still with you?"

"I put her in Mr. Gruber's office."

"Good. Keep her there. Don't say anything for a minute.
I've just called the police, and there should be at least a patrol
unit here in a minute. Send them up to 1507, okay?"

"Police?" He has the presence of mind to whisper the
word. "Why?"

"There's been a shooting, Ray. Did you call Margo?"

"Not yet. I was waiting for word."

"Call her. We have a situation."

"What about the woman?"

"Her name's Molly MacKay. Somebody will have to
tell her that her brother's dead. But wait until the police
show up, okay?"

"Really dead?"

"I'm afraid so, Raymond."

And then I see Gritch because his leg moves and I catch
the movement in the mirror over the desk. He's on the floor
between the bed and the window.

"And, Raymond?" I say. "Call an ambulance, too. I just
found Gritch."

chapter seven

First the uniforms show up. I let them into the suite. Two young men, one tall, one with shoulders like Joe Frazier. They're wearing Kevlar and nine-millimetre Glocks. They tell me to wait in 1507. Gritch is groggy but awake when the paramedics show up a few minutes later. I have to convince them that Gritch isn't the one who's been shot. They seem disappointed. Gritch wants to walk out on his own two feet, but they take him away on a gurney. I tell Gritch I'll be down to see him as soon as I can.

"I think it was the coffee," he says.

After the paramedics leave, I lie back on the bed and feel a sudden stabbing pain when the lump on my head hits the pillow. The smell of Brylcreem. The room starts to waltz. I struggle back to a sitting position as the door opens all the way and a detective comes in, someone I know.

Norman Quincy Weed is moving towards retirement. I met him when I got shot seven years ago. He's a sergeant of detectives now. I guess this case rates one of the big guys.

He's a heavy-set, rumpled man who wears brown shoes with a blue suit and has bad taste in ties, too. He's wearing a wide yellow-and-green-striped job tonight, and I feel a prompt attack of nausea.

"How you doin', Joe?" he asks. "You look like shit. Who hit you?"

I shake my head, which is a mistake. "From behind. Felt like a baseball bat."

"That's what I'd use on a guy your size to keep you from turning around."

"Didn't even hear him. I was in a hurry, banging through the doors down there, and I hit my knee. There was a trolley in the middle of the hall."

I'm sitting on the bed and I pull up my pant leg to have a look. I must have hit something edge-on. There's an abraded welt straight across the shinbone just below the knee.

"Paramedics didn't want to take you in?"

"Yeah, they did. If I feel nauseous or dozy, I'll go. I think I'm okay. Not the first time somebody put my lights out."

"At least you had a fighting chance the other times."

"Not against Holyfield," I say.

"What happened to Gritch? He wasn't drinking, was he?"

"Not a chance. Hasn't had a drink in fourteen years. He'd just had a three-hour nap in the office, and for Gritch that's like hibernation. He thinks there was something in the coffee."

"That pot?"

"Yeah, the cup's on the floor. I didn't touch them."

"Good. What was he doing in here?"

"Watching the door to 1502."

"You were in there?"

"Just long enough to see the man was shot. Didn't touch anything there, either, except the back of the sofa and the doorknob."

"So what about this Buznardo guy?"

"He had money with him. A lot of cash."

"Yeah, I heard. How much cash?"

"Almost two hundred and fifty thousand. All hundreds. Bank wrappers."

I stand and fight my knees to stay that way. "Little holes in him, right?"

"Yeah," Weed says, "five of them. Only one of them came out the back. Popgun — .25, maybe .32. Nothing bigger than that."

"Professional?"

"Bit exuberant for a pro," he says. "But, hey, who knows? Must have had at least one enemy."

"I think you'll find quite a few people who weren't happy with him."

"You were keeping tabs on him?"

"Doing a real fine job," I say, remembering not to shake my head. "I had somebody in here from the time he checked in, keeping an eye on the door. I talked to him a couple of times, over there, and down the hall in the other big suite. He wasn't having a wild celebration considering he was suddenly richer than God. Very quiet, room service for him and his sister, glass of wine with the musicians down the hall. Came back to the room before 1:00 a.m., according to Dan. His sister went out for a while with the band. I don't know when she got back, exactly, but she was pounding on the door at around three."

Weed shakes his head and pulls out a pen and a folded piece of paper. He starts scribbling little notes to himself. "Okay, so who do I have to talk to from this outfit?"

I'm finding it difficult to make my brain work, but Weed is a patient guy. "Dan and Arnie, that's Dan Howard and Arnold McKellar. And Gritch when he wakes up, and the people who were at the party down the hall. I can remember some of them. Washburn is the name of one of the musicians. The sister, Molly MacKay. Let's see, Phil Marsden from room service was in once at least. Maurice the bell captain carried Buznardo's bags. Oh, yeah, his lawyer, Neagle…"

"Alvin Neagle, the legal beagle? My, my."

"Won the case."

"Anybody else?"

"There was a man named Axelrode around for a while. He ran out on his bar tab."

"That's a different squad."

"No, he was up here. He was all over, giving Margo a hard time about security arrangements, nosing around my guys. He was up to something."

"Big guy? Almost as tall as you? Cop moustache, big chest, big gut?"

"He was carrying a gun."

"Was he now? That definitely puts a star next to his name."

"I want to talk to him. Personally."

"If he's involved in this thing, you steer clear," Weed says.

"This is an unrelated matter. He assaulted one of the bar staff."

"File a complaint."

"I'd rather complain in person," I say.

"Anybody else?"

"There's a TV reporter in the hotel. Connie Gagliardi."

"The cute one from Channel 20 with the curly black hair?"

"That's her. She was trying to get an interview. I don't know if she got lucky." All this thinking is making my head hurt. I allow myself a restrained moan. "I've got a lot of explaining to do."

"Hey," Weed says, "you're lucky one of you guys didn't get killed. This was one determined shooter. Drugged your partner, sandbagged you, put five shots into somebody staring straight at him, and got out of the place with a quarter of a million in cash."

"Could have been a team maybe."

"Maybe."

"Seems dumb to me."

"Oh, yeah?"

"I mean, two hundred and fifty thousand is a lot of cash, but this man was worth more than half a billion. And they wouldn't have had to kill him for the suitcase, anyway. He said if somebody wanted it bad enough to steal it, they were welcome to it. I'm serious. He was planning on giving it all away. The whole six hundred million and change."

"And he said that out loud?"

"He made no secret of it."

"I bet some people wouldn't want that to happen."

"I should call Margo, see how she wants to handle things for the hotel. Check on Gritch."

"Listen, don't be an idiot. You've got a concussion. You look like shit. Go see a doctor pretty quick."

"I'm okay," I say. But I'm lying. I feel like he said.

Weed leaves to check on his investigators, and I call down to the front desk. Margo has arrived. I can hear a woman crying in the background.

"Joe? He's really dead?"

"Yes, yes, he's dead, Margo. I'm sorry."

"And Mr. Gritchfield?"

"I think he's fine. It looks like somebody drugged his coffee."

"Or he was drinking."

"No, he wasn't drinking."

"And the money?"

"It's all gone."

"What a mess. Lloyd's going to be so pleased with me. He won't take another vacation for ten more years."

"Margo, it wasn't your fault."

"I don't know about fault, but I sure as hell know it was my responsibility."

"Is there anyone with Molly MacKay?"

"Yes, there's a policewoman sitting with her. What's happening up there?"

"Investigation. They'll take their time. It could be a while before they move the body."

"I've got to go and find rooms for all the guests at that end of fifteen. Some of them want a different hotel, some of them want to be comped for tonight. Call me with any news."

"Will do."

"Oh, Lord, Joe, I completely forgot about you, Raymond says you were knocked out."

"I'm okay."

"You have to see a doctor."

"Soon as they finish with me."

"Promise?"

"Yeah, you bet. I'll get checked out when I go down to Vancouver General to see about Gritch. I'm fine. Really."

All that lying. What a tough guy. I don't feel fine. I have a monster headache. I keep shuffling around 1507, shrugging my shoulders as if I'm throwing shadow punches, scuffing the carpet, building up enough static to give myself a shock when I open the bathroom door. The face in the mirror is looking old this morning. I splash cold water on it and hold a wet washcloth to the back of my head. The lump has topped out at walnut size.

Weed comes back into the room as I'm coming out of the bathroom. "You still look like shit, only now you're wet."

"You move him out yet?"

"Nope. Still taking pictures."

"Want me to have a look? I was in there earlier. I might see something."

"Can you walk?"

"Better than I can lie down."

Weed escorts me down the hall to 1502–1504 and announces our entrance.

"Coming through. Give us a little room. Wounded man here."

Buzz has been covered up.

"There was a Samsonite attaché case behind the couch," I say.

"Nope," Weed says.

"Maybe he moved it into the bedroom."

"Nope."

"It had two hundred and forty thousand dollars in it. And maybe another nine thousand on the desk, give or take. He was handing out hundred-dollar tips. Don't know how many, but they all came from a new stack. They were fanned out right here."

"Also gone," Weed says. "Who knew he had that much cash?"

"Practically everybody."

The door to Jake's bedroom is open. There are cops inside. Uniforms and suits. The room is a shambles, drawers on the floor, mattress overturned, Jake's duffle bag spilled on the box spring, journals and jeans, paperbacks.

"You guys do this?" I ask Weed.

"Nope. Somebody was looking for something."

Weed takes me back to 1507. I take the desk chair, which helps me sit straight.

"I've got to talk to those musicians," Weed says. "What's the name?"

"Redhorn," I say. "Three guys, but there was a room full of people — visitors, other musicians, couple of suits from a record company, a big guy named Bubba, road manager for the group, four or five women. I didn't get the ladies' names, but three of them were singers on Redhorn's latest album."

"CD," he says, as if he's up-to-date on things.

"They played a tune from it, and the three women had their harmonies down like they'd done it before."

"Backup singers?"

"I guess. They could sing."

Weed checks his notebook and releases a long-suffering sigh. "Geez, look at this. Have I got a list or what? At least twenty people roaming around this floor last night that we know about."

"It's a hotel," I say.

"Yeah, well, get your guys lined up so I don't have to go looking for anybody. And anybody else from the hotel — room service, cleaning staff, I don't know what all. You line 'em up and we'll get around to them after I talk to Horndog."

"Redhorn."

"I knew that," he says, walking off down the hall.

I'm about ready to get off this floor. When I get to the elevator, Connie Gagliardi is emerging. Her eyes are bright and she's wearing makeup. The woman with the video camera is still following her. I can't tell if she's wearing makeup; she never takes the camera off her face.

"Ms. Gagliardi?" I say. "I'm Joe Grundy, hotel security. This floor is closed."

"I just want a shot of the hall. Who's in charge?"

"Sergeant Weed. I'm sure he'll talk to you as soon as he knows anything."

The camerawoman is taking my picture. I make a move to straighten my tie, but I'm wearing a damp sweatshirt, so I turn the reflex into a hair-straightening gesture and brush the bump on my head, which should make for a nice picture of a man trying not to wince.

"Can you confirm the identity of the deceased? Jake Buznardo?"

"I suppose I can do that."

"He was shot?"

"Ms. Gagliardi, the police really want to keep this floor clear for a while. If you'll wait downstairs, I'll make sure they talk to you first."

"Mr. Grundy," she says, giving me a twenty-five-watt smile, "I have maybe a fifteen-minute head start on the other channels and you can't guarantee me anything."

Then she spots Weed coming down the hall from the other end, and she and the camera lose interest in me instantly. I figure I'll let Weed deal with it and grab the elevator to the lobby. According to my old Rolex Skyrocket, it's 6:16. I presume that's a.m.

chapter eight

"Joe, I need you," Margo says when I get down. "There's a line of people halfway around the block. I think they're all here for the money. You're going to have to tell them there isn't any."

The uniformed cops at the entrance have been keeping the great unauthorized at bay, but there's grumbling on both sides of the yellow tape when I get outside.

"We'll get the horses down here if it gets any worse," one uniform says. "Some of these guys are starting to get rowdy."

There are about fifty people, mostly men, a lot of them street people, but I can see a few suits and some kids who should be getting ready for school. The sky is still dark. The streets are wet, but it's not raining now, just damp and unfriendly on the sidewalk.

"Hundred-dollar bills in there."

"Shot the fucker."

"I just heard about it."

"Everybody settle down," the uniform in charge says.

"There's no hundred-dollar bills and there's no free money. You just all head on home or wherever you're going. There's nothing to see, nobody's getting inside. I'm serious. Let's start breaking it up, people."

"Not doing nothing, just standing on the sidewalk," someone mutters. "Law against that now?"

Two camera trucks arrive. Channel 20 and Channel 13, competing local news specialists. A few flashes go off. The city papers are represented. I hear my name called and spot a grey fedora with a red feather in the band. A guy named Larry Gormé from the *Emblem* is waving his hat. He's stuck on the edge of the mob. He really wants to talk to me. I give him a shrug and a complicated gesture that I hope conveys regret, a vague promise of personal attention at some unspecified later date, and an urgent need to be elsewhere. More uniforms arrive, and it looks as if things won't get out of hand. It's too damp and chilly for a riot. There's no catalyst, the goose is dead, nothing left but gawking and grumbling. And picture-taking. Won't be the most flattering images taken of the stately Lord Douglas facade.

Inside the lobby we have guest problems. At least ten people are checking out. The quality of the grumbling is more refined in here. It has a self-righteous tone and an undercurrent of recrimination. Someone in the party is a lawyer.

Margo is handling things pretty well, considering. She has Melanie locating other suites in the hotel, other hotels in the area. Raymond D'Aquino is still on duty, hearing complaints, adjusting bills. Lorraine, the hotel operator, is handling calls with her usual aplomb.

In Lloyd Gruber's office, Margo takes a moment to look me up and down. "Can you shower? Can you put on a suit?"

"Right away. I'll be back in ten minutes."

"The police won't let people check out until they've been questioned. Not just the people on fifteen, but anybody who's checking out. And the cleaning staff want to get home, but they're taking names, asking questions."

"They have to."

"Can you just put on a suit and take over some of that."

"I'll be back in ten minutes."

"Joe?" She looks worried. "Did we do it? Somebody from the hotel? Please God say it wasn't somebody on staff."

"I'll find out, Margo."

"First put on a suit." Then she slaps her forehead. "What am I thinking about? Go see a doctor. Immediately. You could have a concussion. You could suddenly fall over."

I take Margo's advice about the shower and the suit and I don't fall over during either procedure. I'm even managing to tie a decent knot in my best tie when Dan comes in looking shaky, not well rested at all. He glances around as if expecting to see a bunch of cops.

"They drag you out of bed?" I ask.

"Seven-thirty. Pounding on the door." He looks around. "Just you?"

"Gritch is in the hospital. He's going to be okay. You already talk to Weed?"

"Weed, his partner, big-haired pain in the ass. He thinks I did it."

"That's just cops. They think everybody did it until they're sure who did do it."

"Yeah, well, they're pretty sure I did it. Told me to sit tight in here. They'd get back to me. They like me for it."

"Because of the gambling debts?"

He stares at me, sighs deeply, scratches himself, then studies the corner where the walls and ceiling meet in shadow. "Well, yeah, sure, because of the gambling debts, like I owe Randall Poy about eighteen thousand plus the interest, which compounds, like, hourly, and he's already threatening my knees, and I could definitely use a suitcase full of cash right now."

"What colour suitcase?"

"What?"

"What colour was the suitcase with the money in it?"

"How should I know?"

"So you told Weed you didn't take it?"

"Yeah, I told him, but I don't think he believed me, and his big lard-ass partner with the Elvis hairdo sure as shit doesn't believe me, and I can't say I blame them, except when they get around to checking things out they'll come up dry because I still owe Randall Poy eighteen K and counting and he's going to break a kneecap for me on Wednesday if I don't make a substantial payment, which I'd be inclined to do if I had some cash to avoid getting a kneecap busted, which doesn't sound like a lotta laughs."

He looks disgusted and scared — with himself and of Randall Poy, I'm guessing.

"Want me to talk to Randall?" I ask him.

"What could you do, boss? Randall's just a businessman doing business. That's how he does business. I know the rules. Shit, I should. I've been trying to bend them all my life."

"I could talk to him about a schedule of payments."

"Won't work, boss. You know how it is. The only way out is forward. I can't pay him back in installments. I couldn't even keep up with the vig that way. I need a score. A trifecta, aces over kings and everybody calls, a small miracle."

"How much is the vig for Wednesday?"

"I can keep my knee for five K."

"I can maybe work something out for Wednesday."

He looks at me, and I can see he's grateful but still disgusted with himself, and still scared. "You think? Buy me a week. Something might turn up."

I pull my chair up closer to my side of the desk and lean across the blotter pad to get as close to him as I can. "Okay, we'll work it out somehow, but you're going to have to tell me some stuff you don't want to tell me and probably didn't tell Weed and his partner."

"Like what stuff?"

"Like about the other apartment."

"What other apartment?"

"The one on East Sixth."

"My mother's place? I pay half the rent."

"Dan, your *mother* has been phoning your wife, complaining about the rent situation and asking her if she has a new refrigerator and if she has her own car. Your *mother* and your wife have been getting real chummy on the phone, talking about Bangkok and how to get citizenship papers and which one of them should dump you first."

Dan looks back up at his favourite corner in the room and shakes his head. "Aw, shit, she got so demanding."

"The thing is, Dan, when Weed finds out about the apartment on East Sixth, and he's going to, because he's a good cop, and if he doesn't, then I'll be telling him because I have to, then he's going to go over there and meet the woman. What's her name?"

"Prana."

"He's going to meet Prana and find out she isn't your mother, that she isn't a legal resident, and that's she been nagging you for a car and a new refrigerator. All of that's going to give them a whole new set of ideas of where the money is, or where it went."

"They won't find it there, either, and they won't find a new refrigerator or a new car, and if they throw her out of the country, they'll probably be doing me a big favour because she's not the same woman I brought over."

He pushes back his chair, stretches his legs, and puts his hands behind his neck. "They change so fast. Couldn't do enough for me. Cooked me special meals, did stuff. You don't need to know that angle, but I'm telling you, that woman could do stuff, not anymore but back then. Now all she does is complain because I'm not as rich as she thought I was."

"Probably not a smart move trying to keep two households going on what you make."

"Two years ago I was rolling in it. I was ahead fifty thousand. People owed *me* money. That's when I took my trip to the Orient to check out the action. I told Doris.

What'd she care? I gave her a pocketful of dough. I'm not cheap, Joe. When I have it, I spend it."

He gets up and goes to the window that looks out on the back street and across at Connor's Diner and the Scientology Reading Room. "What goes up must yada yada, as they say. She's like I brought bad luck back with me from Thailand. Two months after I get Prana set up on East Sixth, I'm scrambling to make my nut and getting deeper and deeper into Randall Poy." He turns to look at me. "If I had the guts, Joe, I would have hit the Buznardo kid for some cash, but I know my luck too well. I know when I'm on a roll and when I can't catch a card to save my ass. I'd never get away with it. You know it and I know it. I'm not smart enough or cool enough. Not even desperate enough, come right down to it. I've been here before. I'll dodge this bus. I always do." He sits back down and rubs his face. "That's a pisser about Prana and Doris being in touch with each other. She's a cool one that Doris, I tell you."

"She loves you, Dan."

"Weird, eh?"

chapter nine

I keep a personal stash in the hotel safe. It builds up. I don't have a lot of expenses. I put three thousand in cash in a hotel envelope. I'll have to liquidate a few of my accumulated paycheques to get more, but I figure it can wait a day at least. I'm sure Randall Poy will be reasonable.

I'm on my way to the hospital with good intentions, but I really need a cup of coffee and an order of toast. I interpret feeling hungry as a positive sign that I'm not about to drop dead from my injury. Molly MacKay is in the Lobby Café, sitting at the counter and dipping a tea bag up and down in the metal pot. She glances up as I come through the lobby door and watches me without a hint of recognition as I approach.

"Ms. MacKay?" I say. "We met last night. I'm Joe Grundy."

"I remember. You were warning Jake about the dangerous people in the world."

"I suppose you've had to tell the police about last night so many times you're fed up."

"I'm just tired, Mr. Grundy, and I'm waiting until I can get my little suitcase and go home."

"Where's home?"

"Roberts Creek on the Sunshine Coast."

"I know it. It's on the way to Sechelt. You've got a ferry ride ahead of you. Do you have a car?"

"I took the bus. There's one at noon, if they'll let me leave."

"I'll talk to the detective in charge. He's not a bad guy."

"Thank you."

Hattie brings me toast and coffee and withdraws just far enough to be polite. The toast is great. Heavy with butter, crunchy around the edges, just what I need. I try not to talk with my mouth full. "Could you fill me in a little bit on what happened after I left the party?" I ask.

"More music. Then some of the record executives started talking about going somewhere to hear a group that was playing. Jake — I always called Buzz Jake — decided he'd had enough for one day, but told me to go along."

"About what time was that?"

"After midnight, I guess, getting on to one o'clock. Anyway, I went, and it was fun. The drummer made a pass at me, but he wasn't the guy I was interested in. I kind of liked that big roadie guy, Bubba, but he disappeared. I didn't get back until after two and the room was locked. Jake wouldn't wake up, so I got scared and went down to the front desk."

"Jake didn't give you a key?"

"He meant to. We left in a hurry. I was having such a good…" She pours tea from the metal pot into her cup and has a sip. "He was too good for this world."

"Your brother?"

"He wasn't a saint, you know. I mean, he did things when he was younger — sold weed, that kind of thing. But he was always … sweet. Sweet-natured. Generous. Shirt off his back. That kind of person. And generous with himself.

Always time to listen to your story or help you fix whatever needed to be fixed. Never in a hurry. Why do you think that rich man left him all his money? He wasn't a stupid man. He wasn't someone who could be conned. He left the money to Jake because he saw the goodness in him."

"How did they meet?"

"An accident, really. Prescott had a lodge on Harrison Lake. He'd pretty much moved there after he found out. And Jake was just travelling, on the road."

"After he found out what?"

"Parker Prescott was dying. He had some kind of inoperable cancer or something, and they'd given him a year or so to live. Jake stayed with him."

"For a year?"

"Five years. Jake got him an extra five years."

"How?"

"Diet, meditation, exercise. I don't know the details. Jake was into alternative medicine, herbs and like that. But mostly he was into peace of mind, meditation. He took Prescott on canoe trips, camping trips, got him out under the sky where he could think and feel and start to understand what was coming. Jake said that at the beginning Parker was really angry about everything, but by the time he started to go he was at peace."

"He must have been very grateful to Jake to give him so much."

"He loved Jake. He made him his son. Adopted him legally. That's why the will couldn't be broken. He made Jake his legitimate heir."

"I want you to know, Ms. MacKay, that I'm very sorry about what happened."

"You couldn't have done anything. You saw what he was like. He wouldn't carry an umbrella. He believed in karma and taking what came along. It wasn't your fault."

"Somebody's to blame."

"Jake would say, 'That's their karma. They'll have to deal with it.'"

"Well," I say, "I'll be poking around, seeing what I can find out. After all, I didn't do my job very well last night."

She glances at the clock on the wall. "Do you think you could talk to your cop friend about me getting home?"

Nodding, I go off to look for Weed and find him talking to a couple of his detectives on the mezzanine landing.

"Like to talk to one of your boys again," he says. "Dan Howard. Found out he's got a serious gambling debt with one of our more efficient money changers."

"Talk to him," I say. "I told him to come clean."

"You heard from the other one — McKellar?"

I shake my head. "He's usually late, but he's really late today."

"I know he is," Weed says.

"I can't see Arnie McKellar involved in anything requiring more than a knife and fork."

"His estranged wife hasn't seen him, and his girlfriend doesn't know where he is. That makes him missing. Puts him at the top of my list."

I remember why I sought Weed out. "Molly MacKay's wondering if she can go home."

"What?" he says, distracted, checking a list of interviews that will take most of the day. "Yeah, she can take off. Her suitcase is in the lobby. We've got her address and phone number."

"You satisfied she was where she said she was?"

"Oh, yeah, they cut a wide swath through the clubs late last night. That Redstone bunch attracts a lot of attention."

"Redhorn."

He smiles. "That's what I said."

"So she can go?"

"I told her she should get some protection."

"What for? Oh…" The apprentice sleuth has grasped one more obvious element. "Now it's hers."

"She may have a claim, that's for sure. Could make her life interesting."

I fetch Molly MacKay's suitcase and escort her and the bag outside to the first cab in line, negotiating through the small knot of reporters still hanging around. Andrew has the cab door open when we get there. He takes the case from me and walks it around to the other side of the taxi. The reporters crowd around, and the cabdriver, Maxine, gets halfway out.

"Keep your hands off the vehicle," she tells the mob. "People trying to earn a living here." She turns to look me over. "Got knocked out again, eh, Grundy?"

"Story of my life. You camp out here all night?"

"My cab. I can run it 24/7 if I feel like it. Anyway, more action here." She grabs my chin and turns my head gently to study the bump. "Now that's seriously gross. You okay?"

"I'll live." I point at Molly. "I think she's going to the bus station."

"Six blocks, whoopee!" Maxine says. She opens her door, and I come around to her side.

"Hey, Max," I say. "Remember that fare you got about eleven-thirty last night? Woman, forties maybe. Very classy."

"I get better tips from winos. Rich people are cheap."

"Remember where you took her?"

"Sure. Shaughnessy. Where else?" She gets behind the wheel. "Watch your back, Grundy."

"Too late," I say.

Molly doesn't look up as they drive away.

The reporters shout a few questions at the departing taxi. I can't believe they expect the cab to stop and Molly to give them an interview. I'm not sure what they're hoping for at this stage of the game. The big story was all filed before 8:00 a.m., and the smart scribes went off looking for representatives of the Prescott Corporation. As Grundy, ace hotel dick, enters his place of business, he mulls over the crux of the matter. There's more than half a billion dollars up for grabs again.

The hotel hasn't quite settled back to its regular rhythm. The staff is maintaining, the guests are wary, their conversations hushed, there's a hum. Andrew the doorman is deigning to exchange whispered words with Maurice the bell captain. That they are talking at all when they can't abide each other under normal circumstances is a clear indication that things are unbalanced.

I walk back to the kitchen to have a look at the room-service order book. When I ordered coffee for Gritch last night, it was handled by Wallace O'Ree at 1:48 a.m. Wallace is at home, and I have to call him there, but he doesn't mind.

"Hi, Mr. Grundy," he says. "No, I'm just looking at a catalogue. Trying to decide do I really need a Shop-Vac or not. Sure would come in handy." Wallace makes clocks out of wood.

"Have the police talked to you yet, Wallace?"

"Just on the phone. They said somebody'd be around later."

"I need to know something about one of your last orders last night. A pot of coffee for Gritch in 1507. It was after one-thirty."

"Oh, sure. I didn't take it up."

"Who did?"

"Phil Marsden. He said he'd take the coffee up to Gritch. That was fine by me. I was ready to go home."

"Phil Marsden took the coffee up?"

"Sure did. That's what I told the policeman on the phone."

chapter ten

The doctor is a nice young man from Bombay named
Ganesh. He says he thinks I'll live. I'm not puking, I'm not
seeing double, my pupils look normal, and I can stand on one
foot without falling over, which apparently is a good sign.

Gritch is in a bed in the hallway on the fifth floor.

"Who's minding the store?"

"Half of Vancouver's finest," I say. "They making up
your bed?"

"I don't even rate a room, that's how critical I am.
There are guys in here with life-threatening injuries — I'm
causing traffic problems in the hallway."

He looks okay to me. "They pump you out?"

"Nah. How you doing?"

"Got one helluva headache," I say. "You?"

"Feh. Best sleep I've had in months. I can get you a pill.
I've got pull with the nurse. He likes me."

"It's easing up."

"Weed says you got sandbagged."

"I should be so lucky. This was hard. And cold. Weed was here?"

"Oh, yeah. That old hound is all over this one. Let me see it." I turn around, and he checks the back of my head without touching it. "Lucky you're walking."

"What about you?" I ask. "They know what was in the coffee?"

"Maybe. They aren't telling me. I figure it was sleeping pills. I didn't fall down. I just thought I'd put my feet up for a minute. That's all I remember."

"I can't figure it," I say. "Somebody going in to shoot Buznardo, why go to all the trouble to drug you first? Why not shoot you, too?"

"Thanks for the thought."

"Why so subtle dealing with you and then blow Buzz away and hit me with a brick?"

"Doesn't look like brickwork to me. More like a baseball bat."

"Point is, we've got three different approaches to the robbery. With you we get subtle, then we get what looks like a cold-blooded killing, and then I get mugged."

"You were the fly in the ointment."

"And then whoever put me down calls the front desk to tell Raymond I'm passed out by the service elevators."

"That was kind."

I probe the bump on the back of my head. "But it's too kind. I just filled a guy full of holes and then I give a damn about some guy I just knocked out? It's like he cares about the hotel employees but didn't care for Buzz at all."

"Sounds like two guys."

"That's what I think," I say. "Who delivered the coffee?"

"Nobody."

"What?"

"I mean it, nobody. I've got the door half open, got a good angle on both doors to the suite, I'm reading the newspaper, a *Seattle Post* I grabbed at the newsstand, and I hear a tray hit the back of the door."

"No knock? No announcement?"

"No. Just that. I recognize the sound, the spoon clattering in the saucer. I know it's my coffee. I figure maybe you brought it up and went off to check something else. Anyway, after a minute, I go out in the hall and collect the tray and have a cup."

"It tasted all right?"

"You know me. I don't like coffee. I just drink it for the caffeine and to keep from drinking anything else. Three sugars, lots of cream. You could hide Listerine in there and I'd never notice."

"How long did it take you to pass out?"

"Couldn't tell you. I guess after the second cup I thought I'd put my feet up and watch the other door through the mirror. Then I thought it would be okay if I just kicked my shoes off and lay my head down for a bit. And that was it."

"You were on the floor when I found you."

"I think I tried to get up after a while. An alarm went off in my head, and I tried to get up."

Just then a burly male nurse with a broken nose and kind eyes comes along and starts checking Gritch over.

"Stick around a few minutes, Joe. I think I'm getting outta here."

"Yeah, we've had about as much of you as we can stand," the nurse says. He glances at me. "You look like you could've used a night in a hospital bed, too."

"I had things to do," I say.

"Mister Tough Guy," Gritch says. "Wonder you don't have permanent brain damage, all the hits you took."

"Who says I don't have permanent brain damage?"

Gritch and I leave the hospital and climb into the hotel car I appropriated. It's nothing fancy, just a sedan we keep around for emergencies and errands. The streets are clean and shiny after last night's rain. At a stoplight Gritch jumps out and gets a newspaper from the corner box. The tabloid *Emblem* has already hit the street with an extra. I bet they had a good time being a newspaper for a change. The front page is suitably garish: HIPPIE BILLIONAIRE SLAIN IN HOTEL ROOM. I spot Larry Gormé's byline. There's a colour insert of Buzz's bagged body being loaded into the back of an ambulance over a half-page image of our very own Lord Douglas Hotel with a red X marking the suite where it happened. They've missed it by four windows.

"I've got a couple of errands to run," I say. "Want me to take you home? The Douglas?"

"I'll hang with you," he says. "Where we going?"

"Chinatown."

Randall Poy is about five feet, three inches tall and weighs around 124 pounds. He doesn't wear lifts or heels. He does wear Hong Kong silk suits tending towards the electric end of the spectrum and Italian shoes to match. Randall is rumoured to hold black belts in several lethal martial arts forms, but I doubt that he troubles himself to do his own crippling these days. For that he has the brothers Chow, Marlon and Mikey, who don't bother with Tai Chi Chuan niceties. Both are bonecrushers with anaconda arms and shoulders like oxbows.

Poy isn't hard to find. He doesn't insulate himself from his clientele. Randall presides in the rosy backroom of the Noodle Palace on Alberni Street. He parks his blood-red Ferrari in the lane just outside the rear entrance. One of the Chow cousins, slightly smaller than Marlon and Mikey, has the job of guarding the vehicle. It's a ceremonial position. No one would dare leave fingerprints on Randall's fender. The Ferrari never moves. Randall has failed his driver's test nine times. There are some things money can't buy.

The main dining room of the Noodle Palace is loud with the clatter of bowls and cups and enthusiastic diners, predominantly Chinese. The walls are decorated with menus as long as scrolls, the calligraphy like action paintings. The backroom is another world. There's no evidence of food. Seven television sets carry satellite broadcasts of most of the sporting action currently taking place in North America. Randall has three cell phones, a BlackBerry, and a MacBook on the table. He's plugged in.

Marlon and Mikey sit at an adjacent table, close enough to empty Randall's ashtray and refill his teacup.

"Mr. Joe Grundy. Good morning, good morning. I hear you got knocked out again."

"That's right, Randall."

"You should learn to keep up your left. That's how Holyfield took off your head."

"I was done with the body shot he started with," I say. "His last two punches were a formality."

"People lost money on you."

"Sometimes people don't think things through."

"I didn't lose money. I never bet on a white heavyweight."

"History will back you up."

"What can I do for you? You like football?"

"I don't gamble."

"Need money?"

"I'm here to give you some money."

"Why?"

"Dan Howard works for me. He says he owes you eighteen thousand dollars. He says you want five thousand this week or you'll hurt him."

"I would never do that."

Mikey and Marlon almost smile.

"I'm glad to hear that. I don't like things happening to my people."

"Your people shouldn't lose so much money when they can't pay their bills."

"I won't argue with you there, Randall. Dan's made some bad decisions lately. I'm hoping he'll straighten himself out."

"How much money are you giving me?"

"I have three thousand dollars in my pocket. I can get you another two thousand by, let's say, tomorrow before lunch. That should square him for a week. After that you and I can work something out on the balance."

"Balances keep going up, Joe Grundy. There's interest."

"I know, Randall. That's why I'm hoping you can ease back on the implied threat of physical injury for a couple of weeks until I can help Dan get his affairs in order."

"Maybe his Thai girlfriend should get a job."

"That's for her to decide, I guess. I'm mostly concerned with keeping Dan from getting himself damaged before he has an opportunity to sort our his personal problems."

Randall thinks it over for a minute. Marlon and Mikey watch the stock market crawl on one of the television sets. Mikey is pushing one flat palm against the other under the table overhang. Dynamic tension. I think his right hand is winning.

"Okay, Joe Grundy," Randall says. "Three thousand now, and two thousand tomorrow morning, okay?"

I put the envelope on the table in front of him. He glares at me as if I've just urinated on his Ferrari's Michelins. He says something to Marlon, who sweeps up the envelope with his left hand and pockets it inside his leather jacket. I get a brief glimpse of a shoulder rig. Marlon relies on more than dynamic tension. Also, Marlon is a southpaw.

"Thank you," I say. "I'll make sure you get the other two thousand before noon tomorrow. And I'll keep you informed on how Dan is going to straighten things out."

"You his broker now?"

"No, Randall, I'm his boss. He works for me. I need him to keep working."

"I don't think people will go to your hotel anymore if they're going to get murdered."

Randall laughs with genuine glee. Marlon and Mikey almost smile again. They're having fun. I have other things to do with my day.

"Okay then," I say. "I'll see you tomorrow."

"That's not necessary. Somebody will come around to see you." He looks directly at me, gaze unwavering, a smile twitching the corner of his mouth.

"I prefer not to conduct personal business inside the hotel. I'll come to see you."

"Okay, but don't be late."

"Randall," I say in my most reasonable tone, "I know you're a businessman, so let's keep this businesslike. I'll make another payment. You have my word on that. I'll make sure Dan applies himself to the problem of getting square with you, and I'll stay in touch until things get sorted out."

I move a step closer to Randall's table. I can hear and feel both Mikey and Marlon gathering their feet under them, but I keep my eyes off them. I look at Randall instead. "Until this matter's cleared up, I'd appreciate it if the people who work for you don't make life difficult for the people who work for me."

"Who wants to make life difficult?" Randall says.

"Good. Then we have an agreement?"

"Have a nice day, Joe Grundy. Learn to keep up your left hand."

"Always good advice." I nod to Randall, then glance at the Chow brothers, who are both watching me. They seem hungry. I wonder if they're allowed to eat their noodles in here.

Gritch isn't in the car. He's dodging traffic, coming back from the convenience store across the street where's he's replenished his supply of cigars.

"How's Randall doing?" he asks.

"I made his day."

"Best noodles in Chinatown," he says. "Steve Gorman and I used to come here, before your time, back when you could eat in the backroom."

"You hungry?"

"Not for noodles. What's next?"

"Have to see a man about a bar tab."

chapter eleven

Our next stop is a seven-storey purple stone office building propping up the corner of Dunsmuir and Hamilton. The cornerstone says it was inflicted upon the city in 1907. I know for a fact that it's been slated for demolition for fifteen years, but the heart of the city keeps shifting and the price of the corner lot remains higher than anyone can be persuaded it's worth. There's only one operational elevator, the other having been sealed and abandoned years ago.

AxeHandle Securities is listed on the lobby directory as having offices on the third floor. I haul my bulk up the two flights, figuring the exercise might loosen me up for any encounter, but when I get there, 303 is locked up tight. Through the pebbled glass I see a heavy accumulation of mail building up on the carpet inside the office door.

I trudge back down to the lobby where Gritch is waiting. "Nobody home," I tell him. "Doesn't look like he's been there for a while."

Gritch points at the directory. "You see who else lives here?"

Alvin Neagle, Barrister & Solicitor, occupies suite 512.

"If we can take the elevator, I'll come with you," he says.

A woman carrying a cardboard box is heading our way as we walk down the fifth-floor hallway. I figure she probably came from 512 because the door is open and I can see Alvin Neagle standing in the outer office filling another cardboard box. Gritch lingers behind to help the woman with her cargo.

"I don't suppose that second elevator has ever worked," he says.

"Oh, it did," she says, "for the first year we were here, but not since then."

The door slides open and he takes the box from her.

"Oh, thank you."

"Moving office?" he asks.

"Oh, it's wonderful," I hear her say as the elevator door closes, "broadloom, air conditioning, a wonderful view."

I head for Neagle's office. "Mr. Neagle?"

"You'll have to make an appointment with my secretary. As you can see, I'm moving today."

"Oh, really? Where are you going to be located?"

He looks up. "Do I know you?"

"Joe Grundy," I say, sticking out my hand. "Hotel security at the Lord Douglas. We met the day before yesterday when you came out of Jake Buznardo's suite."

"Oh, yeah." He shakes my hand without enthusiasm.

"I'm not surprised you don't remember me. You must have been busy."

"I've already spoken to the cops. They were here this morning."

"They've been busy, too," I say. "I guess you couldn't help them very much."

"I didn't see it happen, if that's what you mean." He does a clumsy but secure tape job on the box he just filled, then glances up at me.

"Did Mr. Axelrode manage to catch up to you last night?"

"What?"

"I understand you got into an argument with Jeff Axelrode in the bar last night and that he chased you down the street."

"Who told you that?"

"I have a number of witnesses. Five altogether."

"And what's it got to do with you?"

"A few things. Axelrode ran out on a bar tab. But then, technically, so did you. And he injured one of the servers, who may very well charge him with assault. I'd like to get the matter straightened out, but his office is locked up and it doesn't look as though he's been there for some time."

"Yeah, well, I don't know where he is."

"Mind telling me what your connection is to him?"

"I don't see that it's any of your business."

"I suppose the police have been asking you the same thing."

"Look, I hired Jeff Axelrode to keep Buzz in line. Keep track of him, get him into court on time, like that. I never knew where Buzz was going to be. You can see what a pain in the ass that was. One time we had to drag him out of a rodeo in Big Creek. Then Buzz said no more, said he didn't want Axelrode around. The big dork said something rude to Buzz's sister or something. Anyway, I told Axe to stay out of sight. He was still on the job, just supposed to keep a low profile. He kept a low profile all right. Guy's as subtle as a beer fart."

"He told our acting manager he represented Prescott Holdings."

"You know what private dicks are like, no offence. They'll say whatever they have to say. He was working for me."

"What was your fight about?"

"It wasn't a fight. Expense money, whatever. There's Buzz throwing around hundred-dollar bills, and Axe gets pissed off because I can't give him walking-around money."

"You got any idea where he is now?"

"No. And, frankly, I don't want to know. Right now the more he stays away from me the better I like it."

"Will you be handling Buznardo's estate?"

Neagle makes himself busy, yanking and slamming filing cabinet drawers. "He died intestate. I'm looking at two, three years' work to collect my fee."

The woman returns from her elevator ride. "Mr. Neagle, my car's almost full."

"Right, right," he says, "take this one and get them over there."

She lifts the box that Neagle just sealed and heads back down the hall. Gritch is waiting for her by the elevators.

"I'm sure you'll get paid," I say. "Buznardo's estate will have to go through probate, won't it? Will you be handling that?"

He grabs another cardboard box, puts it on his desk, and begins filling it with law books. "Look, Grundy, is it? I've got a lot on my mind right now. I've got a shitstorm of writs coming down on me, I've got cops crawling all over me, I've got a dead client who left his affairs in a mess, and unless you have some legal status or a subpoena or something, I'd appreciate it if you'd bugger off."

"Okay then," I say. "Maybe we can talk again after you get resettled."

When I get back to the street, Gritch is waving goodbye to the woman as she drives away. He comes back to the car lighting a fresh cigar. "You find out where Neagle's moving to?"

"Nope," I say.

He smirks and puffs. "I did."

We get in the car and I fire up the engine. "Well?"

"You'll love this. The legal beagle's moving into the Horizon Building."

"I should know where that is?"

"It's where Edwin Gowins hangs out."

"And he is…?"

Gritch looks at me as if I'm a moron. "He's one of the head snakes, slugger. You're going to need a crash course in how the Prescott empire was set up."

"I don't care about the Prescott empire," I say. "I want to collect a $16.45 bar tab."

chapter twelve

Back at the hotel, I have visitors. Both brothers. Lenny and Theo. Lenny is with Margo in Lloyd Gruber's office. I can see him through the glass partition giving her a hard time. Theo is in the lobby, pacing around the big rug. Theo is the larger of the two brothers, overweight the way rich people are overweight, with good tailoring and no wrinkles. He always looks as if he's just had a trim and gives off the faint scent of an expensive barbershop.

"Grundy," he says when he sees me coming in, "what the hell happened?"

"Guest got shot last night, Mr. Alexander. You probably read about it." I hold out the newspaper.

"I've seen that piece-of-shit rag," he says. "I mean, weren't you supposed to be looking after that guy?"

"Not exactly. I wasn't his bodyguard. I tried to keep an eye on his money —"

"And you blew that one, didn't you?"

"Yes, sir, someone robbed him."

"And shot him."

"And shot him, too."

Then the other brother, Lenny, comes stalking out of Margo's office. The tough one of the pair, he's a bit short, wears leather jackets, swings his shoulders a lot as if he's loosening up for a fight. He smells of Brut.

"Hey, Grundy, you really blew it this time, didn't you?"

Not much point in arguing.

"I guess so, sir."

"You guess so. If you didn't have the old man on your side, I'd fire your ass out of here so quick your eyes would water."

"Yes, sir."

"Do one thing," Theo says. "Make damn sure none of the hotel staff was involved in the shooting. If this was an outside job, that's one thing, but if we have a murderer on staff here, we might as well close the place down."

"That I can do, Mr. Alexander. I'm sure no one here was involved in the shooting."

"Prove it," Theo says, "to everybody's satisfaction. Old man or no old man, you're hanging by a thread here, Grundy."

With that said the two brothers depart the lobby, staying as far away from each other as they can and exiting by separate doors. They leave me standing in the middle of the big carpet feeling my arms hanging down, fighting the impulse to curl my fingers into cudgels, digesting my medicine, not sure which of the two brothers I'd enjoy dropping more. Probably Lenny.

After a minute, Gritch comes up to me from wherever he disappeared to. "Arnie hasn't shown."

"Keeps getting better and better," I say. "How about Dan?"

"The cops let him go home."

"You should go home, too."

"Yeah, yeah, and miss all the action? I paid for my ticket. What did the brothers want?"

"Make sure I knew I blew it."

"I guess they told you."

"Sure did."

"Straighten up and fly right."

I start walking towards the office. "Mostly, make sure nobody from here pulled the trigger."

"Any question of that?"

"If somebody brought you coffee filled with sleeping pills, that would have to be one of us, don't you think? Who else knew you were getting coffee? Who knew where you were?"

"Who's first on the list?"

"Phil Marsden."

The cops have already gotten to Phil Marsden, and he's fed up. We track him down outside the main kitchen and take him into one of the pantries to talk, and he isn't happy about that, either.

"If I'd known how much trouble that little shit was going to be, I would have told him to shove his hundred-dollar tip the first time. You think I haven't had a hundred-dollar tip before? I haven't served some rich people before? I looked after Bette Midler last time she was here. I took care of Pavarotti, for Christ's sake. I've had so many hundred-dollar tips, better than hundred-dollar tips. I'm not impressed by hundred-dollar bills."

"Even a suitcase full?" I ask.

"I never saw the damn suitcase. All I saw was a bunch of C-notes fanned out on the bureau. I don't know anything about any suitcase. To hear the cop's version I'm in there like Al Capone blasting away in the middle of the night."

"Okay, calm down a second. I need to know what happened at the end of your shift. You had a Thermos of coffee for 1507, for Gritch, right?"

"Right."

"What did you do with that?"

"I gave it to Arnie."

"Arnie?" I say. "What was Arnie doing here? He went home around ten."

"He was in the hallway on fifteen when I went up."

"What the hell's Arnie doing in the hallway at one-thirty in the morning?" Gritch demands.

"How should I know?" Phil says. "Scrounging leftovers off room-service trays. He gives me the creeps."

"So you gave him the coffee and then you went home?" I ask.

"When I get up there, Arnie's in the hallway. He says, 'Who's the coffee for?' I say it's for Gritch. He says he'll take it. He wants to talk to Gritch. I say okay, but I still have to get that room-service thing from Buznardo. He says Buznardo's in the other suite with the musicians. So I go there and Buznardo's nice as pie and they drag me inside for a few minutes."

"Had a beer?" Gritch asks.

"Yeah, I had a beer, so what? Big biker dude practically forced it on me. So, anyway, after that they're all deciding who's going where, and he, the guy, says he's going to take a pass, long day, yada yada, have a nice time, and he walks me back down the hall to the other suite."

"Arnie still around?"

"Long gone unless he was in talking to you."

"Nope," Gritch says.

"Anyway," Phil continues, after a sigh of the deeply put upon, "the guy goes inside, comes out with the signed tab, says he'll have to tip me tomorrow. He must have given his loose cash to his sister or something. I say that's cool, some other time, and get the elevator and go back down. Ten minutes later I'm on my way home."

"No, you're not," Gritch says. "You went to play poker in the chlorine casino off the laundry room."

"For an hour maybe. It's just a little friendly game."

"I know about your Monday night poker game, Phil," I say. "And the Friday night one, too. Did you tell the police?"

"No."

"You told them you went straight home?"

"It was just an hour or so."

"It was just a lie to the police, which they don't like because it makes them have to check things all over again. They're questioning everybody who was working last night. Pretty soon they'll get around to the night cleaning staff and one of them will say, 'Yeah, we were playing our regular little Monday night poker game in the laundry room kitchen.' And the cops will say, 'Who all was there?' Then your name will get mentioned and they'll be all over you again."

"But I didn't do anything."

"See, I'm on your side and I'm making you sweat."

Gritch says, "The cops will take you downtown and make you sit in a room by yourself for an hour, and pretty soon you'll be telling them about more than poker. They'll hear about the escort service you're affiliated with and the two women you ushered up to 903 around midnight."

"Hippie high-rolling asshole," Phil says. "If I'd known how much trouble that skinny little shithead —"

"We heard that already, Phil," I say. "What you do now is find Weed, or one of his detectives, and tell him about the poker game. Then tell him you told me all about it."

"And maybe they won't roast your ass," Gritch says.

Phil goes off in a hurry to search for Weed.

That leaves us with Arnie, who hasn't been seen since last night and was supposed to come in at nine. It's eleven-thirty now. I figure the cops must have picked him up and taken him to the station for questioning. They aren't about to let him roam free for that long unless he's on the run and they're chasing him.

Back in my office, I call Arnie's place and talk to his girlfriend, Janine. Arnie has been separated for three years, but he isn't divorced yet.

"Janine? It's Joe Grundy. How are you?"

"How am I? You want to know how I am? I've had the police here since nine-thirty this morning. They had a search warrant. They practically tore the house apart looking for something. I'm sitting in the middle of this disaster area. It looks like a hurricane went through here. What gives them the right to just throw things any which way they please and never offer to pick anything up?"

"Where's Arnie, Janine?" I look over at Gritch. He's grabbing the end of his tie and pretending to hang himself.

"I don't know. I gave the cops every place I could think of — the hotel, his mother's place in Duncan. What did he do? What's going on? The news said there was a shooting. Jesus Christ, did he shoot somebody?"

"We're just trying to find him, Janine, and make sure he's okay."

"Will you call me when you find him?"

"Of course. And if he calls you, tell him to get in touch right away."

"That's what the head cop said. He left a card. Sergeant Weed."

"I know him. He's a good man."

"Joe, did Arnie do something bad?"

"I don't know what happened, Janine. I really don't. I'll make sure he calls you."

Janine is a small woman. I can see her sitting in the middle of the chaos left behind by the cops searching their home, wondering where to start cleaning, wondering what's happened.

"Arnie's taken off," I tell Gritch.

"Shit," Gritch says. "There goes my shift rotation."

"We're going to need some bodies around here."

"Dan's coming back for the evening," Gritch says, "if his wife hasn't killed him. Or his other lady."

"You're going to need some rest yourself."

"Later. I'll go home, grab a few hours, put on my other suit, and come back."

"Remember that woman who worked here last year?" I ask. "She was good."

"Rachel?"

"That's the one. Rachel Golden. Number's in the desk. Remember her?"

"She said the crease in my pants left something to be desired."

"She's ex-army and highly qualified."

"Yeah," he says grudgingly, "she's competent."

"Let's see if she can come in and take over Arnie's spot."

"Stupid bastard."

"Arnie?"

"Who else?" Gritch says.

The phone rings.

"Joe Grundy?"

"Yep."

"Connie Gagliardi, Channel 20 NewsWatch. I think we bumped into each other last night. You're semi-huge, aren't you?"

"I suppose I am. But then you're rather petite as I recall. I'm sure the height differential is exaggerated."

"Nah. You're a big'un. Anyway, the reason I called is I'd like to interview you for the six o'clock NewsWatch. How about it?"

Gritch is looking through the desk for Rachel Golden's telephone number. I cover the mouthpiece. "It's in the left-hand drawer," I tell him. Then into the phone I say, "I'm pretty busy, Ms. Gagliardi."

Gritch glances up at the mention of her name, then waggles his pudgy hand, telling me she's hot stuff.

"It won't take but a minute," she says. "We can be down there in no time at all."

"I really can't say anything at this stage. We're still trying to figure out exactly what happened."

"One of your staff has gone missing, isn't that right?"

That makes me wince. I hope it isn't common

knowledge yet. "You'll have to talk to the police," I say. "Sergeant Weed…"

"Oh, come on, Joe. You don't mind if I call you Joe? I've been all over the police and they're sick of my voice. Weed's very polite, but as forthcoming as a clam. Just five minutes with you. That's all I need."

Gritch has located Rachel Golden's phone number in the left-hand drawer. One of these days I'm going to tackle the filing system in here.

"I don't have time right now, Ms. Gagliardi."

"Call me Connie."

"Okay, Connie, but I still don't have time right now. You can probably guess that we're dealing with a whole bunch of things. Our system is all out of whack."

"Because one of your guys is on the lam?"

"I don't know if that's the case," I say.

"The police have his description on top of their be-on-the-lookout-for list."

"Well," I say, "you obviously know more than I do. All I know is I have fires to put out and people to report to. Maybe I could see you later, tomorrow sometime."

"It'll be old news by then, big guy."

"You never know."

"I'll stay in touch," she says. "I'm not finished bugging you yet."

"I look forward to it."

Gritch waves Rachel's phone number as if he's fanning himself. "Oooh-la-la. Personal interview?"

"Be careful or I'll sic her on you. Give me that." I grab the card with the phone number from him. It's legible. Just. "You getting hungry yet?"

"I could eat."

"Get us something from the café. Tell Hattie I'll have a BLT." I stand up and put the card in my pocket. "I'd better tell Margo about Arnie."

Gritch leaves his cigar to die in the ashtray and I finish

putting it out but don't flush it because there's a good two inches of toxic material left for him to enjoy. Then I give Rachel Golden a call.

"Sure," she says. "Give me two hours to get there."

"You're saving my life," I say.

"It's mutual. I can't play golf, I don't know dick about begonias, and my husband's just decided to remodel the bathroom. Get me out of here!"

chapter thirteen

"Aw, shit!" Margo says. "Shit, shit, shit!" She seems to be getting the hang of it.

"It's my fault, Margo," I say. "I blew it. I'm the one who sent Arnie up to watch the money."

"There'll be enough blame to go around. Once Lloyd gets back from cruising the Caribbean I'll be out on my ear. The brothers want to get rid of our whole set-up and bring in a private security company."

"Mr. Alexander won't stand for it."

"He might. He doesn't like to get involved in the day-to-day." She shuffles papers. "What a mess. Redhorn's checked out. You'd think they'd have been happy for all the free publicity. We've had four big cancellations. Two conventions gone. Why couldn't some stranger have murdered the guy?"

"Arnie didn't murder him." I say, hoping I sound convincing.

When I return to the office, Gritch is back with the food and on the phone.

"He wants to talk to you," he says, handing me the receiver.

"Joe? Is that you?"

"Arnie? Where are you?"

"I didn't do it, Joe. I swear."

"That's good to know, Arnie. Where are you?"

"I've got cops after me for murder, Joe. I didn't shoot anybody. I just heard about it this morning on the news. I didn't do it. You know who did it?"

"Who?"

"No, that's what I'm asking."

"If you didn't do it, then I don't know who did it, Arnie."

"That's what I'm saying, because I didn't do it."

"Then why did you run away?"

"Because they think I did it and I definitely didn't do it."

"Didn't do what?"

"I didn't shoot the guy."

"But you took his money."

He doesn't answer. I cover the mouthpiece, look over at Gritch, and mouth the words, "You know where he is?"

Gritch shrugs and shakes his head. I signal him to pick up the other phone.

"Stupid, stupid, stupid," Arnie says in my ear.

"You took the money, didn't you?" I say.

"Stupid."

"Was Buznardo there when you took it?"

"No, he was down at the other end of the hall with those musicians. The room was empty."

"Where was I?"

"Listening to music."

"I was down the hall, too?"

"It was a spur-of-the-moment thing. You went down the hall and they invited you in. I waited a minute and then I said, 'What the fuck! I'm going for it.' Then I went in and there it was, behind the couch."

"What did you do with it?"

"Brought it back to the room and stuck it under the bed."

"Under the bed?" I glance at Gritch, who spreads his palms, indicating where else? "And you left it there?" I ask Arnie.

"Yeah. All I needed was a minute to get it out of there. Who's going to look under the bed?"

"What about the cash on the bureau? There was thousands of dollars there."

"I never saw it. Maybe I missed it. I just grabbed the briefcase."

"What did you do to Gritch's coffee?"

"Janine has a prescription for lorazepam, which I was supposed to fill, anyway. I went to the drugstore in the Arcade. That's where I usually go. I put some in the coffee pot."

"How many?"

"Prescription was for thirty. I put in about half. Maybe fifteen."

"Lorazepam is…?"

"A sleeping pill."

"You son of a bitch!" Gritch blurts, breaking radio silence. "You didn't even measure the damn dosage?"

"Gritch? Hey, man, those pills aren't that strong. I figured you'd just nod off. I only needed a minute."

"So let me get this straight," I say. "You wait for Gritch to drop off, then you grab the case from under the bed…"

"Then I go down the fire stairs, back of the big kitchen."

"What time was this?"

"I don't know, maybe two, two-thirty."

"Then what did you do?"

"I had something to eat."

"Yeah, that makes sense," Gritch says. "Steal a quarter-million, deke downstairs and have a sandwich."

"I needed some time to figure things out. I think better when I'm eating."

"You're an idiot," Gritch says. "What did you eat?"

"Mayonnaise. And bread. Bread and mayo. First things I found."

"Yeah, that's what all the big thinkers munch on," Gritch says.

"Then what?" I ask.

"I was in the kitchen, trying to think of a safe place to stash the case. I was thinking there should be a good place around the pantry maybe, and then I heard voices and got nervous, so I grabbed the case. I heard somebody running and I tried to duck behind a door, and then —"

"What did you hit me with?"

"I swear, Joe, I'm sorry. I didn't know it was you. I didn't know who it was. It was dark and somebody was running, and then you crashed into the trolley and I'm just behind the door and I didn't even think. I just swung."

"Swung what?"

"The attaché case. I think I hit you with the corner. I'm really sorry."

"Now we need to talk about the gun."

"Joe, I swear to Jesus, man, I never had a gun, I never saw the guy, I never shot the guy. I didn't even know he was shot until I heard it on the tube."

"Where's the money now?"

"Just talk to the cops, Joe. Tell them I didn't shoot anybody."

"You have to come in, Arnie. You can't run."

"I need time to think this through."

I refrain from telling him he should have done that yesterday. "Nothing to think about, Arnie. You need to turn yourself in. I'll come with you. It'll be okay."

"I just need some time to figure —"

"It's not enough money, Arnie," I say. "If you're thinking of running, it won't get you far enough. You won't get out of the country. You start spending hundred-dollar bills and they'll be on your trail in no time."

"Time. I need a little time." And he hangs up.

"Prick," Gritch snaps.

"He's running scared," I say. "He's got to be going

somewhere."

"Why? You think he has a plan? You think this was a planned thing?" Gritch's contempt bubbles over. "Here's a guy never put two consecutive thoughts together in his life. He runs in and grabs a suitcase full of money and hides it under a bed across the hall."

"Semi-brilliant, so far," I say.

"Yeah, well, after that it gets a little messier." Gritch begins spreading his late lunch over the desk — ashtray, lit cigar, two cans of Canada Dry ginger ale. "He gets his girlfriend's prescription filled, which the cops are bound to track down once they figure out what's in the coffee. He takes the coffee pot from Phil and says he'll deliver it personally, which takes two minutes to find out, even for us. He bops you on the head, which isn't a good plan no matter how you slice it, then runs away into the night like a purse snatcher." Bits of onion and relish spill off the tinfoil onto the desk blotter. "It's the crime of the century," he adds with his mouth full. "Nobody will ever figure this one out."

I unwrap my BLT. Hattie knows how I like it: bacon crisp, tomatoes thick, lots of mayo. It looks as appetizing as Gritch's ashtray. I take a bite because I know I need it.

"It wasn't a well-thought-through plan," I say. "If Arnie could have just taken the money at ten o'clock, it wouldn't be so complicated. The fact that he had to come back after one to collect the suitcase puts him there at a bad time. Is one of those ginger ales mine?"

"Yeah, yeah. I got it for you." He laughs. "So you got kayoed with a quarter of a million. That's almost as much as you got for Holyfield, isn't it?"

Gritch munches, dribbles, slurps, puffs cigar smoke, burps onion. I can't handle any more. I wrap up most of the BLT and file it with the wastepaper. My side of the desk is tidy. I try not to look at his side. My head hurts. And for the life of me I can't figure out how the thing went down.

"Why would he take a gun with him the second time?"

I ask. "I can't make any sense of it. Why would he go back into 1502 if the money's under the bed in 1507?"

"What if the first time in, he sees the money on the side table. Over seven grand maybe. That would be a good score for Arnie."

"Okay, so he grabs it and beats it back into 1507 before I get back from the singalong and before Dan shows up."

"Right," Gritch says. "So there he is, seven thousand or so in his pocket, free and clear."

"Where's the suitcase?"

"Still in 1502."

"Then?"

"Then he gets greedy. He remembers about the suitcase. Or he didn't have time to grab it the first time because he heard something and chickened out, or people were in the hall, whatever. He left it behind, and now he's kicking himself because all he got was a measly seven thousand and there's still almost a quarter of a million sitting in the room. So he goes back to get it."

"And he figures he might need a gun this time?" I say.

"He might. He's stupid enough."

"Okay, then you tell me how it goes down. Does Buzz attack Arnie, try to stop him from leaving with the money? No, he probably tells him to take it and be happy."

"So Buznardo stands there and says, 'Hey, man, go ahead, help yourself,' and someone shoots him five times point-blank."

"That's pretty cold," I say.

"That's pretty accurate, but it's not the work of somebody like Arnie, who's all twitchy and furtive. He'd be more likely to shoot himself in the foot."

Gritch finally starts cleaning up his picnic. He doesn't do a very good job of it. Thank God for maid service, even if our office suite at the back is usually last on their list. Gritch burps more onion and heads for the bathroom. He's got mustard on his chin. I hope he spots it. I don't like giving grooming tips.

"Don't forget," he yells from the bathroom, "there's an army of people who couldn't give a radioactive rat's ass about a suitcase full of hundred-dollar bills. These are guys concerned about the real legacy which, if memory serves, is half a billion."

"Six hundred and eighty-eight million."

"See?" Gritch says. "Now that's *serious* money. That's the kind of money people do cold-blooded murders for. And you don't know half the players."

I sip my ginger ale and have a look at my neglected paperwork.

"Did you get hold of Rachel?" he calls out.

"She'll do the evening shift with Dan. She'll be in at four, she says. When's Dan coming in?"

Gritch comes out of the bathroom, more or less presentable. "Dan's not coming in till six. It'll work out."

"I don't think Arnie shot anyone," I say. "Is there Aspirin in there?"

"Tylenol."

"That'll help." I pass him as I go into the bathroom. When I open the medicine cabinet, I don't remember any of the stuff that's there. Razors and Q-Tips.

"All right," Gritch says, "I'll give you that decisive action doesn't sound like the Arnie I know."

"Think about it," I say. "First of all, with what? A .32-calibre pistol? Where does he come up with one of those between 11:00 p.m., and what, 2:00 a.m.?"

"Okay, that's one. He'd have a hard time getting a piece."

"A very hard time. He couldn't have left the hotel, or if he did, he couldn't have gone very far. And who does he go to? He doesn't have a lot of friends in the neighbourhood. He drops into the Scientology recruiting centre and says, 'Can somebody lend me a gun for the evening?' I don't think so."

"Maybe he had it all along," Gritch suggests. "Maybe he carries a piece and we don't know about it. Maybe somebody else in the hotel has a gun and Arnie knows who it is, or where they stash it. He borrows it, steals it, and the owner won't report it because they're not supposed to have one in the hotel, either."

"That's nice," I say. "The list of suspects just went from one to five hundred and thirty-three."

"And that's just our guys."

"I'm only concerned with our guys. My territory ends at the sidewalk. If somebody out there did the murder, that's their business. I'm hoping one of our guys *didn't* do a murder."

I phone Weed and tell him about Arnie's call. Weed says if Arnie calls again I should tell him to make it easy on himself.

"They think he did it, the murder?" Gritch asks when I hang up.

"Oh, yes."

"Well, who else?"

chapter fourteen

Gritch and I spend the next couple of hours quietly making the rounds, checking people's whereabouts, asking as delicately as possible if anybody knows about any guns kept in the hotel, not that there would be any recriminations, we're careful to emphasize. We tell them we're just wondering. Nobody knows anything about any guns. I figured as much, but you never know. It's a big hotel, and there are people on staff I don't know well.

Rachel Golden shows up at four o'clock. She looks like a soccer mom — suburban hair, smart slacks. She was an MP in the army for the full twenty years, then retired with rank, a stack of commendations, and more than a few medals. Rachel knows how to handle herself, definitely knows how to handle other people. She says she'll work until midnight. She'll come on full-time until we hire someone to replace Arnie. I should have had her guarding the money. She has a pension.

Dan comes in at 6:15. Says he spent the day dealing

with domestic issues. Says I don't want to know, and I'm sure he's right about that.

"Thanks for coming back in, Dan," I say. "I appreciate it."

"Jesus, Joe, what you're doing for me, I'll work all night if you need me."

"Just until midnight," I tell him. "Take tomorrow off."

"I was hoping to stay far away from both domiciles for a while."

"You have to face the music sometime," I say. Like I have a clue about marriage.

"I'll be facing the music for some time, boss. You can count on it."

"That's your business, Dan. You take tomorrow off. Rachel Golden's going to work out a new shift rotation. You know her. She doesn't gamble, she's immune to your charm, and she doesn't need a new refrigerator. She'll give you a call about Thursday. I'll try to make it a late shift."

He tries not to look over his shoulder, but hunches his back defensively as he leans in closer. "Talk to Randall Poy, by any chance?"

"Saw him this morning. He's okay for this week. We'll talk about our next move after I get the hotel business sorted out. It's on my list. Promise."

"I appreciate it, Joe. I really do. I'll make it good."

"There'll be some extra hours here for a while. That'll give you a few extra bucks. Gritch needs to go home, and I need some sleep. You and Rachel stay on top of things until midnight, then I'll be back. Maybe this house will be safe for a few hours."

"Don't worry about a thing, boss. Get some shut-eye."

I leave Dan and take the elevator up to Leo's aerie above the top floor. The Skyrocket says it's 7:05. *Seinfeld* reruns. Leo's very big on *Seinfeld* reruns. He's seen every episode at least a dozen times. When I let myself in, he's eating the kitchen's best steak with Béarnaise sauce and stuffed mushrooms and sipping a glass of the cellar's best Burgundy. On the wide-screen Sony, George Costanza is trying to get an extension on his unemployment benefits.

"This is the one with Keith Hernandez in it," Leo says. "The ballplayer."

"Yes, sir," I say.

"World Series is coming up. We should watch a ball game together."

"Yes, sir. I'd like that."

"Sit down, Joseph. You want some of this steak?"

"No, thank you, sir. I just had a BLT from the Lobby Café."

"Hattie still there?"

"No, she's closed up for the night."

"I mean, she still runs the place?"

"Oh. Yes, sir. Hattie's still there."

"That's nice. I hired her mother. Can you believe that? Woman name of Ellis, Ellis what? Maureen Ellis. Hattie's mother. You ever see her around?"

"I think Hattie told me her mother was in a nursing home now."

"Really? Nice-looking woman, I recall. Friendly."

"Yes, sir. It must run in the family. Hattie's a very friendly person, too."

"You tell Hattie I asked after her mother."

"Yes, sir, I'll do that."

Leo pours the last of the wine into his goblet, tosses the linen napkin onto the table, and leans back to allow me a better view of the Sony.

"I had a phone call from Arnie McKellar," I say.

"Did he do it?"

"He says he didn't, sir. He admits taking the money."

"He did? That's unfortunate."

"Yes, sir."

"Most unfortunate."

"But he says he didn't shoot anybody."

"I hope that's true."

"So do I, sir."

"I'd take it as a personal favour, Joseph, if you could make sure of that. The stealing is bad enough, but we can deal with that. A murder wouldn't be good for the Lord Douglas, not right now." He looks around. "Hand me that humidor, would you?"

Leo opens the walnut chest, bound with brass, lined with cedar, and starts rummaging among his riches. "Still police all over my house?"

"No, sir. They've wrapped up the investigation. We can get back into the suite tomorrow. We'll need to change the carpet."

"We had two guys from California get shot in the Palm Court back in '53," he says. "Did you know that? Before your time, I suppose."

"A bit."

"And just a year after that some poor schnook got caught with a hooker by his wife and she emptied a Colt six-shooter at them — a damn cowboy gun like Wyatt Earp carried. Blew a hole through the door as big as a window. Missed her husband, but she shot off the poor hooker's big toe. That caused a ruckus. We had to replace more than the rug."

"Theo and Leonard want to bring in an outside company."

"Joe," he says, "Theo and Lenny don't make the rules in the Lord Douglas. They don't hire, they don't fire, and if they give you a hard time, just smile and go about your business. This hotel has seen murders before, and it may very well see them again. It's a hotel. We invite a thousand strangers a day into our house and we don't ask them what they plan to do here. They bring their troubles in with them. They take them with them when they leave. Our job is to give them a good night's sleep."

"But it's not our job to rob them."

"True. That's bad. Most of the robberies in here are on

Rolf's wine list. Two hundred and seventeen dollars for this bottle. He'll hear about it."

"Yes, sir."

"This will blow over. We'll weather the storm just fine."

"I'll keep you up to speed on the Arnie McKellar business, sir. In my opinion, he's not the kind of person who could do a murder."

"I hope you're right. I don't like to give my offspring any free ammunition."

"Yes, sir."

"Good night, Joseph. Remember, the World Series is coming up."

"Yes, sir. We'll watch a game together. I look forward to it."

"As do I, Joseph." He turns his attention to George Costanza, who is lying on the floor with his pants around his ankles.

As I let myself out of the suite, Raquel, I'm sure it's Raquel, comes in with a pile of fresh towels and a basket of toiletries. She smiles at me.

"*¿Cómo está noche, Señor Grundy?*" she asks.

"*Muy bien, gracias,*" I reply. Definitely Raquel.

chapter fifteen

Eventually, I get some sleep. Dreamless, heavy, lumped in one position so that when I swim up from the deep, my frame aches and my right arm is dead. The clock radio reads 11:47. That's p.m., I presume. It's dark outside. The street is dry for a change. Connor's Diner is closed, but earnest discussion is still going on in the Scientology Reading Room next door. No panic phone calls have disturbed me. I slept almost five hours — okay, four and a bit, but it should keep me going for a while.

The phone rings. It's Arnie.

"Joe? Is that you?"

"Where are you?" I hold the phone in my left hand, flexing my dead right arm to get the tingle started. "You have to tell me where you are. Nothing good can happen if you keep running. They'll find you, Arnie."

"Joe, I need your help."

"I'll help you, Arnie. I'll come and get you and we can walk into the police station together. I won't let anything happen to you. Just tell me where you are right now and I'll come."

"Wait. Wait. I'm still trying to work out something."

"There's nothing to work out."

"There's something."

My right arm is now buzzing happily, and the fingers of my right hand are flexible enough to hold the receiver to my better ear. Somewhere on the other end of the line I hear a PA announcement, unintelligible, as usual, and then the distinct sound of a BC Ferries whistle.

"Arnie? You at Horseshoe Bay or Tsawwassen?"

He hangs up.

I shower, shave, put on a fresh shirt and my comfortable shoes, and head out for the lobby.

Raymond D'Aquino glances up from what he's doing. "Mr. Grundy, how are you feeling?"

"I'm good, Raymond. Thanks. I thought you'd get the night off."

"I stayed until ten this morning and then I went home. I came on at eleven."

"Thanks for last night, Raymond. I appreciate what you did."

"The whole thing was pretty intense, what with that woman screaming, you unconscious…"

"You handled it well. Credit to the establishment."

"It was really Arnie?"

"Looks like it was Arnie who took the money. I'm hoping that's the worst thing he did. Anything I should know about?"

"Not a thing. Everyone's on their best behaviour tonight."

"I'm going down to Olive's. Call me there if you need me. I won't be long."

Olive is sitting in with the California trio when I walk in. She nods at me over the top of her Steinway and smiles as the sax player does something sweet over her left-hand chords. She answers him with a right-hand run that makes him smile in return. The place isn't full, but the patrons are paying attention to the music, which is fitting because the music is good. Olive is making the California trio sound like the full Basie band.

My favourite corner bar stool is unoccupied.

"What'll it be, champ?" Barney asks.

"Coffee fresh?"

"You bet. Anything in it?"

"Just coffee, Barney. I just woke up."

"Long day, I guess." He puts a mug of straight Colombian in front of me, gives the already clean bar a reflex wipe. "That's harsh about Arnie. What was he thinking?"

"I don't think he was thinking. I think it was a spur-of-the-moment thing. Couldn't resist the impulse."

"But shooting the guy. That was really stupid."

"Well, the jury's still out on that one," I say.

Barney goes down to the other end of the bar to fix a few drinks. I take a second sip of black coffee and feel the thump of Gritch grabbing the stool beside me.

"What are you doing here?" I ask him. "You get any sleep?"

"Sure, sure, I rolled into the house at six-thirty. The wife was out partying with the Tupperware set or something. I turned the ball game and crashed on the couch until she got home. Had a good nap. I'm fresh as a daisy."

"Who was playing?"

"Couldn't tell you, except the sun was shining when it started, and then the shadows got longer, and somebody got beaned. Pitcher got tossed. It was baseball. It's as good as a sleeping pill."

Barney comes back to refill my cup and give one to Gritch. He supplies Gritch with sugar and cream and watches while Gritch scatters grains and droplets all over his gleaming oak surface. By the time the mug reaches Gritch's lips, Barney has wiped the bar, added extra napkins, and disposed of Gritch's cigar stub.

"I was smoking that," Gritch says.

"He called me again," I say.

"Who?"

"Arnie. Twenty minutes ago."

"Son of a bitch," Gritch says. "He say where he was?"

"He wouldn't tell me. I think he was getting on a ferry, or getting off. I heard a whistle. I heard a PA address, but I couldn't make out what it said."

"What does he expect you to do?"

"He sounded excited."

"Scared witless."

"No, his mind's working on something. Like he still thinks he can get away with it somehow."

"Oh, he's a genius all right," Gritch says. "Old Arnie boy is just full of bright ideas."

Olive finishes her set with the California trio and steps off the stand to a generous round of applause. The sax player is clapping, too. He enjoyed himself. Olive acknowledges it all like the queen she is — regal, generous, and fully deserving. Barney has her rum and Coke ready when she slides into her booth with her back to the room like she's disappeared into a dressing room backstage. No one bothers her unless she invites them. She gives me a head shift that says, "Come on over." I pick up my coffee.

"Go visit Madam Queen," Gritch says. "I'll go sit in the lobby."

He rolls out of the place, and Barney tidies up after him with dispatch as I slide into the booth opposite Olive May, who is lighting a Winston from a fresh pack.

"How you doing, Joey?"

"I'm okay, Olive. You sounded good."

"Cuban drummer. Can he drive or what?"

"The sax player's in love with you."

"Instrumental infatuation. He's got six kids and lives in

L.A." She offers me a Winston, which I accept. It's a ritual. "All quiet upstairs?"

"Everything's pretty much back to normal. Except the Governor's Suite's still closed. It needs a new rug."

"I don't know this Arnie guy. He never came in here."

"I don't think he likes music."

"Well, there now," she says, "that should tell you something about the man."

"Gritch always wanted me to fire him."

"I hear Gritch got knocked out."

"No, that was me. Gritch got sleeping pills in his coffee."

"Sounds like the better deal. You okay, sugar?"

"Yeah, I'm fine."

"So what's the matter, Joey? Your forehead is all fisted up and you're actually smoking that thing."

"Arnie says he didn't shoot anyone."

"What about you? You think somebody else did it?"

"It's making me a little crazy. It doesn't add up. Too many loose ends."

"Let the police figure it out. It's not your problem anymore, is it, sugar?"

"Well, yeah, it is," I say. "It happened in the hotel."

chapter sixteen

It's a clear and bright morning. The rain has moved inland. Vancouver has a scrubbed and shiny face. It's a day for getting things done. I put on a white shirt, a paisley tie, the good grey suit, my polished black shoes, and the Burberry trench coat. It's in the back of the closet in a dry cleaner's bag, a gift from Mr. Alexander many Christmases ago that I rarely get to wear. I look okay. A Clydesdale with shiny hooves.

Wallace Gritchfield grabbed a few hours' sleep on the office couch and wants to know where his overnight bag is, with his spare stuff inside.

"I don't know," I say. "The bottom drawer of the filing cabinet is where you usually stash it."

"Drawer's full of files."

"How inconvenient," I say. "Check under the desk in the private space."

"You going courting?"

"I have a date for breakfast."

"You need a boutonniere."

"After that I'm going to see some people. I'll be gone most of the morning."

"I'll notify the media," Gritch says.

"Rachel will be on the job at nine sharp. Dan has the day off. I've got the cell with me if anything comes up."

"The house will survive without you," Gritch says, checking me out. "Nice topcoat."

"It's a Burberry," says the fashion plate.

"Take the safety pin out."

Connie Gagliardi has oatmeal for breakfast, with butter and salt. "It's a family thing. I know it's odd."

"It's unusual," I say.

"My grandfather swore by it. He lived to ninety-three."

"Maybe I'll switch."

"It's an acquired taste, I think."

She isn't wearing makeup, and her hair is becomingly tousled. Channel 20 has a department ready to attend to such details before she goes on camera. She looks younger, and tinier, if that's possible. I loomed over her when we met on the street ten minutes earlier.

"You used to be a fighter, is that right?"

"Yes, that's right."

"Were you any good?"

"White heavyweights who can stay alive for five or six rounds can make a living. I fought a couple of premier guys. Mixed results, but I didn't stink up the joint."

"Did you ever fight for a title?"

"Never got that far."

"I'm not a fight fan. Sorry. Did you get in with anyone I might know? Who's that brute who keeps getting in trouble? Tyson?"

"Never had that privilege. Fought Evander Holyfield on his way up. Gave him a good lick, second round, woke him right up, unfortunately. Anyway, that's how I earned a living until I got too old for it and once or twice caught myself hearing things that weren't there."

"I guess security work would be a logical next step."

"For someone with few marketable skills? Yes."

"How did you make the transition?"

"Along the way I met some people, good and bad, and one of the good ones, an old PI named Louis Schurr, started giving me odd jobs, surveillance, protection. He got me a licence, got me bonded, gave me an alternative to getting my brain scrambled. He's the guy who introduced me to Leo Alexander, who owns, among other things, the Lord Douglas Hotel. Mr. Alexander was in need of a bodyguard and hired me to keep him alive."

"Was he in danger?"

"He never told me exactly what he was worried about, only that he needed protection. One night at a fundraiser somebody fired five shots at him. I managed to stop three of them. The other two missed by a mile."

"Were you badly hurt?"

"There was hospital time involved. I came out of it more or less intact. I don't do many one-armed push-ups anymore and my collarbone has a knot in it, but that's about it."

"Mr. Alexander must have been grateful."

"He's an honourable man."

"He gave you a reward?"

"Sort of."

She finishes her oatmeal to the bottom of the bowl, drains a glass of grapefruit juice, and turns her attention to tea, with honey and lemon. I watch her with some fascination. She reminds me of a wild creature grabbing a quick bite at the edge of the woods, all senses alert, no wasted motion. I'm still working on my first piece of toast.

"I didn't see the interview," I say. "Somebody at the hotel said your piece with Buzz was on the news last night. There any way I can have a look at it?"

"Oh, sure, come out to Channel 20 after ten-thirty, say

eleven o'clock, I'll be free. I'll run it for you."

"Thank you."

"How much time did you spend with him?" she asks.

"I talked to him for five minutes after he checked in, then for a little while when they were listening to music in the other suite."

"What did you think?"

"Good music," I say, "folk rock, I guess you'd call it."

She smiles. "Of him."

"He was pleasant, open, cheerful."

"You think he had a Jesus complex?"

"I don't know," I say. "Some people are so serene they seem remote, on a cloud just out of earshot. I'm not sure I made much contact."

"He was surprisingly articulate during the interview. I was expecting him to be all spacey, peace-love-togetherness, but he made a cogent case for what he was planning to do. It made sense. Not sense in a practical way, but sense on some real level, like he was trying to do something."

"Confound the prevailing paradigm," I say.

"Exactly."

"His sister said he was too good for this world."

"We do tend to chew up our saints. What do you think of the sister?"

"I've got a weakness for red hair," I say. "I think I had a crush on someone in grade two."

"That'll do it." She touches her own dark curls.

"I got the feeling Molly MacKay has a garden and a dog and enjoys sex, food, music, and going barefoot."

"Earth mother type." Connie sips her tea. "I couldn't get to her after it happened. How was she?"

"Very quiet, very tired, very sad."

"And maybe very rich. I'm trying to set something up. I'll go to Roberts Creek if she'll talk to me. Can't get her on the phone. I don't know where she is."

"Avoiding reporters."

She looks up at me and shrugs. "We just do our jobs, right? You stop bullets for people and I chase people who don't want to talk to me."

"Did you ever meet this Parker Prescott?" I ask.

"Nope. Now there was a serious recluse. He dropped completely out of sight. For five or six years no one saw him."

"Except Jake Buznardo, evidently."

"You can imagine what it looked like when Buzz came out of the woods. You remember that guy after Howard Hughes died? Some guy shows up, says he picked Hughes up one night hitchhiking. Claimed Hughes left him all his money."

"Vaguely."

She puts down her cup and tilts her head as if examining the damage to a front bumper. "You've never seen my show, have you?"

"I've seen your picture on the side of a bus."

She laughs. "I shouldn't even talk to you."

"If it doesn't happen inside the hotel, it's not really part of my life."

She shakes her head. "Okay. How much do you know about the Prescott fortune?"

"It's six hundred and eighty-eight million dollars."

"At the very least. There should be more once they add it all up." She picks up the salt and pepper shakers and holds them apart. "Okay, Parker Prescott formed two corporations. Prescott Holdings —" she waggles the salt "— takes in all the money. Horizon Foundation —" she jiggles the pepper "— hands it out. It's a neat set-up. All Prescott Holdings can do is make money. It can't spend it, can't buy anything, can't sell anything. The only thing it exists for is to make cash available to Horizon which, conversely, isn't allowed to earn money, only to spend it."

"What business is Prescott Holdings in?"

"Initially, Prescott made his money in the lumber business, plywood or something. Then he got into mining and transportation, good West Coast industries. Six, seven years ago, he started consolidating, liquidating. It's like he wasn't interested in growing anymore. He just wanted to make sure there was fifty million, sometimes a hundred million a year to funnel into Horizon to keep his favourite charities funded."

"So the whole Prescott empire exists to give money away."

"That's it."

"No wonder he and Jake Buznardo got along."

"But you can understand why the rest of the players freaked. A whole lot of charities and foundations rely on the Horizon Foundation for a big chunk, in some cases the entire chunk, of their budgets. Then up pops this gypsy with a stranglehold on the entire Prescott empire, and he looks flaky enough to upset all their cushy apple carts. Prescott Holdings fought it as long and as hard as they could, but the old man had foxed them at every turn. He'd adopted Jake Buznardo as his legal son and heir, he had psychiatric reports from unassailable institutions attesting to his soundness of mind, and he made it virtually impossible for Prescott Holdings to use their own funds to fight the will. In the end, Wade Hubble was spending his own money."

"What about the other arm, this Horizon Foundation?"

"Horizon always has its nose in the air. They like to give the impression they're above such sordidness. But let's face it, Edwin Gowins was every bit as vulnerable." She checks her watch. It's almost eight-thirty. "I have to get to the shop."

"Who's Gowins?"

Connie gets up, starts to collect her gear. "Edwin Gowins runs the Horizon Foundation. If you ever read a newspaper, you'd have seen him. He loves cutting ribbons."

I stand and make a smooth grab for the check. "He must be very popular. A man who hands out a hundred million a year."

"Very popular," she says.

chapter seventeen

The Horizon Foundation exists to dole out money to deserving charities. From the look of its office building, I figure some of that money must go to window washers. It's the Crystal Cathedral without the pews. Embracing the reception area is a curving trophy wall bedecked with plaques, scrolls, honours, and framed colour photographs of Edwin Gowins being embraced by dignified cultural panhandlers. Not for him the anonymous donation. He likes having his picture taken. Every penny he hands out comes with an oversize cheque and a photo op, and the documented thanks of a grateful, and preferably high-profile, worthy cause. Edwin Gowins has expensive teeth and exquisite taste in haberdashery.

In the middle of the trophy wall, slightly out of place, is a handsome oil portrait in a massive gilt frame. Parker Prescott, philanthropist, humanitarian, benefactor. It's my first good look at the man who started all this. The artist has given him the elevated gaze of a visionary. Made him look taller, too. By all accounts, Prescott was a bantamweight. In the painting he looks like a welter.

Edwin Gowins, the managing director of the Horizon Foundation, has his chancel in what should have been the apse of the high altar. Before I can get in to see him I have to dance my way past a series of politely hostile buffers, all of whom wear nice shoes and wrinkled noses. I don't think I look that bad, what with my Burberry fresh out of the dry cleaner's bag, but when I finally get in to see Edwin Gowins it's obvious there's a higher level of sartorial splendour in the world. I was unaware there were pink alpacas in Peru, but then I've never been to South America.

"Mr. Gowins," I say. "It's good of you to see me, sir."

"Why am I seeing you, exactly? Mr. Gundy, is it?"

"Grundy. Joe Grundy. I work for the Lord Douglas Hotel, where Mr. Buznardo was shot two nights ago."

"I prefer the Park Royal."

"Yes, sir, that's a nice place, I'm told."

"But you still haven't answered my initial question. Why am I seeing you?"

"I'm unofficially looking into Mr. Buznardo's murder. On behalf of the hotel."

"You wish to minimize your liability, is that it?"

"I'm concerned that one of my employees may be charged with something he didn't do."

"Unofficially looking into?"

"Yes, sir, though I do know the investigator in charge. Detective Sergeant Weed. And I'm keeping him informed of my efforts."

"I've already spoken to Detective Weed. I'm sure he can fill you in."

"He has, sir. I know you were nowhere near the Lord Douglas on the night in question."

"Nor any time in the past five years that I can recall."

"Yes, sir. I'm just trying to get a clearer picture of how Mr. Buznardo's death will affect your foundation."

"It won't impact our foundation in the least, Mr. Gundy."

"I'm sure that's a relief."

He looks at me with less than complete favour.

"If Prescott Holdings' funds had been diverted, it could have caused a disruption," I say as if I know what I'm talking about.

Gowins wafts an airy wave over his immaculate desk. He's shooing away a gnat. "The corporate and legal set-up is much too carefully structured to be dismantled by some spaced-out tree hugger with a Messiah complex."

"He did have radical plans for the future of Prescott Holdings."

"That would have had no influence on Horizon, Mr. Gundy. The two entities have an arm's-length relationship. Our funding is based on a strict formula relative to their corporate earnings. They earn the money, we spend the money. They aren't allowed to spend, we aren't allowed to earn. It's quite simple."

"I understand that, sir, but if Prescott Holdings stopped earning money, there wouldn't be anything for Horizon to spend."

He gives me a thin smile and caps his thousand-dollar fountain pen. "I find that highly unlikely." He closes his desk binder of Spanish leather as he stands. I think my time is up.

"So you weren't particularly concerned about the change at the top of Prescott Holdings?"

"Immaterial as far as Horizon is concerned."

"And the CEO of Prescott Holdings, Wade Hubble? His departure wouldn't have altered your relationship with Prescott Holdings?"

"I seriously doubt that Wade Hubble would be removed from his position, Mr. Gundy. His stewardship has been exemplary, if a trifle parsimonious of late."

"Did you discuss the situation with him?"

"Mr. Hubble and I avoid contact, personal or professional. It's part of our agreement."

"Who do you deal with at Prescott Holdings, sir?"

"Mr. Gundy, I think you may be entering an area far removed from the interests of the Lord Douglas Hotel. The Prescott Holdings/Horizon relationship is no concern of yours. Both entities are represented by established law firms. You're welcome to seek an appointment."

"I've already talked to one of your lawyers."

"Really? Which one would that be?"

"Alvin Neagle."

"Neagle?"

"Alvin Neagle, Jake Buznardo's lawyer. I understand he's joining the Horizon legal team. I suppose his familiarity with Buzz's legal status will be of value."

"Good day, Mr. Gundy. Next time please make an appointment."

"I will, sir. Thank you for your time. And it's Grundy, sir, Joe Grundy."

"Of course it is."

He sits back down and opens his binder of Spanish leather, dismissing me without so much as a nod. I resist the impulse to back out of the room.

Edwin Gowins's next appointment is waiting in the outer office. She's wearing taupe today, cashmere it looks like. Her ash-blond hair is curbed at the temples by heirloom tortoiseshell clips. Her shoes and handbag match. She's still out of my league.

Nonetheless, I say, "Hello again."

"Again?" she says without a glimmer of recognition.

"We met briefly outside the Lord Douglas Hotel two nights ago. And before that I saw you get out of an elevator. I believe you were visiting Jake Buznardo." Amazing how the ace hotel dick can put two and two together if he's given a few days.

"I'm sorry," she says, not sorry at all, "I don't recall."

"That's my fault, ma'am. I should have introduced myself. My name's Joe Grundy. I'm in charge of hotel security."

"Really?" She doesn't look too impressed.

"I was just talking to Mr. Gowins about the possible repercussions of Mr. Buznardo's murder."

"How nice for you," she says, turning away in response to a discreet cough from a well-favoured young man with spiked blond hair and a jacket almost as fine as the number Gowins had on.

"Mrs. Ingraham? Please go in. Mr. Gowins is expecting you."

"Thank you, Jeremy," she says, and leaves me standing on the purple carpet.

She turns at Gowins's burled walnut office door and looks back at me. "For the record, Mr. Grundy, I wasn't visiting Mr. Buznardo that night."

Oops. First slip. "Sure you were, ma'am. He gave you a hundred-dollar bill and you threw it away in the elevator. I guess you found it insulting."

"As I do you, Mr. Grundy. Most insulting."

She enters the inner sanctum with most of her shell intact, but I think I spot a hairline crack. A tendril of ash-blond hair has come loose. She won't like that.

I turn to the handsome young man behind the desk. "Jeremy?" I say. "That was Mrs. Ingraham? Did I get that right?"

But my time in the Crystal Cathedral has elapsed. He doesn't even trouble himself to sneer.

chapter eighteen

"I have to tell you, Mr. Grundy, that I am shocked by your ineptitude. And that of your staff. What can I say? A drunk, a gambler, a murderer, and a thief. You should rethink your hiring policy."

That's Wade Hubble talking. He's making me follow him down corridors and in and out of elevators, busy moving among his subjects, dispensing blessings, barking orders. A man of substance. A Borgia on a tour of his provinces.

I've tracked him down at the Prescott Holdings offices through a leap of sleuthing inspiration that told me the CEO of Prescott Holdings might be found at Prescott Holdings, and I was fortunate to arrive at the executive level as he was parading along the outlying carpeting accepting the accolades of his loyal subjects, who appreciate that Wade Hubble has repelled the Visigoth and secured the borders of the kingdom. Whether any of them infer that Wade Hubble personally bumped off the invader isn't for me to say, but I get the distinct impression they'd be proud to think so.

Wade Hubble's Roman beak cleaves the air like the prow of a ship. He'd be at home in a toga. I'm not exactly rubbing elbows with the man. He has a scrum of suits and haircuts following closely, and I have to work at maintaining a position in his wake. Now and then one of my questions gets through to him and he pauses in his more important duties to grant me a barb.

"And to top it off, the entire organization is being run by an over-the-hill prizefighter who never won a prize. It appears that your sole claim to fame is that you stopped a bullet meant for Leo Alexander seven years ago."

"Mr. Hubble," I say, "I don't want to take up your time. I'm sure you have important things to attend to. I was hoping you could direct me to Mr. Axelrode's office."

"Never heard of him."

"Oh. He introduced himself at the hotel as being associated with your company in a security position."

"Mr. Grundy, you're on the wrong floor. You'll find the security offices on the ground floor. I'm surprised they let you up here."

"They may have been distracted by all the reporters trying to get up to see you."

"Yet somehow you managed it."

"I'm big, but I'm shifty," I say modestly.

He looks me over as if I'm a piece of fish he's considering for lunch. "Please shift yourself back down to the lobby."

"I will, right away, sir. I really do need to see Mr. Axelrode."

"What for?"

"I need to straighten out a few hotel matters. An unpaid bill —"

"I don't deal with bill collectors."

"And a pending assault charge."

"None of this has anything to do with me."

"It does if he was working for you at the time."

He's given me far too much of his time already. He

starts walking again, handing off memos, scheduling important meetings.

"I suppose Molly MacKay will inherit Mr. Buznardo's estate," I say.

He stops, turns, gives me a thin smile. "I'm still not willing to concede that Mr. Buznardo ever had an estate, but whatever the situation, Parker Prescott's interests are safely back with the board of directors."

Half an hour later I'm on a log staring blankly at the business section of the *Emblem*, columns of numbers and acronyms as incomprehensible to me as cuneiform, and not nearly as pretty. The sun is behind me, warming the back of my neck. The North Shore glows. The freighters at anchor in English Bay gleam like cruise ships. Gulls wheel, mergansers dabble close to shore, a rangy retriever chases a Frisbee along the wet sand, quick clouds pile up against the Coast Mountains.

Norman Quincy Weed, wearing his red-and-blue tie, walks towards me across the grass, carrying a bag of popcorn. "How's the head?"

"I slept, I ate, looks like I'm gonna live."

"What'd he say he hit you with?"

"The money."

"At least it wasn't a cheap knockout."

He strolls down to the water and broadcasts the entire bag of popcorn. Gulls and crows and ducks converge. He leaves them to sort out who gets what.

"Haven't found him yet?" I ask.

"It's the manhunt of the year. You figure he caught a ferry?"

"I heard a ferry. He was near a ferry. He could have been getting on, getting off, hanging around reading brochures."

"Horseshoe Bay," Weed says. "The one last night was from a payphone at the terminal. You figure he'll call again?"

"I'm carrying a cell. He's got the number."

"The log wet?"

"I'm sitting on a newspaper. You can have the sports section."

He sits on the hockey scores and stretches his legs. The popcorn has been divvied up, but not equitably. "The Mounties are all over the big island. If he's over there, they'll find him." He stands to adjust his section of the newspaper and sits again. "I had a knot under there."

"Want the business section?" I have it in my hand. "It's thicker."

"Even Dan Howard's not stupid enough to play the Vancouver stock market."

"I wanted to find out how Prescott Holdings' stock was doing."

"Not publicly traded," Weed says. "You'd have to know all the companies they own pieces of, and how all of them are doing. Prescott Holdings has its fingers in more pies than it has fingers."

"I don't think I'm smart enough to figure out what's going on, anyway," I say.

"Join the club. It'd take a team of forensic auditors a year to sort out their set-up. That's assuming someone found evidence of a crime that would justify opening up their books. Lucky for me that's not my department. I'm working the who-shot-the-billionaire angle."

"Still think Arnie did it?"

"Give my guys an hour in a room with him and I'll know for sure. It's a strange one. Big mess in the bedroom, no struggle in the other room, nothing knocked over. Shooter got real close. Like the victim maybe knew who he was."

"Buzz was a laid-back kind of guy."

"So I hear," Weed says. "Also he was a wee bit stoned. Marijuana and wine. THC and alcohol in his blood."

"You did an autopsy?"

"Ongoing. Got the blood work back. There's going to be other stuff."

"Some other drugs?"

"Nope." Weed has yet to find a comfortable perch for his rump. He takes the business section from me and adds it to his cushion. "Medical examiner doesn't think the young man was very well."

A brief image of Buzz wincing when he stood up flashes in my head.

The rangy retriever is tireless and hasn't stopped running since I got here. His Frisbee-throwing trainer sends him on yet another deep route. The dog gallops in our direction wearing a demented grin, defies gravity, and snatches the disc in midair. He grants us a moment to admire his prowess before loping back down the beach with his prize. The retriever is a picture of vitality, but all I can see is Jake "Buzz" Buznardo coming out of the hotel bathroom wearing a towel, his Jesus beard still dripping, his pale-skinned torso, ribs showing, chest hairless, something bad going on inside.

We stand and I collect the newspaper sections and walk them to a trash basket. "We're getting crowded off the front page," I say.

"Well, you got lucky. The Middle East blew up, some sports celebrity got caught with his pants down, and there's a serial rapist working his way through Richmond." He tosses his popcorn bag on top of the newspaper. "That's a nice trench coat."

"I had a breakfast date."

"Jesus! With a woman?"

"Connie Gagliardi."

We start walking back from the beach, heading for Denman.

"She's too short for you," Weed says.

"Too young, too."

Weed climbs into his car. "Probably going to release the body tomorrow. His sister's having him cremated. There'll be some kind of wake, play music, scatter the ashes, like that."

"Scatter them where? Roberts Creek?"

"Here. Out there." He points at the Kitsilano side of the bay. "Point Grey somewhere, near the university. Wreck Beach maybe to entertain the nudists. The sister never left town."

"Where's she been?"

"Hanging out with that rock-and-roll band, Redphone," he says, smiling before I can correct him.

"I'll get in touch if I hear from Arnie again."

"Next time you hear from him he'll probably be in a lock-up somewhere," Weed says. He starts the car, then organizes the seat belt to his satisfaction.

"Norm, on the off chance Arnie didn't do the murder, my money would be on Axelrode. He was lurking, he was carrying a piece, he was poking his nose into everybody's business, he had a hard-on for Buzz. I think you should be looking for Jeff Axelrode."

"We're looking for him. What can I tell you? We've got his name on the list. We'd like to talk to him. We expect to talk to him once we find him. When we find Arnie, we'll talk to him, too. One of those guys has the money. Maybe they were in it together. Who knows? We'll locate them and we'll talk to them."

"Is it okay if I look for him?"

"Who? Axelrode? No, it's not okay if you look for him. You work inside the hotel. That's what you do. You stay inside the hotel and everything will be fine. When you step outside the hotel, you're in my house."

"I'm a private citizen. I should be allowed to move about the city like everyone else."

"You're allowed. Merely constrained."

chapter nineteen

Channel 20's studio is in Burnaby. It takes two phone calls from the guard at the gate before I'm allowed to get lost in the Channel 20 parking lot. I was told that visitors are allowed to park in Section 7, but I can't find Section 7 to save my life, so I park in Section 6 where the spaces aren't allocated and the vehicles aren't Porsches or Mini Coopers. After that I find a fire door propped open by a square wastebasket functioning as a community ashtray and promptly get lost in endless back halls, wandering without a clue for at least a mile.

I arrive at a reception area from an odd direction, according to the surprised look on the receptionist's face. She tracks down Connie Gagliardi for me by phone. I'm given specific and detailed directions for this final leg of my journey and arrive without incident on the third floor, where Connie is waiting for me. She's wearing her on-camera look: flawless eye shadow and two-tone lips. I think I like her face better without makeup, but this is good, too.

"The scuttlebutt precedes you," she says. "Some giant is thundering up and down the halls searching for Connie. My secretary thought I should hide."

"I try not to thunder," I say, "but I think I got desperate when I hit my fourth dead end."

"You came in the back way."

"And I parked in the wrong section."

"I'm glad you made it. Want to sit down?"

"Do I look done in?"

"You look thirsty."

"I admit to that."

"Stay close," she says. "It's just as confusing up here."

Connie's secretary seems relieved to see that I'm not a deranged water buffalo bent on destruction, and she supplies me with a frosty Evian and a shy smile.

"I've got it set up in my office," Connie says. "It's the raw footage. It got trimmed and edited before it went to air. I had Redhorn playing one of their songs at one point, but the mix was so bad we left it out. They were hoping for a plug for the new CD. I'll make it up to them. You can fast-forward through those sections. The meat of the interview begins about halfway through."

She gives me a remote and points out the play and fast-forward and rewind buttons. I appreciate the instruction.

"I'll leave you with it for a while," she says. "I have an interview to do in Studio 3. If you get brave, you can track me down there. It's the studio after 1 and 2. Otherwise I'll be back in about forty-five minutes."

Connie's secretary, whose name is June, is kind enough to show me a second time how to operate the remote, and then waits with me for a moment to make sure I've grasped the basic principles.

The tape starts with some bumpy images. I recognize a few of the faces — the record executive, Carno I think his name is, and Barnett somebody, "the best record producer on the West Coast," Washburn, the young guy with the old face, and J.J., the guitar player sitting beside the long-haired soprano. The broad shoulders of Bubba, the road manager, block the frame for a moment until the camera pans and locates Buzz and Molly sitting together.

Redhorn performs a song. The guitar sounds out of tune. The camera moves around the musicians but always returns to Buzz and Molly on the couch. Buzz leans forward, nodding his head to the beat. Molly relaxes against the back of the couch at an angle halfway behind her brother's shoulder. I can't see her face.

With June's help I fast-forward to the interview. It was taped in Redhorn's second bedroom. Buzz sits on a chair. CONFOUND THE PREVAILING PARADIGM is readable across his chest. Molly is partially visible on a vanity bench. I glimpse the back of her head reflected in the mirror as she brushes hair back from her face. Music comes from the other room. Every now and then Buzz pauses for a moment, his gaze getting distant as he listens to the tune. Or maybe he's eavesdropping on the music of the cosmos.

Connie's voice is audible off-camera. "Why do you think Mr. Prescott left you all his money?"

"I'll have to ask him when I see him," Buzz says, and he chuckles.

"What are your plans now that the courts have ruled in your favour?"

"It's no secret," he says. "Park asked me one day, 'What would you do if you had half a billion dollars?' I told him I'd give it away, and Park said, 'All of it?' I said I'd give it away to anybody who asked me, for any reason. I wouldn't even ask why, I wouldn't make them tell me a story, I'd just keep handing it out until it was gone."

"What was his reaction?"

"It cracked him up. He thought I was nuts. He said I didn't understand what money could do. He said he already funded charities to the tune of fifty, sometimes as much as a hundred million dollars a year, that the money went to all kinds of good causes. That he had set up his entire financial structure so his good works would carry on after his death."

"But you didn't agree with that system?" Connie asks.

"Hey, I thought that was a pretty good idea, too. I didn't try to talk him out of it. The way he set up his companies makes a lot of sense."

"Then why change things?"

Buzz takes a deep breath, and his gaze elevates a few degrees as if he's standing on a lookout watching a particularly interesting sunset. "I see this vast financial structure of Prescott Holdings, and the vast administrative structure of the Horizon Foundation, and I see eleven million dollars a year in overhead, and salaries, and bonuses in the tens of millions per annum. I see an army of departmental heads, and accountants, and overseers, and expensive legal talent, and I see that barely twenty-three percent of the profits of Prescott Holdings actually gets to the people it was meant for. Sometimes less. I see that a substantial portion of the funds that *do* get handed out is going to support the arts and heritage projects."

"You think the money's being wasted?"

Buzz shakes his head and laughs. "Sometimes I think most money gets wasted."

"What would you do differently?"

"Give people a good meal, or a pair of jeans, or a few bucks to get them through the weekend. I can't fix the world. I won't make judgments about whether someone needs money more than someone else."

"How do you intend to do that?"

"Starting tomorrow, I'm going to begin giving away Park Prescott's money to anyone who gets in line to take some. I won't be giving away much at a time, and I'm not interested in listening to hard-luck stories. Everybody has a hard-luck story. I won't get into who's more worthy than someone else. I'm just going to hand it over. I'll do it on the street if I have to."

"Gonna be a long lineup," Molly says. She leans forward into the frame and pats her brother on the chest with the palm of her left hand. Her head is tilted with love and bemusement, as if listening to the cooing of an infant.

Buzz is serious. "I can give a hundred dollars to each person I meet so they can get themselves a new coat, or buy their kid a week's groceries. Rich people won't bother lining up to get a hundred dollars. It won't mean anything to them, but it'll mean something to someone who's broke or behind in his electric bill."

The music stops in the other room. A phone is ringing. Someone knocks at the door. Buzz stares at something off-camera. At that point the interview is cut off. There are a few clips of Connie taping her reaction shots, and then blank tape.

When I look up, June is standing in the doorway. "More water?"

"No thanks. Which elevator do I take to get to Studio 3?"

"Connie says I should take you there."

June tells me she's hoping to get into production. She'd like to direct. At the moment she's working on a low-budget movie with a bunch of film students.

"We shoot on the weekends," she says. "The director wrote the script. It's way loony, but it's good experience. You want to be in a movie? You'd be great."

I decline with thanks as the cell phone in my pocket rings.

"You'll have to turn that off before we go in," she says.

"That's okay. I'll wait out here until Connie finishes. Thanks for getting me here."

"You sure you don't want to be in a movie? You could play one of the alien soldiers. I don't know if we have a costume that would fit you, though."

"Hello? Who's that — Gritch?"

"Joe? It's Larry Gormé."

When last seen, Larry was waving his fedora at me.

"So you give interviews out at Channel 20 and you won't talk to me?"

"I wasn't avoiding you, Larry. Yesterday was kind of busy."

"How about today?"

"Yeah, well, I've got things to do today, too."

"Like hanging out with the little bingo caller? Watch your back, big guy."

"She did me a favour."

"Meet me for lunch and I'll pull the knives out for you."

"All right," I say. "Give me half an hour. That place across from your place."

"Not there," Larry says. "Too many assassins. Go to Buckles. You remember where that is? On Davie?

"I can find it."

Connie comes out of Studio 3. She glows and hums like a tiny reactor. I've seen the same look on good athletes. She has her game face on. "You made it."

"I had a guide."

"Step into my parlour." She holds the studio door open for me, and I take two steps forward. "Sit right there."

I look around. The chair she's offering me is beautifully lit from three directions. There is a camera pointed at it. There's a clip-on microphone attached to a cord draped over the back of the chair. "Oh, Lord," I say.

"Come on, I did you a favour. You do one for me. It'll only take a minute."

"I don't take good pictures."

"That's so lame. You look fine. You're wearing a nice tie and you haven't dribbled butter on it. Sit down."

A young woman who smells of warm sandalwood powders my face and does something to my hair, a young guy with a headset clips the microphone to my lapel, Connie sits in an identical chair in a somewhat warmer pool of light and arranges herself in her element.

"Any time, Felicity," she says.

Red lights go on, a buzzer sounds, and I catch a glimpse of my face on a monitor off to the side. I don't look like a mass murderer. More like a moose caught in the headlights.

Connie looks directly at one of the cameras and starts right in. "The shooting death of Jacob Buznardo in the early hours of Tuesday morning was a tragic final curtain to a courtroom drama that had raged for nearly two years. In an exclusive interview recorded just hours before the shooting, Buzz, as he preferred to be called, told this reporter that he intended to give away the entire fortune, conservatively estimated at half a billion dollars and possibly higher." She turns to look at me. "I'm talking with Joe Grundy, who is chief of security at the Lord Douglas Hotel. Thanks for coming in, Joe."

"I was in the neighbourhood," I say.

"You discovered Mr. Buznardo's body, is that right?"

"Yes, I did." I'm sitting tight, like a kid waiting to go to confession. I attempt to appear more relaxed by crossing my ankles, but that feels stupid.

"One of your staff at the hotel, Arnold McKellar, is high on the list of suspects, is he not?"

"You'd have to talk to the police about how high on the list he is."

"You can confirm he went missing the morning of the shooting at the hotel?"

"That's right. We haven't seen him since then."

"But he's been in touch with you by phone on two separate occasions since then?"

I smile. "You do get around, Ms. Gagliardi."

"But is it true? He has called you?"

"I've spoken to him, yes."

"Can you tell us anything about what he said?"

"I don't think I can say much. The police have all the information I could give them. I don't suppose I'd be breaking confidence if I told you he says he didn't do it."

"Do you believe him?"

"I hope he's telling the truth."

"Do you have any idea where he is?"

"Not a clue."

"Do you have any theories about what happened to Mr. Buznardo?"

"I'm not much of a theory guy, Connie. I don't think it was too smart of Arnie to run off, no matter what he did or didn't do. I hope he's smart enough to turn himself in. I hope he's okay."

"You have any reason to suspect he might not be okay?"

"No. I'm merely speaking as his boss. I feel a certain measure of responsibility for him."

"And, of course, a certain responsibility for what happened at the hotel."

"Well…"

"After all, as head of security, it was your job to watch out for Mr. Buznardo, wasn't it?"

"Technically, no. It wasn't. Once a guest rents a room it legally belongs to him for as long as he occupies it. We weren't acting as his bodyguards."

"But you were keeping an eye on the situation?"

"The hotel was concerned about the large amount of cash he had in his possession. We thought it might attract unwanted attention."

"And, as it turned out, it did. From one of your employees."

"That's what it looks like," I say. I'm trying not to squirm, trying not to let my annoyance show.

"Was there anything in Mr. McKellar's background check that indicated he might have been capable of something like this? Robbery, possibly murder?"

"Nothing I'm aware of, Ms. Gagliardi. And, as the investigation is still ongoing, and charges haven't been laid, I don't think public speculation is appropriate."

"Are you involved in the ongoing investigation?"

"No, I'm not. I have no legal authority to operate outside the hotel."

"How about inside the hotel? Are you cleaning house?"

"Things are pretty much back to normal."

"Except that one of your employees is a fugitive."

I'm not sure that a response is either appropriate or particularly warranted. I look her straight in the eye with what I hope is an unwavering and guileless gaze. Her eyes are brown, dark, almost black, like her hair. Her firm chin is uplifted, her expression expectant. I have nothing to offer her.

She glances over her shoulder. "Cut."

Red lights blink out, a buzzer sounds, the pools of light are doused around our chairs, and for a moment I can't see much. When things are in focus again, I see her face about a foot below mine, smiling at me with what seems like approval.

"You handled that pretty well," she says.

"Considering I was ambushed."

"Aw, you were warned. I told you I wasn't finished bugging you."

"You also said it would be old news by today."

"It is, but you never know. Once they catch up with your boy it could get interesting again."

We weave our way past cameras and lights, stepping over cables and dodging technicians as they ready the space for what might be a cooking show. There are food smells in the air. My stomach rumbles.

"Let me buy you lunch," she says when we make it to the corridor. "You got breakfast. The cafeteria isn't bad."

"I'd like to, but I have a job to get back to." I give her my most charming smile. "Housecleaning."

She smiles back. "Some other time then."

"Thanks for letting me see the tape. I noticed right at the end there was a phone call or something and somebody knocked on the door. You remember what that was?"

"Buzz's lawyer showed up. He wasn't happy we got the interview and didn't want it on the air. He wanted Buzz to hold off making any announcements."

"What did Buzz say?"

"He said it was a done deal."

chapter twenty

Larry Gormé drinks his Molson from the bottle, holding
the neck with his thumb and three fingers, pinkie raised like
a man sipping tea. He sits at the counter with his fedora on
the stool beside him, saving me a space.

"So? You a TV star yet?"

"Do I look like one?"

"You're wearing makeup."

"Had my hair professionally combed, too."

"A beer?"

"Just a cup of coffee, Larry. I have to get back to the
hotel."

He signals the counterman, who cracks him another cold
one and gives me a cup of caramelized coffee. What I really need
is a sandwich. Something to keep me going through the rest of
the day. Pastrami would be good. I have a look at the menu.

"So, Joe, can I ask you a few things? On the record?"

"I hate being quoted in the paper. I always sound like
an idiot."

"Bullshit. When I was doing sports, you were good for a quote."

"I sounded like an idiot all the same, and that was something I knew something about."

"You know something about this Buznardo business."

"Wish I did."

"Come on, you were there. When did you get so cagey?"

"Since everyone in the world started taking shots at the hotel."

"No shots at the hotel. Scout's honour. I like the Douglas. I used to drink in the Press Club back in the old days, I was there the first night Olive May came to play. I don't take shots at the Douglas." He sips his beer. "What's happening with Arnie?"

"He's made himself scarce, Larry. That's all I know."

"I hear you got in to see Wade Hubble. I haven't been able to."

"I'm wearing my good trench coat. I pretended I had an appointment."

"What did Hubble say? Off the record."

"Off the record? He said get away from me, scum of the earth. I paraphrase."

"Piece of work, isn't he? Hubble? Thinks he's Rupert Murdoch. Must piss him off that he can't wheel and deal with the big boys." Larry looks disgusted. "Hated to see that Buznardo kid go down."

"Yeah, I liked him, too."

"Liked? Shit! He was my big ticket!" He turns to me, his eyes intense, like those of a frustrated terrier whose excavation has hit a sewer pipe. "I was on that story for two years. Not all the time. It wasn't that kind of story. But every time they showed up in court, every time somebody made a statement, I was there. I heard all the testimony, know all the players. Now that it's a big murder, certain hot shots on the city desk think it should be their private hunting preserve. Fuck 'em. I'm the one with the files."

There's no pastrami on the menu. I see a hamburger heading for the other end of the counter, but I'm not tempted.

"The story was just about to get really good," he says. "I was going to ride it like an express."

"The Big Giveaway Story?"

"That was just the catalyst, the opening salvo. The serious action was going to be when the kid got a look at Prescott Holdings' real set of books."

"Why? What's going on there?"

"We may never know now that your idiot pal Arnie McKellar stopped it in its tracks."

"He says he didn't do it."

Larry peers at me. "You talked to him?"

"He's called me. Twice. Connie Gagliardi knew all about it."

"She's got a friend at headquarters."

"She's a charmer."

"At least she can write. If she weren't so pretty, she could work for a newspaper."

"It's a real drawback."

"So what did he say?"

"Not much."

"Come on. I bet you told her what he said."

"That's what I told her. He says he didn't do it. Wouldn't tell me where he was. I told him to turn himself in. Said he needed time to think things through."

"Shithead! Robbed me of a great story." He takes a deep swig, pats his pockets reflexively like a former smoker, has another pull on the bottle. "You believe him?"

"Believe who, Larry?"

"Arnie McKellar, Wanted Man. I thought he'd be good for a cycle or two yet. Today he's below the fold. Tomorrow he'll be on Page 3 unless they catch him. So you believe him? Did he do it?"

"Off the record?"

"Aw, shit, man, I'm a reporter."

"And I'd be speculating," I say, "which is something I'm not particularly good at, and I don't want to read my infantile spit-balling as considered opinion. I'm swimming in sharky waters here. I don't know any of the players and they're probably all ten steps ahead of me, brushing out their tracks."

"Sharks don't leave tracks."

"Let's move to a table," I say.

"Have a beer."

"All right. It's got to taste better than this coffee."

"People don't come here for coffee."

I grab a corner booth with windows at my back and to my left. The street outside has lost its shadows, the sky is getting lower, darker, and a wind is making dust and litter swirl along the sidewalk gutters. Larry slides in opposite with bottles clanking in one hand and two bags of Planter's salted peanuts for sustenance.

"That's it for the sunshine," he says. "There's a Squamish starting to blow."

I have a sip of cold ale. It tastes good but reminds me that I haven't eaten. I snatch one of the bags of peanuts and start thumb-wrestling the packaging.

"Buznardo was a fool," Larry says. "One of God's divine idiots. He didn't have a clue how the world was run, didn't particularly give a shit. You want to give away half a billion dollars? Go ahead. Drop in the bucket. Probably get torn to shreds handing it out, but don't let that stop you. Shit, drop hundred-dollar bills out of a helicopter, stuff them in mailboxes. In a year it's gone and nobody remembers what they did with the money." He takes the peanuts from me and rips the top off the bag with a quick zip, spilling them out onto the tabletop. I get my share. "Look, face it, he was wacko."

"I never saw him without a smile on his face," I say through a mouthful of peanuts.

"He was stoned. And wacko."

"People liked him."

"Not everybody. Wade Hubble isn't heartbroken Jake Buznardo won't be pissing on the broadloom anymore."

"Made a few people nervous, I guess."

"Nervous? Ha! Hubble was shitting bricks. Just when he thought he was going to be a real player, Buznardo cuts him off at the knees."

"I'm sure he's well compensated."

"Oh, sure. Hubble gets more than half a million bucks a year basic, plus bonuses, plus who knows what. He does okay, but he's not running an empire, which is what he thinks he should be doing. I mean, shit, there he is sitting on that big fat cash cow and he can't do anything with her. All the profits go to Horizon."

"That's the way the companies were set up."

"I think he was making some moves under the radar, amassing a war chest. But then the shit hit the fan."

The peanuts are gone. The second bag is under Larry's elbow.

"Buzz Buznardo, Wade Hubble's worst nightmare," Larry says. He has a big pull on his beer but doesn't release the peanuts. "The Monday morning of Parker Prescott's funeral, this long-haired freak shows up at Prescott Holdings with Alvin Neagle, of all people, by his side, and says, 'You're all fired.' Naturally, they threw him out of the building, but the old legal beagle was ready for them. Boom! They're hit with subpoenas, writs, cease operations, assets frozen until further notice. We're going to court, baby!"

He looks expectantly at me, but I'm still working on the top half of my bottle. "Damn, that was a good story! Two big-ass law firms come down on Buznardo like a ton of shit, from all sides — he's a degenerate, he's a dope dealer, he's a homosexual, he's a cultist, he got Parker Prescott hooked on psychotropic drugs, he fucked with his mind. They dragged it out as long as they could. I got twenty-three pieces out of that court case."

He gets up and crosses to the counter. I grab the second bag and look for the magic zipper. Small packages defeat me. Larry returns with two more bottles, no more peanuts.

"What's the matter with Prescott Holdings' books?" I ask.

"Who says anything's wrong with Prescott Holdings' books? Tomorrow morning, it'll be business as usual. In both camps."

"You ever talk to the other camp?"

Larry snorts and wipes Molson off his upper lip. "Edwin Gowins! Now there's a smoothie. Starts off appraising furniture for antique auctions, winds up the darling of the preservation set. If he had his way, the city would be upholstered and he'd pick out the fabric. He gets to give the money away. Who knows how much sticks to his fingers?"

"He wears nice jackets."

"You got in to see him, too? Jesus, you've been busy. What are you up to?"

"Just poking around, Larry. Making a nuisance of myself, evidently. I've been scorned at least four times today, and it's not even lunchtime."

"You've been to Prescott Holdings and you've been to Horizon, is that right? And you and Sergeant Weed are tight."

"Are you writing this down?"

"You see me with a pencil?"

"I'm trying to keep one of my guys from being charged with a murder he says he didn't do."

"Why? Hubble and Gowins would probably kiss his ass if they could. Everybody's getting rich."

"Except the needy."

"The needy! Shit, this is a welfare state. The needy have it made. Socialized medicine, homeless shelters, job training, welfare, free needles, free condoms, food banks, hostels. I know panhandlers who make more money than I do. And they don't pay taxes. There's a bag lady who makes enough to spend the winter in Hawaii. Fuck the needy. *I'm* needy. I'm the guy with the mortgage and the two kids in school and the wife working at Wal-Mart and the taxman up my ass." Larry signals for another beer and then remembers that he brought a backup. He waves the counterman off. "You think Horizon's money goes to feed the homeless? Check the corporate donor's list for the symphony, the opera, the galleries, museums. Those are the needy souls Horizon deems worthy of handouts. The homeless don't give you a private box for Rigofuckingletto."

"I'm going to take off, Larry. I'm neglecting my real job."

"Yeah, all right. I'm going to sit here and think for a few minutes of what a great story it would be if Wade Hubble and Edwin Gowins got arrested for murder. Jesus, that would be sweet."

chapter twenty-one

Shaughnessy is old money. Heritage House isn't a palace, exactly, but it's close enough. It has a turret. There's a moving van in the driveway. Two movers, a man and a woman, are loading a padded package the dimensions of a queen-size mattress.

Grace Ingraham stands on the front steps watching the operation. When she spots me approaching, she appears to grow taller, her head lifts, her shoulders pull back, her elegant neck lengthens.

"I didn't expect to see you again, Mr. Grundy."

"I apologize for dropping by unannounced, Mrs. Ingraham."

"Yes," she says. "Don't tilt that," she tells the movers. "Perpendicular, please."

She turns and goes inside. The door has been propped open. There's a protective runner covering the doorstep. I follow her.

Entrance hall, foyer, vestibule, call it what you will, it's long enough to bowl in. The grand room to the left has bay windows and Chinese rugs. It looks empty. There are bare spots on the walls. The French doors at the far end are open. They lead me into a garden. Grace Ingraham is moving away from me down a curving flagstone path. She pauses to examine a fading rose. With a precise pinch she amputates the bloom and drops it to the ground.

"Are you moving, Mrs. Ingraham?"

She turns to me with a look of annoyance. "Of course not."

"What about the movers?"

"Some things are going into storage. We rotate the collection regularly."

"You have a beautiful home."

"It's not mine, Mr. Grundy. It belongs to HAPS."

"I'm not familiar with that group."

"The Heritage Architectural Preservation Society. I'm the executive director."

"But you live here?"

"I have an apartment, yes. What do you want, Mr. Grundy?"

"I'm trying to talk to everyone who was at the hotel on Friday night."

"In what capacity?"

"I have no official status, Mrs. Ingraham. I expect Sergeant Weed has already spoken to you."

"No."

"Perhaps he's unaware that you were in contact with Mr. Buznardo. I was."

"I told you before —"

"Please, Mrs. Ingraham, I'm not looking to make things difficult for you. I'm sure the police will get around to speaking to you sooner or later. You should maybe call them before they do."

She hugs herself as if against a sudden chill and walks past me, heading for the open French doors. "I don't see how I could possibly help them."

I follow her. "But you can see why they might be interested. You're connected in some way to the Horizon Foundation, which certainly had a vested interest in what Jacob Buznardo was planning."

She stops at the French doors and turns to me. "The room reeked of marijuana smoke."

"What time was that?"

"He was preparing to take a shower. He didn't have the decency to find a robe."

"So that was just before I saw you coming down in the elevator. Say about eight o'clock in the evening?"

"He didn't have the common courtesy to give me his attention. And that odious little lawyer of his, bustling about like a tom turkey with his ridiculous hair…"

Inside the grand room the movers are removing something else.

"That piece is under-insured," she tells them. "Be very careful."

"What did you want to see him about?"

"I was hoping Mr. Buznardo would give me reassurances that HAPS could continue its operation the way Parker established it."

"You knew Mr. Prescott?"

"Of course I knew him!"

I've hurt her feelings, but she recovers quickly.

"He took a personal interest in the society. It was our creation. We built it together."

"I understand he became very reclusive. Did you see much of him in the years before he died?"

"I hadn't seen him in … a number of years. He stopped seeing anyone. We … we remained in touch."

She walks across the room to reassure herself the movers are taking proper precautions. I turn to look back at the garden. There are no new roses.

Grace Ingraham follows the movers out of the room, and

I trail them down the bowling alley and onto the front porch.

"Thanks for your time, Mrs. Ingraham. I apologize if I've complicated your schedule. You had a busy morning."

"I believe things will get back to normal before long."

"When you saw Jake Buznardo that night, did he reassure you about the future of the society? Did you think it would be looked after?"

"He was a fool! Parker Prescott didn't build a fortune to have it dissipated by an infantile sociopath."

"Why didn't Mr. Prescott make provision for the society in his will?"

"He did. I'm certain he did. Before that filthy drug addict destroyed his mind."

"You think that's what happened?"

"I know that's what happened. I knew what was going on in Harrison. That degenerate cut him off from everyone he knew, from everyone who cared about him. Marijuana, poisoned mushrooms — God knows what he put in the man's body. Park was always such a fastidious man, a temperate man."

"Maybe they just became friends. A lonely old man without long to live…"

"It didn't have to be that way." Her voice betrays her need to wail and the rigid control required to hold the pain and loss inside. "There were people who cared about him. He didn't have to spend his last years associating with … *that*." She stands aside to let the movers return for another item.

"It must have been difficult for you to ask someone you despise so much for money."

She doesn't wish me a good day.

chapter twenty-two

I get back to the Lord Douglas after three. I order a sandwich from the kitchen and tell them to deliver it to my office. It won't be pastrami — hard to get good pastrami in this town — but the kitchen makes a fair steak sandwich. I'm really hungry, so it should keep me going for a few hours.

"You're fired," Margo says when I walk into Lloyd Gruber's office.

"I am?"

"Or you can retire, I guess. Who needs you? Rachel Golden really is gold. She's calm, efficient —" Margo looks at me "— she's *here*."

"We're lucky to get her," I say.

"What's happening with Arnie?"

"Still no word," I say. "Before I forget, can you cash these paycheques for me? I've endorsed them."

She glances at the cheques. "One of these is from last April."

"Is it still good?"

"Sure." She shakes her head. "When do you need it?"

"I should have done this yesterday."

"I'll take care of it."

"Thanks."

"You buying a car or something?"

"Making payments on a Ferrari."

She gives me a look. "Sure you are. This is for Dan, isn't it?"

"Just a loan."

She opens the desk drawer to put the cheques away and grabs a brown envelope. "Oh, somebody left this for you."

It has my name on it but is otherwise unmarked, sealed with both glue and Scotch tape. "No name?"

"Just yours. Melanie found it on top of her computer an hour ago." She hands me Lloyd Gruber's personal Jensen silver letter opener.

"Sure I'm authorized to use this?"

"Probably not. Lloyd called ship-to-shore from somewhere around Nevis. Wants to know if he should fly back. I told him we have things under control." She stands. "We do have things under control, don't we?"

"You bet." I open the envelope and pull out a cardboard sandwich, roughly five by eight, inside of which is a 35-mm black-and-white print of two men sitting in the stern of a sailboat. On the reverse side is written: "June 14, Nanaimo." I hold out the picture so Margo can see. "Recognize either one?"

"Wouldn't know them if I found them in my soup."

"The big one with the sunglasses and the Tilly hat, that's Wade Hubble. I recognize the Roman nose."

"The other one?"

"Not sure," I say. "He's got his shoulders turned, but ... could be."

"Could be?"

I check inside the envelope, front and back of the

cardboard sandwich. No note, no phone number, just a slightly out-of-focus snapshot of two men sitting in the sunshine, sipping something expensive, no doubt.

"I've got a sandwich waiting," I say.

"If Arnie calls this afternoon, tell him he's fired."

"He probably knows that."

"I just want it to be my last official act before Lloyd cans my butt."

"That won't happen. Leo Alexander likes you. He says you remind him of his first wife."

"Do we know what happened to her?" she asks.

When I get to my office, Gritch and Rachel Golden are there. Rachel is at the desk, working on what looks like an improved shift assignment chart. I always meant to do that. Gritch sits on the leather couch with his coat open and an unlit cigar between his teeth.

"No matches?" I say.

"I insisted," Rachel says. "No more five-cent cigars on my watch."

"I'm chewing this in the interest of office harmony," Gritch says.

"Margo says you handle the job better than I do, Rachel. She tried to fire me."

"She can't do that," Gritch says. "You're a made man."

"I'm enjoying myself," Rachel says.

"I have to change this shirt. Anything I need to handle?"

"Everything's under control, boss," Gritch says.

I look at Rachel.

She tilts the new chart so I can see how it all fits together. "I've hired those two boys from Moonlight Security. They're solid. They wear plain suits. They'll be around all night."

"The Mormons," Gritch says.

"Sounds good," I say.

When I come back from my shower wearing a fresh shirt, a blue one this time, my sandwich is waiting for me.

"That blue looks good on you," Rachel says. "Don't dribble steak juice on it."

I take a careful bite of rare steak and horseradish sauce, leaning over the plate and keeping a napkin handy.

"That reporter Gormé called again," Gritch says.

"I saw him," I say.

"Yeah, he said that. He called just now. He's downstairs. Has some other stuff he wants to talk about."

"He say what?"

"Nah. Being very coy. Sounds a bit squiffy."

The phone rings, and Rachel answers it.

"He had more than a couple," Gritch says. "Take it from an old piss-tank."

"You back, Joe?" Rachel has put the caller on hold. She's pointing downward.

"He still in Olive's?"

She nods. "Want to talk to him?"

"Tell him I'll be down as soon as I finish my lunch. All he ever eats is peanuts."

"The boozehound's staple diet," Gritch says.

Olive's is almost empty when I walk in. Kyra is alone behind the bar. The sound system has Errol Garner turned down low. In the far corner Larry Gormé sits across from a woman wearing scarves, pins, pearls, rings, and a hat that would decoy exotic birds. She is short and stumpy, has disobedient hair and no natural eyebrows. She looks like an Easter basket.

"Now there's something you don't see every day," she says as I approach the table.

"What's that?" I say.

"A building in a suit."

"Moira Eddowes," Larry Gormé says, "Joe Grundy."

"Sit down. Please," she says. "I'm getting a crick in my neck."

"You want a beer, Joe?" Larry asks. He's finishing a pint of domestic.

"If I have a beer, I'll want a nap."

"Coffee it is." Larry goes to the bar for drinks.

"Where do you like to nap?" Moira asks.

"Here at the Lord Douglas."

"How convenient." She twinkles at me and tugs at a few yards of florid silk held in place by a brooch of amethyst grapes.

Kyra follows Larry back to the table with a tray bearing coffee, beer, gin and tonic. Her hair is pulled back with a black velvet ribbon and braided like a rope down the length of her spine.

"Hi, Joe," she says. "Cream and sugar?"

"Black this time," I say.

"There'll be no napping today," Moira says.

"Probably not," I say. "Thanks, Kyra. How's Laurel's wrist?"

"Sprained. It'll be okay. Would anyone like a menu?"

"Anyone hungry?" I ask.

"Not for bar food," Moira says.

"It's the same menu as the Palm Court," I say, defending the Lord Douglas's grub.

"I've eaten at the Palm Court. Your chef is far too fond of cumin."

"No menu, thanks, Kyra," I say. "Like your hair like that."

"Most men do," she says.

"Of course men like it," Moira says. "It's a hackamore."

"What's that?" Kyra asks.

"A bridle, reins, a harness. You're wearing your own restraining device. Provides a good grip for dragging you back to the den."

"We don't have a den," Kyra says.

Kyra retreats, Larry reseats, Moira has a taste of her gin and appears to approve of that at least.

"So, Moira," Larry says, "tell Joe about the auction."

"Make a note of this name," she says. "Graydon Goulding. He's an appraiser and auctioneer at Tuffleton's Auction Gallery. You'll want to talk to him."

"About what?"

"About Moorcroft teapots and Jensen silver and walnut tables."

"I don't know much about antiques."

"Of course you don't, dear," Moira says, "but Graydon Goulding does, and that's why you should speak to him. He's sold quite a few interesting pieces over the past few months — rare books, prints, Japanese and Chinese porcelain."

"I take it those things are worth money."

"Some of them are extremely valuable. I myself would have happily committed a small murder for a certain imperial jade necklace that went for over eighty thousand dollars. There was a Tiffany lamp that sold for thirty-two thousand. A very small Fragonard that brought a hundred and twenty thousand."

"So far that's over two hundred thousand dollars," I say, proving that sometimes I can add more than two and two.

"Much more," she says. "How about a million dollars or more in the past three months?"

"All that from the same source?"

"Bingo, big guy," Larry says. "Take a guess. You being a detective and all."

"Shaughnessy. Heritage House. There was a van picking up some paintings. She said they were going into storage."

"Maybe till Thursday. Tuffleton's is having another auction."

"The preservation society is selling off their collection?"

"Not *they*, dear heart," Moira says. "*She*. The chatelaine of the manor, the keeper of the keys, the mistress of the hoard."

"The Ice Maiden," Larry adds.

Moira waggles her empty glass at Kyra.

"Okay," I say, "Grace Ingraham has been selling valuable antiques. They're her personal items, right?"

"Well, now," Moira says, "here we enter a muzzy area, don't we, sweetie? What's hers? What's theirs? Who gets the money?"

"You think she's stealing from the society?"

Larry finishes his beer just as Kyra arrives with Moira's gin and tonic and a refill for my coffee.

"Put it all on my tab," I say. "Okay, Kyra?"

"The whole thing?" she says.

"Since they walked in the door."

"In that case, make the next one a double Black Bush, straight up, water back," Larry says.

Kyra's look to me is just a flicker. My nod to her is just as fleeting. She goes to get the Irish whiskey.

"You've met the woman?" Moira asks.

"Yes, I have," I say. "I didn't charm her."

"Well, you wouldn't, would you? You're much too, ah, rough-hewn, shall we say?"

"You didn't drive up in a Bentley," Larry says.

"There was only one man good enough for her," Moira says. She gives her voice a melodramatic cadence. "The dear, dead, departed Parker Simon Prescott. The man whom she loved beyond all reason, the man to whom she has devoted the past twenty years of her life."

"The man she killed her husband for," Larry says.

"She what?" I say.

"I'm sure that's just a scurrilous rumour," Moira says, "but those are the best kind, aren't they? The accepted version is, she *left* her husband, and he had the exquisite good manners to kill himself."

Kyra unobtrusively slides a whiskey in front of Larry. He stares at it for a long moment. "Remember when this was the Press Club, Joe?" he says. "Before your time, mostly."

"Hap Reynolds brought me in here a few times," I say.

"Hap!" Moira says. "We had such a thing for a week and a half."

"Grace Ingraham," I say, hoping to keep the conversation on the main road, "she and Park Prescott had a thing?"

"Theirs was monumental, dear heart," Moira says. "Hap and I had a fling, those two had a scandal. It was delicious. Older man, self-made, wealthy, quite presentable, a bit rough around the edges as attractive men often are —" she twinkles again "— but he knew how to use a fork, and best of all, he was available, a recent, very recent widower, fresh on the market." She pauses to refresh herself. "She, considerably younger, married, unfortunately, but beautiful, if one likes willowy blondes with good bones and trim ankles. Personally, I can't abide them, but no denying it, she was a Thoroughbred. Married to a CBC producer named Greg Ingraham, maker of earnest documentaries about totem poles and sockeye salmon."

"Poor schnook never saw it coming," Larry says. He still hasn't touched the glass of whiskey.

"He was her starter husband," Moira says. "He got her into show business circles, which she parlayed into the theatre set, the dress circle at the symphony, and invitations to gallery openings. Along the way she established herself on committees, fundraisers, benefit concerts. Didn't take her long. She looked good, spoke well. She wasn't born into money, but she carried herself like an aristo. And somewhere along the way, some black-tie affair to which she neglected to drag along hubby, she met Park Prescott and glimpsed the promised land."

Larry picks up the whiskey glass and catches some light streaming in from the street-level window, a reflection from the glass-fronted building across the street refracted in the cut-glass base, dancing on the amber surface.

"He was doing a picture about a ghost town in the Cariboo," Larry says. "Ingraham was. He got a prize for it. He told me."

"She got the big prize," Moira says. "Park was smitten with 'Hello.'"

"He never did another thing after that," Larry says. Then he nods, as if to the memory of his friend, and knocks back the Irish.

"Hanged himself," Moira says. "A particularly elaborate gibbet, wasn't it?"

"I've got to hit the head," Larry says. He stands carefully and walks, too steadily, in the direction of the john.

"He has wife problems at home," Moira says.

"He didn't mention."

"Not a divorce. Nothing like that. They just can't stand each other. Have you ever been married, Mr. Grundy?"

"No, Ms. Eddowes. I'm what's known as a confirmed bachelor."

"Call me Moira, please."

"Prescott and Ingraham were together for twenty years, you said?"

"They were together for fourteen years. And then, as you've probably learned by now, Park Prescott removed himself from society and went off to die alone in the woods. She maintained the facade that they were still a couple, but it was purely an act. By all accounts she never saw him again."

"Odd thing for a man like that to do, isn't it? Leave his entire operation in other people's hands and become a hermit. You'd think he'd at least want those he loved by his side."

"Who knows how people will react when they get the word that their time is up? Anyway, he didn't think he was going to live that long. The doctors told him he had six months. He got his affairs in order, said goodbye to the people he cared about, including the Ice Maiden, I'm sure, and went off to live in a cabin — a very nice cabin, I understand — to face the end looking at water and mountains. Then along comes this hippie with a bedroll and a guitar and asks if he can sleep on the beach for the night. Five years later Park's still alive, doing yoga, eating roots and berries, learning bluegrass banjo. Whatever else that young man was, he was a true healer."

"And Mrs. Ingraham? He continued to support her?"

"She was well taken care of. She had the directorship of the preservation society, she had a position in society — not the one she wanted, of course, but not bad."

"She wanted to be Mrs. Parker Prescott?"

"Of course she did," Larry says, slipping into his seat, "but she was still married, wasn't she?" The front of his shirt is wet. "Could you get your friend with the hair to bring me a coffee? I just threw up twenty dollars' worth of booze, sorry."

"You need some food."

"Not yet. My stomach's fucked."

"How about a glass of milk?" I suggest.

"Yeah, maybe."

I get up and walk to the bar. "Glass of milk, Kyra. I'll take it."

"He okay? He looked white when he walked by."

"I don't think he's eaten today."

"She's right, you know." Kyra hands me the milk. "That woman? About the sycamore?"

"Hackamore."

"Whatever. Joyce loves to yank on this hair."

I carry the milk back to the table. Larry is weeping. "Drink this," I tell him.

"Okay," he says, snuffling and slurping like a little boy.

I turn my shoulder to give him some privacy and face Moira, who doesn't appear at all sympathetic. She pulls a wad of Kleenex from her beaded bag and tosses it in front of Larry. "Wipe your snot. Man your age should have learned how to drink."

Larry wipes his nose and sips his milk.

"After Mrs. Ingraham's husband died," I say, "Prescott could have married her then."

"It began as a grand affair," Moira says. "Hard to

sustain that kind of magic. They ran away to Paris. They ran away to Florence. They ran away to a private beach in the Bahamas. For a year and a half they flaunted and flouted and flew first class to all the very best bedrooms the world has to offer."

"And Greg had to eat shit every day," Larry says. He has a milk moustache. "Sitting in his shit-hole cubicle at the CBC while his wife rubbed his nose in it. One thing having your wife play around discreetly — fuck, at least you can look the other way. It's something else when everybody in the fucking world knows you're a cuckold. It finished Greg. He couldn't stand it. He took himself out of the picture."

"And so Grace and Park's grand passionate affair ended on a sourish note," Moira says. "There was an investigation. There was a period of mourning."

"The bitch wore black for six months," Larry mutters.

"And after a suitable stretch as a merry widow," Moira says, "she expected to become Mrs. Park Prescott."

"But she couldn't drag the old boy to the altar," Larry says. "Somewhere along the line he got wise."

"And now she needs money," I say. "She wasn't provided for in the will."

Larry grins. "He cut her out! Better late than never. He found out what she was."

"What was she?" I ask.

"Conniving, opportunistic, cold-hearted, emasculating, gold-digging, social-climbing, back-stabbing…"

"Don't leave out thieving," Moira says.

chapter twenty-three

It's viewing day at Tuffleton's Auction Gallery. Five wide rooms of furniture, paintings, and collectibles, open for inspection to roving bands of bargain hunters, dealers, decorators, and collectors, all of them stalking the rooms with open catalogues, murmuring and making notes in the margins. In the cavernous backroom, the loading doors are open wide and a cube van is being relieved of a grand piano wrapped in protective blankets. The man dancing around the periphery of the operation fits Moira Eddowes's description of Graydon Goulding: "He's a wisp, but a pretty one." A perfectly knotted half-Windsor matches the foulard puffing from his breast pocket. He wears a yellow waistcoat.

"Mr. Goulding?"

"Yes?"

"My name's Joe Grundy. I believe Moira Eddowes called you?"

"Yes. Hello."

"I don't want to take you away from your duties. It looks busy today."

"It's always like this. Things are supposed to be in place for viewing day, but there are always last-minute arrivals, and space is at a premium."

"I'm interested in some items that might have come from —"

"Shh," he says, raising a manicured finger to his pursed lips, "let's not mention any names out loud, shall we?"

He leads me on a serpentine tour through roped-off neighbourhoods of gilt and veneer and ormolu and marquetry. The walls are occupied by portraits, landscapes, saints, and pagans, all in frames. He speaks in the cagey pitch of conspiracy.

"First, Mr. Grundy, I must assure you that Tuffleton's is scrupulous about ownership, provenance, legitimacy. In fifty-four years we have had only a very few, inadvertent — and before my time, I might add — instances where we've received and/or sold goods whose ownership was called into question."

"I'm not investigating the auction house, Mr. Goulding."

"I understand that. I wanted to make our position on this very clear. Every item that a certain party has consigned to us comes with full documentation."

"I'm just trying to get an idea of how much material from that certain party may have come through this place in, I don't know, say the past two years."

"Conservatively, I'd say over a million dollars' worth of quality items."

"And the ownership? Was it one person, or was it a society?"

"Both. That is to say, each piece bore the imprint of the, ah, certain society to which you allude, but the provenance showed that the items were, in fact, the personal property of the certain individual and had been on extended *loan*.

And this was made very clear in the documentation — on extended loan to the society in question."

"So the society in question returned the items to the certain individual who was then free to dispose of her personal property."

He winces at my use of the gender-specific pronoun and looks around to make certain none of the murmuring foragers has overheard. "That's correct," he says, leading me into another room. This one is airier and has tea sets and upholstery. "The individual has decided to liquidate some of —" he checks behind him "— *her* collection, a substantial portion of her collection."

"I realize, Mr. Goulding, your personal code won't let you be indiscreet, but maybe you could give me a little hint about why the certain individual is doing this."

"The way I understand it, the society we've been talking about hasn't been properly funded for some time. Certain creditors, mortgagers, and the like have started calling in their markers, so to speak. Perhaps the individual in question is simply trying to keep the society solvent until certain issues are resolved."

"I don't suppose you know what those issues are?"

"The way I understand it, Mr. Grundy, is that when a certain *other* person's claim on a, shall we say, high-profile estate went to probate court, all the assets were frozen. As a result, many of the groups that relied on that source are in serious financial straits."

"I've been to their offices," I say. "They don't look like they're hurting."

"I imagine certain levels of management are secure." He sniffs. "I hear that one of the senior executives recently purchased a forty-two-foot, ocean-going, ketch-rigged motorsailer."

"Nice boat."

I have a sudden image of another boat. Grundy, master sleuth, has remembered something he's been staring at for years. I even remember her name: *Emily Blue.*

There's a pay phone in Tuffleton's foyer, and it's simpler to dig for coins than to fumble with my cell phone.

Gritch answers. "What's up?"

I check my watch. It's almost five o'clock. "When do the Mormons get there?"

"They'll be here at six," Gritch says.

"Good. Can you camp out until I get back?"

"Sure. Where are you going?"

"Arnie's estranged wife — what's her name? Lloyd's sister-in-law."

"Adele."

"Adele. Right. You have an address there?"

"Rachel's got everything in stacks and folders. She's working on a system. If I touch it, she says she'll kill me. Somewhere in Kitsilano. You're not going there?"

"I might."

"What for?"

"I had a thought."

"About Arnie?"

"It's just a thought."

"Call Weed."

"I will if anything starts to add up. Listen, damn, do me a favour. Call Randall Poy. I was supposed to drop off some cash and I got turned around doing this other stuff. Just tell him I'll be in tomorrow for sure."

"He loves that kind of talk."

"I know, but tell him I'd appreciate it. As a personal favour."

"I'm on it," he says. "Call Weed."

I don't call Weed. By a process of convoluted reasoning and rationalization, I half convince myself that I'm merely lending a hand to an ongoing investigation by dropping in on an old acquaintance who I think might be able to point me in the right direction. I don't bother taking it any farther than that since it will inevitably lead me back to the obvious: I should call Weed.

Arnie McKellar's estranged wife lives in Kitsilano, over the Burrard Bridge, ten minutes from downtown. She has a dog.

"He won't bite."

"Hi, Adele. Joe Grundy, from the hotel."

"Of course, Mr. Grundy. Henry! Settle down."

"Could I talk to you for a minute?"

"He's all upset. We've had policemen in and out. I had to lock him up."

I hold out my hand for Henry to sniff. He doesn't bite it, I'll give him that.

"I don't know where he is, Joe."

The dog trails her closely and watches me likewise. She goes inside and leaves the door open for me to follow. I step into the front hall but leave it at that. She's in the middle of the sedate living room with the protective wolf-dog guarding her knees.

"I've told the police. I haven't seen him or heard from him for months. Janice, or whoever it is he's living with —"

"Janine."

"Her. She'd have a better idea where he might be."

"Adele, I'm trying to find him before he does something really stupid."

"Stupider than shooting somebody?"

"He says he didn't do it."

"You've spoken to him?"

"He phoned me. He didn't say where he was. While he was on the phone I heard a ferry whistle. Does he know anyone off the mainland, on the big island maybe, or one of the other ones? Or the Sunshine Coast? Anyone up there?"

"His mother lives in Duncan. The police know that. If he went there, they'll already have him."

"That's it? His mother?"

"Oh, Lord, I don't know. I don't know who his friends are, or if he even has any friends anymore."

"You ever take a ferry ride with him?"

"No. Well, not for years. We went to Victoria once. Years ago. It was nice. Well, the hotel was nice. But he wouldn't be hiding out at the Empress, would he?"

"Not likely."

"We used to go over to the big island on Lloyd's boat. Haven't done that for years, either. Picnics. Day sailing. Couple of times overnight. Anchor in a cove. I'll say this for Lloyd. He tried. He really tried."

"Does Lloyd still have a boat?"

"I think so."

"Do you know where he keeps it?"

"He always picked us up somewhere. Horseshoe Bay Marina, the Bayshore, I don't know where he had it. That was such a long time ago."

"Thanks, Adele. I have to go. I'll let you know when I find him. I'm going to make things as easy for him as I can."

"He killed somebody. I just know it. I hate that son of a bitch so much you couldn't even begin to know how much I despise him." As her voice rises and her anger becomes manifest, the wolf-dog's ruff gets thicker and his ears begin to flatten. "His daughter won't speak to him. She thinks he's a loser. Isn't that a great way to think about your dad? She's eleven and she calls her father a loser!" Henry moves towards me slowly, dropping his shoulders like a good fighter. "And if he'd made even a token effort … She's got a good heart. She would have met him halfway."

"Adele, I've got to go."

Outside, the cell phone defeats me again. Battery problems, big-finger problems, ineptitude — I can't make the damn thing work. I find a pay phone on a corner with a view of English Bay: whitecaps rolling in, high tide hitting the rocks, strong wind tearing the spray. I call Margo.

"Lloyd Gruber's boat. Do you know where it is?"

"Joe? Where the hell are you?"

"I'm doing my job, Margo. I need to know where Lloyd keeps his boat."

"How should I know?"

"You're in his office right now, aren't you?"

"Yes."

"Look across the room. What do you see?"

"Okay, there's a painting of a boat."

"Cross the room and look closely at the stern of the boat."

"Joe! What in heaven's name is going on?"

"I'm trying to find Arnie."

"Why? That's for the police to handle. You have no business —"

"Margo, go and look at the painting. Do it right now, please, because I have no time to waste."

"All right, all right. It says ... wait ... *Emily Blue*."

"Bingo. Is there a word underneath *Emily Blue*?"

"Yes. It's *Nanaimo*."

"Thank you. I'll be back tomorrow."

"Joe?"

"Yes, Margo?"

"Don't do anything crazy, okay? Don't be a big he-man hero guy."

"Not me, kid. I'm retired."

chapter twenty-four

The crossing from Horseshoe Bay to Vancouver Island takes two hours. The ferry sails into Departure Bay, Nanaimo, at 9:34 p.m., according to my Rolex Skyrocket. It's dark as I drive off the *Queen of Cowichan*. As soon as I can, I get out of the traffic surge and find a service station. I fill up, check the tires, and decide I can live with the front left five pounds under where it should be. Inside the convenience store I pay for the gas and get a map of the area. The woman behind the counter shows me where the marinas are: the big one at Departure Bay, the one behind the hotel, the one farther down the coast, the one farther down … I should be able to spend the night looking at marinas.

I start with Departure Bay. The wharfinger is helpful.

"Never heard of it," he says.

That was simple. Next on the list is Newcastle Marina, and I luck out. I don't have to ask anyone anything. I see *Emily Blue*, out of the water, upright on a cradle, protective blue plastic tarp covering the wheelhouse and cockpit. I park the car and take a walk around the boat. It's impressive standing on its keel. The waterline on the hull is above my head. There's no ladder hanging down. No light. I rap on the hull. Fibreglass. There's no echo. I'm not reaching high enough.

"Don't think it's for sale," a voice behind me says.

I turn to see a nautical pair. The man is lean and creased and bald as a brown egg. The woman has short-cropped silver hair and rosy cheeks. They both wear yellow-and-blue sailing togs and look as if retirement agrees with them.

"Must be rough out there," I say.

"We ran for home hours ago," the man says.

"I'm not looking to buy it," I say. "I know the owner."

"Lloyd's not around," the woman says. "They went on a cruise."

"That's right. He's my boss. He'll be coming back this week. He asked me to check on things, make sure she was all right."

"Was he worried about something?" the man asks.

"Not really. He's been away for two weeks. It's his first real vacation in almost ten years, and I think it made him a bit nervous being away. You know how he is."

"He's anal-retentive."

"His laces are pretty tight," I say.

"Man doesn't know how to relax. He had us over for a barbecue one night last year and never stopped fussing with things — the propane, the citronella buckets, the bug zapper, the smoke alarm…"

"I've never been to his place," I say. "Hear he's got a great view of the city from up there."

"Up where?" the man asks.

"West Van," I say.

"I meant the cottage," the man says.

"On Gabriola," the woman adds.

As it turns out, anal-retentive Lloyd Gruber is also antisocial Lloyd Gruber. I sure as hell have never been invited for a weekend of sailing and barbecue at his secret hideaway on a Gulf Island. But then I've never been invited to his home in the city, either. Lloyd and I aren't exactly friends. He's been general manager for six or seven years now, since Abe Victor retired with great ceremony. Abe was GM of the Lord Douglas for twenty-five years, respected by the staff, appreciated by the guests. Lloyd, his assistant for eight of those years, stepped into a big pair of shoes.

The last ferry to Gabriola is 10:55 p.m. The first one back to Nanaimo in the morning leaves at 5:45. I'm going to be there overnight. I'll have to find a motel. The pay phone near the ferry dock has an intact phonebook. He's listed: "Gruber, Seagirt Road."

The phone rings four times on the other end, then the answering machine clicks on and I hear Lloyd's unctuous, hesitant tones. "You have reached the Gruber residence. If you wish to, ah, leave a message for Jennifer, Christian, Scott, or Lloyd, do so at the tone, and, ah, please, the time of your call, as well. Thank you." Then a beep.

"This is Joe Grundy. Arnie, are you there? Pick up the phone if you're there." Nothing. "Arnie, I'm coming over on the next ferry. Pick up, Arnie." I listen to dead air until the closing beep cuts me off.

What the hell I'm doing on a ferry to Gabriola Island on a dark and stormy night is a question for which I have only the most basic answer — *checking Lloyd's cottage.* Arnie could be halfway through Alberta by now, heading for Montreal for all I know, but if that's the case I've got no hope, anyway. I only get one idea per problem, and seeing it through is all I know how to do.

I sit behind the wheel on the open car deck as the *Bowen Queen* rocks and slaps its way past Protection Island and into the more serious chop of the open strait. Swells that were ignored by the big ferry from the mainland are giving this glorified water taxi a pounding. Salt spray rattles off the windshields of the first cars in line as I step out onto the deck. A few hardy souls — dedicated smokers — watch the lights of Nanaimo Harbour dwindling astern. A man with a dog stands near the bow, facing the wind and spray. He looks as if he's enjoying the trip, chin up, legs apart, a come-and-get-me stance. The dog, a Chesapeake Bay retriever, stands the same way. She looks as if she's enjoying everything, too.

"Getting rougher," I say as I come up behind them.

The dog wags her tail and smiles at me. She's in her element. The man turns his head. He has a black beard and impressive handlebar mustachios. "First real Squamish of the season," the man says.

"Your dog seems to like it."

"Like sticking her head out a big car window."

"It's my first time going over. My map's a bit hard to read. I take the North Road to get to the North End?"

"No, no. You want Berry Point Road. Just up from the ferry you make a hard left. How far you going?"

"What is it? Ah, Seagirt Road."

"That's almost at the end. Almost to Berry Point. Only about five klicks. If you reach Surf Lodge, you've passed it."

Half an hour later I'm passing Surf Lodge and searching for a place to turn around. I make my U-turn at a viewpoint ringed with broom and blackberries. From there I spot the lighthouse on rocky Entrance Island. The clouds are moving off the moon, the northern sky is clear and black, and Polaris is where it should be.

Then, half a klick back the way I came, Seagirt Road shows up as a tight right-hander down a dark lane lined with tall trees and gateposts. Lucky for me the residents are proud to announce their locations with personalized signs, and THE GRUBERS is easy to read on the lacquered cedar slab at the gate. The cottage beyond is dark, and I hear surf pounding against the rocky beach on the far side. I park the hotel car outside the unlocked gate, get out, and swing open the gate. The curved drive ahead is surfaced with cedar bark chips. Another car is half hidden under an arbutus tree. When I get closer, I see that its front seat is littered with candy bar wrappers and soiled paper napkins.

The building is timber-framed and one level. It faces the water with an expanse of glass, cedar shake roof, and native stone chimney, with a wooden deck overlooking the rocks and the open water. It's dark inside. The sliding door is ajar, and I'm inside without much noise. I stand in the darkness for a moment, listening, sniffing the air like a night creature. There has been a fire in here recently. I can smell the lingering scent of wood smoke. After a moment, I make out the oversize fireplace at the end of the room. There's a glow to the ashes.

"Are you there, Arnie? It's Joe Grundy. I'm alone. No gun."

No flashlight, either, of course. The peerless hotel dick wasn't thinking too far ahead. But I find a light switch before long, and after that the search takes about twelve seconds. Arnie is sitting in a leather wing chair in front of the smouldering ashes in the hearth. A pistol lies on the floor near his right hand, and there's an exit wound through the top of his skull. The bent and blackened metal frame skeleton of an attaché case is buried in the ashes. On the coffee table there's an empty bottle of Wild Turkey. No glass.

The telephone is on the wall behind the kitchen island. I call 911, get put directly through to the island's RCMP detachment. A firm voice tells me to wait by the front gate for the Mounties to get there. After that I stand in the middle of the room for a long moment, touching nothing, looking everywhere. There's blood on the blade of the ceiling fan above Arnie's head. There's a broken glass at the back of the fireplace. There's a brown McDonald's bag stapled shut and clamped between Arnie's splayed feet. I wonder about his last meal. Did he order the McNuggets or the Quarter Pounder with Cheese? Did he have fries with that?

I resist the further urge to scout the place for clues and evidence. None of my business, bad policy, and I probably wouldn't know what I was looking at. When the RCMP cruiser shows up, I'm sitting in the hotel car with the door open, wishing I had one of Olive's Winstons to drag on.

chapter twenty-five

The Mounties know all about Arnie. He's been on their big list since he went missing. They don't know a hell of a lot about me. I spend an hour explaining who I am and what I'm doing so far from home, after which I'm escorted to the Malaspina Motel and told to visit the detachment as soon as I get up. It's 2:00 a.m. when I get my first look at a bed. The phone rings before I can take off the Burberry. It's Weed.

"Hi there, Sherlock. What's up?"

"I found him."

"Oh, I know you found him. I had a long conversation with a certain Corporal Riggins, who seems mildly annoyed that some hotel dick stumbled over their body."

"Sorry they woke you up."

"Hey, they're happy now. They've got a crime scene to process, evidence to collect. Don't be surprised if your name isn't mentioned in the press release."

"That would suit me just fine."

"Why didn't you call me if you knew where he was?"

"I didn't know where he was. I was looking for Lloyd Gruber's boat. I thought Arnie might be aboard."

"That was a good thought. You should have called me."

"Gritch said the same thing." I hate explaining myself, especially when I'm on shaky ground. "You know what you guys are like. I didn't want you scaring people just because I had a half-baked idea."

"It wasn't that half-baked."

"I wanted a chance to talk him into giving himself up."

Silence on the other end of the line. I pull aside a cheesecloth curtain and see dark pines bending in the big wind sweeping up the strait.

"What did it look like to you?" Weed asks.

"The Mounties can give you a fuller report than I can."

"In their own good time. I can get your version while it's fresh. Did it look like a suicide?"

"Looked like he burned the attaché case and the money in the fireplace, then ate some takeout from McDonald's, drank a full bottle of Lloyd's bourbon, and had a bullet for dessert."

"He burned the money?"

"The attaché case was in the fireplace pretty much burned up except for the frame. There were burned bits of hundred-dollar bills in the ashes, plus a broken glass."

"How was the body positioned?"

"He was in a chair in front of the fireplace. Gun on the floor near his right hand. Small-calibre auto. I didn't get close enough to see the make."

"He right-handed?"

"I have to think." I get a quick flash of Arnie signing his daily report. "Yep."

"Make sense to you?"

"Suicide never makes sense to me," I say. "I'm an ex-Catholic. Suicide is a sin."

"Even for an ex-Catholic?"

"*Especially* for an ex-Catholic. Sin's one of the few things you take with you when you leave."

He laughs. "Thank God I'm agnostic."

"The last time I talked to Arnie, when he called from Horseshoe Bay, he sounded like he was working on a plan."

"What? An escape plan?"

"He said … wait a second … he said … okay, *I* said something like, 'Tell me where you are and I'll come and get you.' And he said, 'I'm still trying to work out something.' And I said there's nothing to work out. Then he said there was something."

"Something?"

"Like there was something else he could do, or something else he was trying to, I don't know, wrangle."

"I guess it didn't work out," Weed says.

I catch the 10:05 ferry off Gabriola and get to the terminal in Nanaimo just in time to watch the 10:30 departure to Horseshoe Bay heading out of the harbour into strong blue water. The next sailing is 12:30.

"Where the hell are you?" Gritch asks when I call.

"I'm in Nanaimo. I'll be back at the hotel by, say, 2:45, something like that." The Squamish has scoured all trace of grey from sea and sky. The air vibrates like crystal; the Strait of Georgia snaps whitecaps in the wind. To be dead and miss a morning like this. "Arnie's dead. Looks like he shot himself."

Silence for a few beats, then a heavy sigh on the other end. "Stupid bastard."

"I've been talking to Mounties all morning."

"What do they want?"

"I found the body."

"Oh." I hear a match flaring, a puff, a bronchial rumble. "You should have called Weed."

"He agrees with you."

"Stupid bastard."

"Who? Me or Arnie?"

More puffs.

"You know," he says, "those Moonlight guys aren't Mormons, after all. They're Presbyterians. That's even worse. They take one look at you, they *know* you're predestined for Hell. They don't even bother to hand you a tract. Far as they're concerned, you're already doomed. It's depressing."

"Everything okay in the house?"

"You kidding? With the Calvinists marching, and the cops lurking, and Sergeant-Major Golden on parade, we've got nothing but model guests. It'll be a relief to see Dan's mopey face."

"When's he coming in?"

"Rachel's got him down for 2:00 p.m. He should be here when you get here."

"Did you talk to Randall for me?"

"Oh, yeah, sure I did. Randall said, 'Tell Joe Grundy the clock is ticking.'"

"Did you say I'd consider it a personal favour?"

"Randall said he doesn't do personal favours."

chapter twenty-six

The ferry pulls into Horseshoe Bay at 2:08, and it's another ten minutes before I'm on the Upper Levels Highway heading for Park Royal and the Lions Gate Bridge into Vancouver. I still can't get the cell phone working. I think I'm doing it wrong.

At 2:45, more or less when I said I'd be there, I wind my way up to Parking Level C and hunt for the hotel's reserved space near the skywalk. The parking garage has open sides, the wind is funnelled down the row of cars, and I can feel the air compressed and swirling as I climb out of the Ford. The parking garage echoes with chirping tires and beeping horns, and over those expected sounds I hear a human voice, familiar, talking fast, a note of pleading.

"Wait a minute, wait a minute, this was all supposed to be straight ... wait ... no, I'm not going down there. Wait, goddamn it!"

There's an automatic entrance to the skywalk that slides open when motion is detected. The door is opening and closing and opening again as three figures, two of them large, one of them skittish, dance back and forth across the range of the sensor.

I see them now. It's Dan Howard trying to avoid the Chow brothers.

"Hey, Mikey," I say loud enough to reach them. "Hey, Marlon. Hold on a minute."

The Chow brothers turn to face me, and Dan makes a break for it through the sliding door to the skywalk, running for the hotel. Marlon and Mikey turn to follow.

"Don't go in there, fellows," I say as firmly as I can. They don't listen. Both of them chase Dan into the passage, and I have to go after them.

On the mezzanine level there's no sign of them. Then I hear a clatter from one of the banquet kitchens.

There are no cooks in the kitchen. It's empty except for Mikey and Marlon and Dan Howard, who's lying on the floor between a stainless-steel prep table and the big double sinks. Marlon looms over him. Mikey stands back a few feet, waiting to be entertained.

"Mikey, Marlon," I say in my most reasonable tone, "leave him alone. I don't want any of this brought into the hotel. Tell Randall I'll be over this afternoon. I got held up, but I'll be there shortly. Go tell him."

That's when Mikey pushes me.

My record is an honest one: thirty-six wins, eleven losses, and two draws. Twenty-three of my wins were knockouts. Three of my losses were also knockouts. I got out-pointed six times and was robbed twice. One of the draws I should have won; one of the draws I should have lost. It was a career of sorts. I always gave an honest account of myself, came into my fights in good shape, trained hard, treated it like a job of work, and went to work every day for fourteen years.

My first manager/trainer, Morley Kline, gave me a decent jab to work behind. It kept me alive a lot of nights.

My right hand hurts people when it hits. I never fought for a title, but I kept them honest on their way up, on their way down, or on their way up a second time. "Get Grundy," the promoters used to say. "He'll give you an honest undercard. The crowd likes him."

That was me, "Hammering" Joe Grundy. Honest heavyweight of reputable credentials. And while I may not have been able to handle Evander Holyfield, most men, even large ones who practise dynamic tension and lift heavy things, aren't really equipped to deal with a trained professional going to work. Left jabs splatter their noses and right hooks bruise their livers, and yes, I'll admit it, an occasional head butt and elbow does ancillary damage.

Mikey tries hard to get me wrapped up, but his arms are too short and heavy. I break his jaw and close his left eye while I'm slipping out of his clinch. When he pauses to consider his next move, I drop him with an overhand right that no professional would have let me get away with, but Mikey's left ear is so inviting I have to do it. I feel the other side of his jaw go soft, and he hits the kitchen floor hard enough to rattle some pots.

Marlon, meanwhile, is taking out his gun. I think his leather jacket is too tight, or maybe it's a new rig, but he doesn't get it unholstered in time. I relieve Marlon of his pistol. It's a nice one, a Glock. Mikey doesn't have a gun.

As I help the two of them find their way back to the parking garage, I give them a message. "Tell Randall I'll deliver his installment. I'll pay him a visit real soon."

I got off lucky. The skin over the big knuckle on my right hand is split and will probably take a month to heal, but the fingers all move the way they should. I take the clip out of the Glock and check the chamber, then stuff the components into separate pockets.

I'm back in the kitchen as Dan gets up from behind the prep table. He looks at me and says with wonder, "Both of them?"

"Forget them, Dan. Are you okay? Kneecaps all right?"

"Yeah, yeah, they just threw me down. They hadn't really got started."

"That's good. Get cleaned up. Use the bathroom in my office. Don't go through the lobby."

I locate the first-aid kit in the kitchen. Chefs always keep a good supply of Elastoplast around. I find a bottle of peroxide and a patch that will fit over my knuckle, then go to a sink and rinse out the split. The peroxide foams and stings, cold water washes off the blood, a clean paper towel dries my hand. I fumble with the bandage to get the backing off. My hands are shaking from the adrenaline. Dan takes the bandage from me and covers the split knuckle.

"Both of them?" he repeats.

"Don't make a big deal out of it, Dan. Just get yourself straightened out."

"But Jesus..." he says.

"Randall made a mistake sending them here."

"Randall's going to be pissed."

"He'll think a bit about his next move, and I'll pay him another visit before he comes to a decision. I don't like personal business interfering with the operation of the hotel."

"I'm sorry, Joe."

"No. That's okay. I told Randall how it was. He chose not to listen."

When Dan and I enter my office, Gritch asks, "What did you do to your hand?"

"He kayoed the Chow brothers," Dan calls out from the bathroom. "Both of them."

"Is that so?" Gritch says.

"I was provoked," I say, emptying the clip, dropping the bullets into a hotel envelope, and sealing it. I pull Marlon's Glock out of my other pocket and slip it, the empty clip, and the package of cartridges inside a heavy brown envelope. I scrawl "Sergeant Weed" on the outside with one of Rachel's Magic Markers and throw it in the office safe. My hand feels as if it's stiffening up. "I've got to grab a shower. You fit to work, Dan?"

"Yeah, I'm fine," he says, coming out of the bathroom.

"What time did you get here?" Gritch asks.

"I was just pulling into the parking garage when they jumped me. Maybe fifteen minutes ago."

"Means you were half an hour late," Gritch says. "Rachel had you down for two."

"I had a fight with Doris," he says.

"Sergeant Rachel runs a tight ship," Gritch says. "Don't be late again."

Dan looks over at me. "Rachel Golden running things now, Joe?"

"Dan," I say, "if you look on the wall beside the desk, you'll see a shift schedule. It's got your name clearly marked and underlined and the days you work and the time you're supposed to be here. If you want the job, do the job. And I'd appreciate it if your personal life didn't leak into the Lord Douglas every day."

Dan hangs his head. "I just asked if she was in charge."

"Go to work, Dan," I say. "Save your money, pay your debts, straighten out your life."

Dan slouches out of the office to start his shift. Gritch marks him down on the schedule as "in" and also "late."

"You usually cut him more slack than that," Gritch says. "You going Presbyterian on me?"

"It's the adrenaline wearing off. Makes me cranky."

My right hand hurts like hell. Fingers stiffening, knuckle swelling. I flex my fingers and make an involuntary noise.

"Let me see that," Gritch says. "You sure it's not broken?"

"It's not broken. It was a straight shot. I didn't hit a tooth or anything. It's just split right on top of the big knuckle. It pulls open every time I make a fist."

"Stop making a fist," he says.

"Get me a bucket of ice, will you? I'll grab a shower."

Half an hour later I'm showered and sweet-smelling, and my right hand is buried to the wrist in a tub of crushed ice.

"Black Jack gets back from his fishing trip on Monday," Gritch says. "That'll ease things." The phone rings, and Gritch answers it. "Security."

I pull my wounded paw out of the melting ice and dab it dry with a fresh hotel towel. The split looks clean enough. The swelling has gone down, but not all the way.

"Dan's working, Doris," Gritch says. He looks at me, waggles the phone. "You talk."

I pick up the other phone with my cold right hand. "Doris, it's Joe Grundy. Can I help you?"

"Where is the son of a bitch?"

"He's working, Doris. I can have him call you when he takes a break. Is it important? He said you two had a fight or something."

"I haven't seen the bastard for two days."

"Oh." The best I can come up with.

"He's been staying with his other wife."

"That's not what he told me," I say.

"Dan lies like other people breathe, Joe. Haven't you figured that out yet? You tell him his suitcase will be on the front porch. Don't bother to knock. The locks have been changed. I'm going to stay with my sister in Edmonton until I decide whether to divorce him or cut off his dick."

She hangs up. I hang up. I look at Gritch. Gritch hangs up.

"We may need another guy," Gritch says. "Danny boy's getting to be more trouble than he's worth."

"Let's give him until the end of the week," I say. "See if he can get his act together."

"You don't listen to me a helluva lot, do ya?" Gritch says. "I warned you about Arnie, I told you to call Weed —"

"You're the voice of good sense."

"Damn straight I am."

"I should listen once in a while."

"I got the solution," Gritch says. "Tell Rachel to give Danny boy the gypsy's warning, and if he screws up again, *she* can fire him and you can continue to be the easygoing dunderhead we know and love."

"Yeah, all right. Tell Rachel Dan's on probation."

"Thin ice is more like. She won't stand for any of his bullshit."

"I'm going to grab a sandwich," I say. "I had a bowl of chowder on the ferry, but I didn't finish it. My guts are all annoyed."

"Finding dead bodies will do that to you."

chapter twenty-seven

Before I make it to the Lobby Café, I check in with Margo Traynor.

"I hear you found the boat," she says.

"Yep."

"So that's the end of it."

"I guess."

"Did he leave a note?"

"I don't know, Margo. I didn't search the place. I called the Mounties and they took over. I'll ask Weed when he gets back. He's gone over to talk to them and have a look at the scene."

"Lloyd's cabin," she says.

"Big cabin. Must be two thousand square feet. Right on the water. Very nice."

"Yes, Lloyd's going to be so glad to get back. A murderer, on the hotel payroll no less, breaks into his two-thousand-square-foot cabin and commits suicide. Cops all over the place. He'll love that. Plus we're getting sued."

"Who's suing us?"

"I don't know yet. But somebody. Theo was on the phone earlier. He wants my head, your head, Lloyd Gruber's head, maybe even his father's head."

"Leo says this stuff blows over. Just do your job."

"I'm doing my job, damn it! You do yours for a change!"

"Point taken," I say, turning to leave.

"Wait." She opens a drawer. "I cashed those cheques for you." She holds out the envelope. "What's the matter with your hand?"

"It's fine. Just a scratched knuckle."

"I told you not to be big-shot hero guy."

"This was unrelated."

"Go away now," she says. "I have work to do."

"This will blow over."

"All the same, I'm getting my résumé updated. If I don't get fired, I may quit."

"Don't do that."

"Go away now."

Leo listens to my report. "Why would he burn the money?"

"I don't know, sir."

"They might have cut him some slack if he returned the money."

"Yes, sir."

"Assuming he hadn't killed anyone."

"I think that might be difficult to prove now."

"That's unfortunate," Leo says. "My sons are making the most of things. They'd like to take the Lord Douglas off my hands."

"They honestly think they can run the place better than you?"

"They don't want to run the place, Joseph. They want to tear it down. The Lord Douglas is worth more as a hole in the ground than it is standing. It's a big footprint. Almost a full city block. Prime midtown real estate. The land it sits on is worth, conservatively, a hundred million dollars. The building that would replace the Lord Douglas, should it disappear, could be twice as high. It could hold a multiplex cinema, a shopping mall, a parking garage, a million square feet of retail space, and it could generate a yearly gross income of over fifty million dollars. Naturally, Theo and Lenny want to get their hands on it. Theo already owns the parking garage across the street. My sneaky boy Lenny has also bought himself a sizable interest in the vacant lot to the north of us. You see, my sons already have the Lord Douglas sandwiched. And they're tired of waiting for me to die."

"But you own it."

"We're being sued for a hundred million dollars, Joseph. I don't think the case has merit, but that kind of hit would stake me out for the tigers."

"Should I be getting a lawyer of my own?" I ask.

"Wait a while, see what it looks like when the dust settles. My opinion, this is posturing. Nobody knows how any of this will resolve itself. It could take years."

"Who exactly is suing us, sir?"

He laughs. "Everybody. Prescott Holdings, Alvin Neagle, Molly MacKay, the Horizon Foundation. It'll take months to decide who gets first kick at the cat. Oh, yeah, also, what's the name of that musical group, Joseph? Redstone?"

"Redhorn."

"Is that it? I don't know who they are."

"What are they suing us for?"

"Publicity, what else? It's a circle dance. Everyone's suing everyone else. Neagle is suing for negligence, malfeasance, half a dozen other nuisance claims. Mostly he wants to recover his fee for handling Buznardo's case for two years. He's also suing Prescott Holdings. And Molly MacKay is suing Prescott Holdings as well as us."

"What do our lawyers say?"

"It varies. They're trying to determine if Arnold McKellar was an employee of the hotel or an employee of JG Protection — that's you. If the latter, you can expect to be sued, as well."

"How serious do you think it is, sir?"

"Our law firm is going to earn its retainer for a change."

"If JG Protection can take the load, it will make things easier on the hotel."

"You want to stop another bullet? No, I wouldn't miss this for the world. This should all be very interesting. We're going to have a ringside seat, but we're not the main attraction. There's still a half-billion-dollar estate up for grabs. Prescott Holdings wants to muddy the water." Leo lights a cigar. "Want one?"

"No, thanks."

"Don't worry, Joseph. I've been sued by bigger gonifs than this crew."

"Is there anything I can do about the lawsuits?"

"Get a good seat. Prescott Holdings is claiming they lost money. They'll have to prove that. That means they'll have to open their books. If they come after me, I'll have Aaron Kuperhause, the accountant from hell, probing their corporate colons like an alien proctologist. I don't think they want that. In fact, I don't think their books can stand a great deal of scrutiny right now."

"Then why hit us?"

"Counterattack. They didn't have much choice. Miss MacKay has filed for probate. She claims her brother left her everything before he was killed. Prescott Holdings can't fight it off the way they did the last one. Buznardo won that round and was declared the heir. They can't refight that. It's up to Ms. MacKay to prove her claim in probate court. Alvin Neagle strikes again."

"Does she have a will?"

"I don't know what she has. If she's his sole living relative, she has a case."

"Neagle's handling it for her?"

"Neagle's going to get a fee out of this thing if it kills him. Meanwhile, Wade Hubble is sitting on a land mine. He can't get off or it'll blow up." Leo takes a deep, satisfying puff on his panatela. "And don't you worry about the hotel, Joseph. The Lord Douglas is a rock. Wade Hubble is just the tide coming in." He smiles. "I want to see what flotsam he drags in with him."

When I get to the elevator, Raquel is getting off. She's carrying a half-dozen crisp white shirts on hangers. *"Muy buenas tardes, Señor Grundy. ¿Cómo está?"*

"Muy bien, gracias, Raquel. ¿Y usted?"

"Bien, gracias. You have a good accent."

"I used to travel with a welterweight named Angel."

chapter twenty-eight

At 9:30 I'm back in the office. The Presbyterians are on the job. Gritch still hasn't gone home.

"If you're crashing here tonight, use the little room," I say. "My bedroom smells of Brylcreem and cheap cigars."

"Don't need your room. I took a lease on the infamous Room 704B."

"There is no 704B."

"Son, there are places in the Lord Douglas no one but me and the long-dead architect know about. I could sleep in a hundred spots in perfect comfort and absolute anonymity and no one would have a clue where I was. You've been here, what? Seven years? You still don't know where the thirteenth floor is."

"It isn't," I say. "It's one of your 'lore of the Lord Douglas' tales."

"You go on believing it, pal. 704B isn't even my first choice. It's just the only one with a phone jack."

"What do I dial?"

"Dial 7004." Gritch starts unwrapping a fresh package of foul cigars. He has a smug look on his puss.

"Okay, I'll bite."

"What?" he says, all innocence.

"The thirteenth floor. Where does it hide?"

"Between twelve and fourteen, naturally."

"There is no 'between' twelve and fourteen."

He shakes his head sadly. "You know how twelve and fourteen have that short side by the service elevators?"

"No."

"You've been here seven years and you've never noticed there's a wall beside the service elevators on twelve and fourteen?"

"Okay, yeah, this is an irregular building. I figured air shafts or something."

"It's the thirteen floor, which you can only get to by a back stairway from the eleventh floor. There used to be private 'meeting' rooms up there. It's been closed off for twenty years at least."

"Closed off how?"

"They blocked off the stairwell."

"Private meeting rooms, huh?"

"Some of our more illustrious city fathers had private meetings there, and not with our city mothers." He scratches a match, prepares to befoul the room. I blow out the flame. "Hey."

"Here. Leo sent you a cigar."

"Beauty." He sniffs it. "What's he say about the fifty lawsuits?"

"We talked about it. He says he's not worried."

"Lenny's worried. There's a message on the machine."

I click it on.

"Grundy? This is Lenny Alexander. This whole shitty situation is your frickin' doing, you know that? You understand that? I want you outta there. I want that bowling ball asshole buddy of yours outta there. I'm going to shut down the whole cheesy amateur night in Hooterville bullshit —"

I click off.

"Bowling ball asshole — that'll be me," Gritch says. "It goes on like that a lot more."

"How about the other brother?"

Gritch snorts. "Hell, Theo's laughing. Anything that makes the old man look bad makes Theo happy."

"Theo only thinks he's smart. He's no match for his dad."

"How much we being sued for altogether?"

"Millions. I've just heard about them, I haven't seen any papers. Leo says we may get sued, too. I mean, JG Security. Technically, Arnie wasn't a hotel employee. He was working for me. I'm incorporated. They can come after me if they feel like it."

"You got ten million?"

"A few paycheques I haven't cashed yet."

"That should cover it," Norman Weed says. He's standing in the office doorway. His purple tie is loosened.

"Want some coffee, Norm?" I ask.

"No, I want a drink. I'm off-duty. I want to go downstairs, listen to Olive May sing 'Bye Bye Blackbird,' and have at least three rum and Cokes."

"Go ahead, Joe," Gritch says. "I've got an expensive cigar to smoke. The boys from Moonlight are marching under the banner of good behaviour. I know where to find you."

Weed leans over the bar to scrutinize the shot of me in my trunks with my dukes up. He looks at me and smiles slyly. "You look like you could still go a few rounds."

"Rum and Coke for the sergeant, Barney. Coffee for me."

Barney puts the beverages in front of us. He serves the Coke in a separate glass bottle. Barney keeps several vintage green Coke bottles on ice, mostly for Olive and preferred customers, fills them fresh from the gun, and serves them with ice crystals clinging. He's old school.

Barney moves away to provide for a couple farther

down the bar. Weed adds most of the Coke to his rum and ice, gives it a stir, has a taste. Olive is making her entrance from the backroom. A sudden patter of applause is heard from two tables near the stage.

"Wore it just for you, sugar," I hear her say to a man who appreciates her blue silk shirt. Her bass player, Jimmy Hind, is already on the stand. As Olive makes her way to the piano, he gives her a walking beat. The pattering applause grows around the room as other patrons respond to the strong tempo from the stand-up bass. Olive slides onto the piano bench, and her right hand runs a silver ribbon around the time signature. The three instruments, bass, piano, and Olive's dark, beguiling voice, become one beaming chord.

"Where would you be without me, mister?" she sings. "Where would you be without me?"

"Mercy," Weed says.

We listen for a while, and when the conversation resumes, we pitch it below the level of the music.

"Seen Randall lately?" Weed asks.

"Had a chat with him yesterday morning."

"Everything straightened out? Him and Dan?"

"We've come to an arrangement. Dan's working it out."

"What happened with his girlfriend?"

"Not really any of my business," I say. "He'll have to pull up his socks."

"That's a bandage on your right hand."

I turn to him with the most inscrutable expression I can muster. "And I've got a Glock nine-millimetre in the office safe in an envelope with your name on it for whenever you want to pick it up. I don't know if it's registered."

"Marlon's?"

"Only if it's registered."

"You see Olive's new CD cover?" Barney is back. He picks up a plastic jewel box from the CD collection beside the sound system and puts it in front of Weed. Olive is sultry in a red dress and red fingernails, her left hand touching her hair, her right hand caressing piano keys.

"*Songs in the Key of Ellington*," Weed reads. "She sell them here?"

"You keep that one," Barney says. "Early Christmas present."

Barney moves to the other end, Norman Weed listens to the music, his fingers tap the plastic case. He keeps terrible time.

"You haven't asked about my trip," Weed says.

"You eat the chowder on the ferry?"

"What ferry? People of my rank fly in helicopters."

"So?"

"So, unofficially a suicide. They haven't signed off on it yet, they're having too much fun. They're going to process the ashes from the fireplace to get an estimate of how much money got burned. They have a lab that just loves to run tests like that. Last I saw they were vacuuming the fireplace."

"I saw a hole in the top of his head," I say. "What did he do — stick it in his mouth?"

"Under his chin." Weed points to a spot below his jawbone.

"Straight up?"

"Angled. Right to left."

"And you saw the blood on the ceiling fan?"

"They've got the ceiling fan down."

"Same gun used on Buznardo?"

"That we don't know yet, but we will soon. Looks like the same size — a .32."

"What was in the McDonald's bag?" I ask.

"Oh, that. Ah … let's see. Two Big Macs, large fries, milkshake."

"It was still stapled shut?"

"Yeah. He didn't get around to eating it. It was all still wrapped up." Weed signals Barney for a refill. "I guess he wasn't as hungry as he thought he was. Probably got there, started drinking —"

"Made a fire, don't forget. Must have got a pretty good fire going to burn up the case that much."

"Right. He gets there, makes a fire, sits down, starts drinking —"

"'Makes a fire' means getting wood from the woodpile outside, kindling, getting it started."

"He was lighting it with hundred-dollar bills."

"That takes a while."

"So?"

"So, he probably bought the Big Macs in Nanaimo. There's no McDonald's on Gabriola. He doesn't eat them on the ferry, he doesn't eat them in the car, he breaks into Lloyd's cabin, starts a fire, and starts drinking bourbon and burning paper money."

"So?" Weed says again.

"So that takes a while. From the time he buys the food in Nanaimo until the time he shoots himself has to be two hours."

"So?"

"So, Arnie was a glutton." I sip some coffee. "He weighed over three hundred pounds and he was five-nine, no more than that. He ate all the time. You don't think that between Nanaimo and the ferry ride and the cabin and the booze and the burning he would've reached into the bag and helped himself to a little sustenance?"

"How should I know? He was running scared, he was living on booze and fear. Maybe he lost his appetite."

"The car was full of wrappers and empties. He'd been living in it for thirty-six hours. Looked like he'd been eating the whole time."

"Maybe he was full."

"Arnie was never full."

"What are you trying to work out?"

"It just strikes me as odd that there was an unopened bag of food between his feet when he shot himself."

"He was being Egyptian," Barney says. "Wanted to take some grub for his journey into the next life."

He places Weed's fresh drink in front of him and wipes the bar. Then we all listen to Olive for a moment: "You and me against the world. Sometimes it feels like you and me against the world…"

Weed tests his drink, nods, rubs his face with the palm of his hand. His voice is weary. "People do weird things when they reach the end of the line."

"And he didn't leave a note," I say.

"How do you know that?"

"Did he leave a note?"

"No. Didn't find one. So? Lots of them don't leave notes."

"Arnie was a whiner," I say. "And a complainer. The world was against him. People were always screwing him over. I'd expect him to leave a manifesto."

"I'll inform Corporal Riggins of your concerns when I speak to him in the morning," Weed says. He's starting to sound tired of this. He came for the music.

"When will you get autopsy results?" I ask.

"Hell, we're still arguing over who should get the body. I say he belongs here. The Mounties think he's all theirs. Higher ranks will negotiate."

"Find out for me if he drank a full bottle of Wild Turkey bourbon, will you?"

"Already got a prelim on his blood. He had a two-point-seven."

"Jesus," Barney says. "Sounds like a full bottle to me."

"That's good shooting," I say, "for a drunk, I mean. One bullet straight up. He could've messed the whole thing up with a load on like that, wouldn't you say?"

"Also had a mess of those things he gave to Gritch," Weed says. "Lorazepam."

"So he's not only shit-faced, he's asleep," I say.

"Maybe it was taking too long," Barney says. "The alcohol

and the pills. Maybe he didn't want to wait any longer."

"Yeah, well," I say, "somewhere in his car will be a ferry ticket from Nanaimo to Gabriola. It'll say what time he went over. That McDonald's bag had a register check stapled to the top. That'll say when he bought it."

"Yeah?" Weed says.

"I'm just thinking out loud. I'm sure the Mounties are all over this stuff. They'll have an inventory — what was in the car, what he had in his wallet, what was stapled to the McDonald's bag."

"I'm sure they're being very thorough," Weed says.

"Okay, then, so you'll know in a day or two. And you'll have a post-mortem on what he ate and when he ate it."

"I'll let you know," Weed says.

"I'd appreciate it."

"Oh, yeah," Weed says, "on the subject of autopsies. We got the full report on young Mr. Buznardo."

"And?"

"And he was a very sick young man."

"How sick?"

"Cancer. Pancreatic and liver. He was going out fast. Pathologist said he had maybe a month, maybe six weeks. Not long. He'd had it for a while. Years maybe. But it caught up with him."

"He must have known about it."

"No way he couldn't have."

"Thanks for the exclusive, slugger," Larry Gormé says, sliding onto the stool next to Weed. "A heads-up would've been nice." He's had a few.

"And you know, Larry," I say, "it was the first thing that popped into my head after the Mounties were done with me. Gee, I should call Larry Gormé. I just can't seem to make my damn cell phone work."

"What's with him?" Larry asks.

"He's grumpy," Weed says. "He broke his knuckle."

"It's not broken. It's split."

"On which one?" Larry asks. "Mickey or Marlon?"

"He's not copping to it," Weed says.

"Guy I know works Chinatown says the Chow brothers are a little bent out of shape," Larry says. He waves at Barney in a sign language Barney obviously understands, because he immediately starts drawing a pint of something. "The Mighty Chows ain't mighty anymore."

"Let's not shout it from the rooftops, okay, Larry?" I say.

But Larry's warming to his theme. "Mikey has his jaw wired shut. For obvious reasons he's not talking about what happened. Marlon has his hand in a cast. His left hand. He's a southpaw, isn't he?"

"I believe he is," Weed says.

"Story is he got three fingers caught in the door of the Ferrari."

"Can we change the subject, please?" I say.

"He is grumpy," Larry says.

"I'm not grumpy. Okay, I am a bit grumpy. Half of my day shift is either dead or being harassed by hostile collection agents who have the gall to start beating up my employees inside the hotel, plus the Lord Douglas is getting sued by everybody and his uncle, plus ... a very nice kid was shot on my watch. Yeah, I'm grumpy."

Barney delivers Larry's pint in a frosty glass, raises an eyebrow at Norm, and gets a nod in return. Then he gives my coffee carafe a quick shake to make sure I'm adequately supplied and turns away to grab the rum bottle and a fresh glass. Olive is exploring the possibilities of "Satin Doll." The street entrance opens and in walks Connie Gagliardi. She smiles at me from the landing.

"Bet he doesn't grump at her," Larry says.

I cross the room to greet her. Her hair is jewelled with raindrops and her cheeks are pink. She smells of ozone and negative ions and West Coast weather. "Hello" is about the best I can manage.

"You look happy to see me," she says.

"I do?"

Her coat is wet when I help her out of it. I hang it in the cloakroom off the landing on a wooden hanger, brushing droplets off the shoulders. I glance up to see her watching me.

"Raining?" Lame.

"Just started," she says.

"Would you like to sit at a table?"

"Hell, no, I want to sit at the bar with you guys."

I escort her to the bar. "Norman Weed you've met, I know. Connie Gagliardi."

"Hello, Sergeant. Hi, Larry."

I shift down one stool so she can sit between me and Norm. She orders a glass of house red. Norm and Larry are giving her the bulk of their attention, but both manage to shoot me a glance of speculation.

"I hear it's been ruled a suicide," she says.

"It's not official yet," Weed says. He looks sternly at me. "There'll be an inquest. That could take a while."

"But it puts a capper on the Buznardo case?" Connie asks.

"Works for me," Weed says. "Grumpy here probably isn't finished beating himself over the head."

"Are you grumpy?" she says. "You don't look grumpy."

"He's putting on a happy face because he thinks you brought a cameraman," Larry says. "He looks good on television, don't you think?"

"Oh, Lord," I say. "Was I on?"

"Six o'clock news," she says. "The man who found both bodies. Of course you were on. I had an exclusive interview. We ran it. Some of it. The part where you squirmed was good."

Olive finishes up her set to a rolling wave of appreciation. Weed claps his hands together as enthusiastically as the rest, even though he missed most of the set. Poor bastard had to listen to me root through other people's trash without a clue what I was looking for.

"And now I must be off," Weed says. "Helicopter lag, you know. Ms. Gagliardi, nice seeing you again."

"And you, Sergeant Weed."

"Call me Norman, please."

"Connie," she says.

Weed tosses cash onto the bar.

"I've got it," I say.

"Nah," Weed says. "I didn't have a good enough time to let you pick up the tab. Now I'm going to be thinking about Mickey D's all night." Weed salutes Barney, blows a kiss to Olive, and heads up the three steps to the street entrance.

"What about Mickey D's?" Connie says.

"Arnie's last meal," I say.

"Oh."

"Well, children," Larry says. "I, too, must leave you now. And I'll let you pick up my tab, slugger, because I had a fine time. No wait. That was in 1983."

Larry leaves, doesn't blow kisses to anyone.

"Boy, I sure know how to brighten a room, don't I?" Connie says.

"I wasn't very good company."

"Want me to leave?"

"I'd be very happy if you didn't do that, but I should warn you that I'm feeling morose."

"Morose, you say?" She smiles. "Then we definitely need a table."

An hour later, during Olive's second set of the night, Connie and I have moved closer to the stage. Olive is almost above us now. We have a table on the far side of the stand, in shadows, in a corner, with a candle. Olive sings "Lush Life" while Connie tells me in a quiet voice how she hopes she won't be seeing very much of me.

"I'm ambitious. I'd like to be posted in Washington, or London, or in some hot spot with bullets flying."

I find myself staring at her face, gazing into her dark eyes. I've seen that look before. She's a warrior. "Bullets flying?" I say.

"I look good in a flak jacket."

"Wear a helmet. It's a dangerous world."

"Want to tell me about your hand?" She's cradling my hand in both of hers, like a book.

"Just a bruised knuckle."

"Your hand is swollen."

"It's sore, but I'll ice it down. It'll be okay."

"But you're not going to tell me about it."

"I'm going to try to avoid showing up in the papers, or on the six o'clock news, or in police dispatches for a while. I'm going to steer clear of hot spots with bullets flying. I have a hotel to look after."

"That's what you were doing, weren't you?"

"I was trying to clear Arnie of a murder. It was bad enough he stole the money. Now it looks like the hotel is going to take some big hits."

"And you, too?"

"It could happen."

Just then one of the servers, Lisa, comes towards us. "Joe? Sorry. There's a phone call for you."

"Gritch?"

"No, it's one of the maids. Raquel, I think."

"Excuse me," I say to Connie. "I have to take this. I'll be right back."

Barney is holding the receiver out to me.

"Mr. Grundy. It's Raquella. Raquel. Can you come up here, please? Mr. Alexander has fallen down. *!Venga en seguida!*"

"*Immediatamente.*"

"*Muchas gracias.*"

I make a quick trip back to the table. "I'm sorry. I have to go. My boss is ill."

"Is there anything I can do?"

"No," I say. "I have to look after this."

The elevator is slower than usual. People want to get on at nine, but I tell them there's an emergency and close the door in their faces. I hope I seemed apologetic. I probably looked fierce. The little boy hid behind his mother's legs.

"Come in, please." Raquel's hair is loose, her dark eyes worried.

"Where is he?"

"In the bathroom. He fell down."

Leo is lying in an awkward position, half in and half out of the rub. His left leg is bent over the rim of the tub. His head is on the floor.

"He hit his head."

"Have you called an ambulance?"

"No. I just called you, and I put his robe over him. I don't want to move him. I thought maybe you could carry him to the bed."

"No, I'd better not move him. Get another blanket. Don't let him get cold. Is there a rug under him?"

"The bath mat."

"Get a blanket."

Leo has a phone in his bathroom. Handy. Raymond is in the office. "First we need an ambulance for Mr. Alexander in the penthouse. Then get his personal doctor, Dr. Kronick. Tell him to get to the hospital. Vancouver General probably."

"What happened?" Raymond asks.

"He fell down and hit his head. He may have a broken leg. I don't want to move him."

"Is he alive?"

"Yes, he's breathing. Just do it. Ambulance first. If you can't find the doctor's number, call Margo. Right away. Better call Margo, anyway."

The paramedics come and move him gently onto a spinal board, with his head immobilized, his legs securely belted, and his arms bound around his chest. Then we take him to the fifteenth floor, around to the service elevator, and straight down to the kitchen and out through the back. The ambulance pulls up to the loading entrance.

"You taking him to General?" I ask.

"Yep," one of the paramedics says. "He'll be there in four minutes."

"His doctor will meet you there," I say.

I go back downstairs and check Olive's to see if Connie is still there. Barney points at the street entrance. "She left ten minutes ago, champ,"

I climb up to the sidewalk, even though I know she's gone home. The street is almost deserted. A steady downpour drenches me, but I stand there, anyway, absorbing the rain.

chapter twenty-nine

Sunrise. A chill west wind with attendant drizzle has kept Wreck Beach nudist-free. Molly MacKay is careful to point the urn away from the wind. The ashes disperse like smoke curling across the chop. I catch myself framing a petition to no one in particular that particles might make it to the anchored freighters in the bay and carry bits of Buzz to far-off lands and other seas. I'm standing on a sloping rock, above and behind the assembly, at the bottom of a steep path down the bluff. There are more people than I expected, a dozen or so. I recognize some of them. Near the water J.J. is under a broad umbrella playing bottleneck guitar for the soprano with the haunting voice. Her silver hair is dancing and her song is pulled away from me. I can barely hear it on the wind.

> "Oh come angel band
> Come and around me stand
> Oh bear me away on your snow-white wings…"

Bubba, the big road manager, has his arm around Molly's shoulders, and she leans against him as they rejoin the little congregation. There are hugs and kisses all around and someone starts another song. It seems like an inappropriate time for me to be bothering her with more questions. I turn to see Connie Gagliardi and her camerawoman sliding down the path.

"You might have told me you knew where it was going to be," Connie says.

When she hits the sloping rock, I put out a quick arm to keep her upright. The camerawoman has wisely worn Reeboks and stays vertical on her own.

"You wore the wrong shoes," I say.

"You could have mentioned the location." She smacks me on the shoulder. "Are you getting any of this?"

"It's a nice picture," the camerawoman says. She has a clear plastic bag protecting her camera.

"Have they done the ashes yet?" Connie asks.

"They just blew away," I say.

"Shit!"

"Shush," the camerawoman says, "I want some of this song."

Connie stands beside me, and we listen for a moment to the tune, to the wind and the gulls crying, to the choppy waves smacking the rocky shore. She has her footing now and doesn't need support but still she holds my arm.

"Melancholy weather," she says.

"Shush," the camerawoman hisses.

Connie lets my arm go and picks her way carefully down to the beach with microphone in hand. The camerawoman turns her head to look at me without taking my picture. "She watched one of your old fights last night."

"Mercy," I say, "where would she come up with one of those?"

"Sports archives at the station."

"Did I win?"

"I don't know," she says, turning her head to peer through the viewfinder again. "I wasn't invited."

The camerawoman follows Connie down to the beach. I stay where I am, above and behind.

It *is* melancholy weather, appropriate to my current disposition — my boss in a coma, my right hand throbbing like a gumboil, my job in jeopardy, no answers. I don't even know the questions anymore. And I haven't done any of what I set out to do. Arnie is still the murderer of record, and Jeff Axelrode hasn't paid his $16.45 bar tab. Maybe it is time for some changes. I've been much too comfortable at the Lord Douglas, too comfortable for too long. Might as well be wearing slippers and a cardigan the way I've been shuffling around lately, operation going to hell in a handbasket, sloppy procedure, suspect workforce. The scorecard doesn't look great.

And then something starts happening down on the beach. While I was indulging myself in rue and recrimination, Bubba the road manager has gotten himself into a tussle with a big man I didn't see arrive. Jeff Axelrode is trying to talk to Molly MacKay. She doesn't want to talk to him and is seeking the protection of the musicians and the mourners who have started to disperse. Bubba bars Axelrode's way, moving side to side like a cutting horse. Axelrode attempts to bull his way past, and Bubba gives him a two-handed shove, the kind that cops give when they slam you against a wall. Axe shoves back. He, too, is familiar with the cop shove. It looks from here to be an even match.

Connie's videographer is in candid camera heaven, gliding around the periphery of the scuffle, grabbing reaction shots. Connie tries to get a microphone near Molly, but Buzz's sister is shielded by backup singers and record producers. Axelrode loses his footing on the rock and now stands on the sand, looking up at Bubba and the musicians. He shouts something at Molly and retreats with as much dignity as his righteous anger will support, heading up the slope at an angle to where I'm standing. I climb with him, parallel and near enough that when we reach the top of the bluff we're within conversation range. He shouts, anyway.

"Get the fuck out of my face, Grundy. I'm not in the fucking mood."

"I need to talk to you about Arnie."

"That piece of shit. He's dead."

"Someone else was there."

"Prove it." He gets into his car, and when I step closer, he points a gun out the window at me. "I'm serious, Grundy. This is not a day to piss me off."

"It's about your bar tab."

"What the fuck are you talking about?"

"You and Alvin Neagle ran out on your bill the night Buzz was shot."

"Get it from Neagle. He's the one with all the fucking money." He has to put the gun on the seat beside him to start the car and jam it into reverse.

"You on the run, Axe? The police are looking for you."

"Mind your own business, Grundy."

"Arnie getting killed is my business."

"Arnie McKellar fucked with the wrong people. Just like you're doing, asshole."

He puts a ding in the hotel's sedan when he backs out. That's another bill I'll have a hard time collecting.

At the other end of the parking area people are getting into cars. Molly is nowhere to be seen. Connie is coming towards me. The woman with the camera is getting into the Channel 20 van. She doesn't look our way.

"Is Molly still down there?" I ask.

"Just left," Connie says.

"Did you hear what that man wanted?"

"Dee got a lot of it on tape. Come and watch it later."

"No ambush?"

She smiles. "You've had your fifteen minutes, big fella. How's your boss doing?"

"He's still unconscious."

"What do the doctors say?"

"They don't know. He could wake up any minute. He's not hemorrhaging, his brain function is good, and his vital signs are okay. I'm hopeful."

"Good," she says.

There's an awkward pause.

"Ruined our date," I offer.

"Was that a date? Felt like a date for a minute. But you didn't ask me out."

"No, it was your doing."

"So? Ask me. I've been carrying the freight in this thing so far."

"You're too short for me," I say.

"I have heels."

"You're too young for me."

"I looked up your bio. You've got a few good rounds left, bud."

"And you're what? Twenty-eight?"

"What a charmer. Still, just for the hell of it, you should ask me out sometime." She turns and heads towards the Channel 20 van.

"Which fight did you watch?"

She looks back at me.

"Dee, your camerawoman, said you watched one of my fights."

"Dionee. That's her name."

"I don't think she cares for me."

"She has a protective streak."

"Which one did you watch?"

"I've seen three. That's all we had."

"I'm surprised there are that many."

"Your fight with Mr. Holyfield was on pay-per-view. We only had a highlight package."

"Not my finest hour."

"You kidding? It was magnificent. Of course, you did

get your clock cleaned, but you were stalwart doing it."

"How about dinner?"

"I wouldn't want to keep you up past your bedtime."

"I'll have a nap," I say.

chapter thirty

I hear Lloyd Gruber's annoying alto voice before I reach the front desk. Melanie gives me a wide-eyed look and an elaborate shudder as I approach. The Groob has returned. She nods in the direction of Lloyd's office. I can't see Lloyd yet, but Margo is visible through the glass partition, standing at attention, chin firm and eyes brave.

"Fine state of affairs! Cut my trip short. Come back to find this operation in shambles ... and ... and find policemen crawling all over my ... my private property. A stack of lawsuits a foot high…"

Margo shouldn't have to face the storm alone.

"Welcome back, Lloyd. That's a nice tan."

"Oh, it's you, Joe." Lloyd is always a bit fidgety when I'm in his space, possibly because I outweigh him by fifty pounds. One of the fidgets is reflexive watch-checking. Lloyd is big on timetables. "It's nine-fifteen. I expected you fifteen minutes ago."

"I had a funeral to attend."

"Oh. Anyone we know? Knew?"

"The hotel guest who was murdered. You didn't get a chance to meet him."

"Ah, well, I'll get right down to it. Obviously, you've heard about Mr. Alexander. Of course you have. You attended to him. He's okay, isn't he? I mean, he's … he's comfortable? How is he?"

"He's not conscious yet."

"You mean he's in a coma?"

"Technically, I guess, but his doctor says there's lots of brain function going on."

"Do they know when he'll wake up?"

"No, sir, they don't."

"That's because he's in a coma." Lloyd bustles about his office, straightening, adjusting, wiping, desk, bookshelves, furniture. You'd think Margo had trashed the place.

Margo stands clear of his housekeeping. She turns to look at me. *Get ready.*

"It looks like he'll be needing a new hip," I say. "They can't do much until he wakes up, of course."

"That's a shame," Lloyd says. "And, of course, you'll be attending to him, I mean, while he's in the hospital."

"I'll be doing whatever he wants me to do, yes."

"Which, ah, brings me to the next order of business. With, ah, Mr. Alexander out of commission, so to speak, Mr. Alexander the Younger, that is, Mr. Theodore Alexander, the son, is, ah, assuming control of the hotel's operation, as of —" he checks his watch "— twenty minutes ago. He's sent me a number of directives. The first of which, and you should be aware that this is not in any way, ah, a reflection of my personal views — I would prefer to consider the situation more fully — but, in light of what's happened here while I was away, and with Mr. Alexander Senior unable to direct things personally, the Lord Douglas is, on specific orders from Mr. Theodore Alexander, terminating its relationship with, ah, with JG Security as of the end of business hours today, Friday, at which point the, ah, hotel will expect you to clear your office of all personal effects."

"When, exactly, is the end of 'business hours' at the Lord Douglas?" I ask. "We're pretty much a 24/7 operation, aren't we?"

"Ah, let's say, today, end of today, midnight."

"I have a contract."

"According to Mr. Theodore Alexander, you have a personal services contract with Mr. Leo Alexander and not with the hotel per se. Now I don't care to get into what that means in terms of your severance package, or any of that. That's … that's between you and Mr. Alexander Senior. But as he is no longer capable of, ah, managing the hotel, and whatever personal services you may be required to provide for him in his present condition would seem to, ah, divert your attention from your responsibilities here at the hotel, Mr. Alexander's son, Theodore, thinks it will make more sense to, ah, relieve you of your obligations here. The first order of business, conveyed to me personally by Mr. Theodore Alexander, is that another security system will be put in place by the beginning of the week."

"What happens between midnight and Monday?"

"I assume Mr. Theodore Alexander is making arrangements for temporary security."

"Just a friendly reminder, Lloyd. *You* are supposed to be managing the Lord Douglas, not Theo. You work for Leo Alexander."

He flinches at this, or maybe he just flinches every time I speak. He turns his back and gives his attention to straightening frames on the wall. "Mr. Theodore Alexander expects you to vacate your residence, as well, but I'm sure we can be a bit more flexible about the deadline for your departure."

"Be careful, Lloyd," I say. "Mutiny is a hanging offence." I follow Margo back to her office.

"Joe, I'm so sorry."

"What about you, Margo? You going to be all right?"

"Nobody's said anything so far. I'm not … who knows what's going to happen."

"None of this was your fault."

"Joe," she says, "I can run a hotel. Given the authority, I could run this place very well. But part of running a hotel is handling things like what happened here this week."

"You did great. I'm the one who messed up."

"I don't suppose Lloyd has mentioned that *he's* the one who made you hire Arnie?"

"I'm sure he'll have to mention it to someone at some point."

"I think you're getting a raw deal."

"Don't worry about it," I say. "It's not over."

Gritch is steamed. "So that's it. We're out of a job?"

"Looks like it."

"They've been waiting for this like a pair of vultures."

I leaf through the overnight reports. Rachel Golden and her new recruits have things running smoothly. If Theo Alexander has half a brain, he'll hire Rachel to take over.

"What are you going to do?" Gritch asks.

"Go to the hospital. See how Leo's doing."

"I mean if we're out of here."

"I don't know. I could rent an office, I guess. Freelance security work. Personal protection. It's all I know, really."

"Can I smoke cigars there?"

"You shouldn't be smoking cigars here."

"Okay, should I not smoke cigars in the new office the way I shouldn't be smoking cigars in here?"

"You're asking me if you can smoke cigars in this new office that I don't have?"

"I'm asking if I should start looking for other work."

"What other work can you do? Your talents are as limited as mine."

"Match made in heaven."

The phone rings. When I answer it, Weed says, "You are a bastard, you know that?"

"Hi, Norm."

"Thorn in my side, pain in my ass."

"I'm fine, too. Thanks for asking."

"Corporal Riggins says they would have figured it out, anyway, that he didn't need me phoning him at 7:00 a.m. to drag his head about ferry tickets and McDonald's receipts, that they had all that stuff ready to look into."

"I'm sure they did."

"Nonetheless, in the interest of interagency co-operation, and assuaging my raging headache, not to mention the pain in my ass, they checked the relevant documents first thing this morning."

"And?"

"And it looks like Arnie must have bought those burgers in Nanaimo three hours after he arrived on Gabriola."

"Neat trick," I say.

"So you're a bastard and we're currently looking for his delivery man."

"I don't think McDonald's has home delivery." I hang up and stare blankly at Gritch. I'm not really looking at him, just using his dome to stay focused.

"What's up?" he asks.

"Arnie didn't shoot himself."

"What do you mean?"

"Or he had help. I don't know. There was someone else there. Someone brought him some food. Someone else was there when it happened."

"You started packing, Grundy?"

Theodore Alexander is standing in my office doorway wearing about eight yards of fine wool worsted and a rep tie from a regiment he never belonged to, or a school he never attended.

"Hello, Mr. Alexander. No, I haven't thought about it."

"Better get organized. A new outfit will be here in a

couple of days. I want a smooth transition."

"I'm sorry, sir. I don't take orders from you. Your father hired me, pays my salary, I do what he wants."

"He's no longer in charge."

"He is as far as I'm concerned, sir."

"Look, Grundy, you're out. Your whole team of fuck-ups is out. I want this office vacated by tonight."

"Mr. Alexander, I was given a direct order by your father, the man who owns this hotel, that I wasn't to take orders from anyone but him. Until he tells me I'm fired I will be doing what he hired me to do, which is look after his interests. I'd appreciate it if you didn't do anything contrary to your father's wishes."

"You're outta here, Grundy. Count on it. I'll change the locks, put guards on the door if I have to."

"You'll be paying for these services yourself, will you, sir? The security budget requires my signature."

"Go fuck yourself."

"Give my regards to your brother, sir."

Gritch closes the door while Theo is still fuming. I hear him stomping away, muttering as he goes.

"Has-beens and drunks, thieves and murderers. Fuckin' loony-tunes!"

"He's got a point," Gritch says.

chapter thirty-one

Lions Gate Hospital is across the bridge of the same name in North Vancouver. The weather hasn't improved since Jacob Buznardo's dawn memorial. I pull into the visitors' parking lot just in time to see Alvin Neagle, still wearing his blue polyester suit and bad comb-over, bustling along a line of cars, fumbling with keys and briefcase and a stack of file folders. When he decides on a vehicle, I pull up to his bumper, blocking him in. He glances up with annoyance, then backs up two steps when he sees who is getting out.

"Good morning, Mr. Neagle," I say as pleasantly as I can muster. "Joe Grundy. Nice to see you again."

"Get away from me, Grundy."

"That's exactly what Mr. Axelrode told me a couple of hours ago."

"I don't want any trouble." Neagle opens his car door and tosses the files and the briefcase onto the passenger seat.

"Mr. Axelrode wasn't quite as peaceful. He pulled a gun on me."

"That's nothing to do with me. You should inform the police."

"I intend to."

"I have nothing to do with Axe Axelrode. He is no longer in my employ."

"Who's he working for now?"

"Just move your car, Grundy. I'm late as it is."

"Certainly, sir, but if I could have just a moment more of your time."

"What do you want?"

"To start with, there's the matter of your $16.45 bar tab from Monday night."

"What?"

"You and Mr. Axelrode ran out on your bar tab. I'd like to collect."

"Talk to Axe."

"He said I should take it up with you. He said you were the one with all the money."

Neagle fumbles with his wallet and tugs out a reluctant twenty-dollar bill. He puts it on his car's hood and pushes it towards me as far as he can reach without actually touching me. "There. That cover it?"

I grab the bill just as he lets go, and before the wind can carry it off to Chilliwack. "I'll get your change, sir."

"Keep it. Keep the change."

"I'll make sure Barney gets the gratuity, and I thank you on his behalf."

"Now will you move your damn car?"

"I just have a couple more questions, sir, if you'll bear with me. I understand you've taken offices in the Horizon Building. Are you now in the employ of the foundation?"

"I don't think that's any of your business." He climbs behind the wheel and buckles himself in.

"But you've met Mr. Edwin Gowins, the managing director?"

"What if I have?"

I slip between the two cars to stand close to his open window. "Forgive me if I'm a bit confused about the legalities here — this isn't my area of expertise — but doesn't that suggest a conflict of interest? You're the attorney of record for the late Mr. Buznardo, and you're involved, at least to some degree, with one of the parties who'd love to see any outside claim dismissed. And yet you're also representing Molly MacKay and her claim. That's a lot of balls you're juggling."

"As you say, Grundy, this isn't your area of expertise." He decides on the correct key.

"Nonetheless…"

"This is all none of your business. You're a hotel dick chasing a bar tab. You've got your money. Leave me alone." He turns the ignition. His starter motor sounds reluctant.

"There's also the matter of my employee's murder," I say.

"Murder? You talking about McKellar?"

"Arnie McKellar, yes, sir."

"He killed himself."

"The police aren't so sure about that. They think he may have been murdered."

Neagle shuts down his engine. He looks pale. "They know who did it?" he asks.

"No, but the list is short and your friend Axelrode is right at the top."

"Shit!" He bangs his hand on the steering wheel, letting off an unexpected beep that causes someone two rows over to look around. "That fucking Axe! I hire him, out of the goodness of my heart, to keep tabs on Buzz. Before you know it, he's making deals with Wade Hubble, feeding him inside information, playing both ends against the middle."

"So Axelrode was working for Wade Hubble and Prescott Holdings?"

"At least. Who knows how many people he was shafting."

"And who are you working for now, Mr. Neagle?"

"Privileged information. Talk to your boss. He might clue you in."

"Mr. Alexander? You've seen him?"

"He just woke up, Grundy. I have a feeling he wishes he was still asleep."

I'm spending a lot of time in hospitals lately. All the hushed voices and antiseptic aromas make me uneasy. As I negotiate my way with much care between food and medication trolleys, I spot Raquel coming towards me, eyes bright and glistening.

"Señor Grundy! It is so good, you coming now. *¡Un lindo milagro!* He's awake!"

"I just heard. How is he?"

"He is asking about you. Come. Please."

Leo Alexander, as befits his station and his bank account, has a private corner room at the end of the hall. Raquel escorts me to the open door, and then I feel her hand slip off my elbow as she backs away.

Leo doesn't look too bad. He isn't hooked up to anything that beeps or breathes. That's always a good sign.

"How are you feeling, sir?"

"Joseph, glad you came by."

"They're keeping the pain down, are they?"

"A nice nurse gave me a shot of something very comforting. How are things in my house?"

"There have been some changes."

"Oh?"

"Theo has announced that he's taking over as managing director. He's replacing JG Security as of today and bringing in some other outfit."

"He thinks he's kicking you out?"

"Yes, sir."

Leo laughs. "That boy. Subtle as a belch, isn't he? Can't wait until they throw dirt on my face. Where's his brother?"

"Haven't heard from Lenny, sir. I figured he was in

agreement with what Theo was doing."

"The last thing those two agreed on was how much they disliked my second wife. Maybe it was my third. But they both want me out of there, that's certain." He winces. "Lift the bed up a little, would you, Joseph? Thank you." Leo tries to get comfortable by shifting an inch or two.

"Should I get the nurse, sir?"

"No, I'm fine. I could use a cigar, but that will have to wait." He rolls his neck.

"I saw Alvin Neagle outside, sir. Anything I should know about?"

"Molly MacKay, through the good offices of Alvin Neagle, has hit us with a civil suit in the wrongful death of her brother. That one might get sticky."

"That makes me a bit sad. Her brother would never have done that."

"Just her lawyer making sure she covers all the bases. Who knows how her claim will play out."

"There's been another development, sir."

"What?"

"It looks like someone was with Arnie McKellar when he died."

"Is that so? Helping him do the job?"

"Could be, I guess. But Arnie was very drunk and sedated and probably not in any shape to make an informed decision."

"You think he was murdered?"

"It certainly seems like a possibility."

Leo reaches for the juice box on his breakfast tray. I help him to get a sip, then hand him a napkin. He wipes his lips and looks at me. His eyes are clear, his mind is working fine. "It would be to our benefit, vis-à-vis the civil suit, if it could be proved that Arnie didn't shoot the man when he took his money."

"Yes, sir. The police are still working on it."

"I know they are. But I'd feel more comfortable knowing

that someone who had the Lord Douglas's interests at heart was also looking into things."

"I'll stay with it, sir."

"Thank you, Joseph." He reaches out to shake my hand. "We have to look after my house. We're being assailed on all fronts." His grip is firm, his veins are blue, the skin is bruised and yellow around the intravenous needle in the back of his hand. "Is Mr. Gruber going along with this Theo business?"

"Yes, sir. He's the one relaying the orders."

"Mr. Gruber shouldn't be taking orders from anyone."

"There's nothing I can do for you here?"

"I'm well taken care of," he says, glancing towards the door where Raquel stands half out of sight but fully present. "Look after the Lord Douglas, Joseph. I'll be fine. I'm going to be in here a few days, maybe a week. I need you to watch my house."

"What should I do about Theo?"

"I've told you. Theo doesn't give the orders. Do the job I hired you for. I'll attend to Theo."

"Very good, sir."

chapter thirty-two

Lloyd Gruber is so thrilled at the news of Leo's recovery that he spills tea all over his freshly organized desktop. "He did? That's, ah, wonderful, I'd better get over there."

"You might want to call Theodore," I say. "Let him know things have changed."

"Is Mr. Alexander, is he, ah, capable? He's aware?"

"Oh, he's fully aware, Lloyd."

"I'm sure he'll understand that certain provisions had to be made…"

"Might have been a bit premature," I say, not to rub it in too much.

Margo is genuinely happy about the latest development. And she's also on top of the situation. She's arranged flowers, get-well cards from the hotel staff, a schedule for visitors, and a statement for the press. Margo has also ordered Rolf Kalman in the Palm Court to begin a shuttle service of decent food across the Narrows and onto Leo Alexander's dinner tray.

"Can you think of anything else?" she asks me.

"I think you've got everything covered, Margo."

"How about clothes? Books?"

"He's got Raquel looking after those things," I say.

I leave Lloyd and Margo and head back to the office to relay the good news. Black Jack Burke has checked in by phone. Rachel has him on the speaker, and Gritch is sitting on the couch, raising his voice to be heard.

"Hi, Jack," I say as I hang up my jacket. "How's the fishing?"

"Hey, Joe," he says. "I'm looking out at the second best fishing river in the world."

"What's the best?" I ask.

"That's the one I haven't found yet, but this one's plenty great."

"You missed all the excitement," Gritch says.

"I don't think so," Jack says. "I locked onto a steelhead on the Ash three days ago. This guy would have taken a round or two out of you, Joe."

"Big fish?"

"Who knows? I never saw the son of a bitch. Twenty pounds easy, maybe thirty. He dragged me half a mile, nearly drowned me twice, wrapped my line around a tree, and took my little lure home for his trophy wall. You got anything to match that?"

"Geez," Gritch says, "let's see now. Arnie's dead, somebody, maybe Arnie, murdered a guest and stole a quarter of a million bucks, Leo Alexander just woke up from a coma, and oh, yeah, we were all fired this morning but that might not stick. Over to you, Jack."

"I stuck a hook through my earlobe," Jack says.

I grab the morning shower I missed rushing off to Buzz's wake before breakfast, which also reminds me that I haven't been eating at all regularly. My stomach rumbles as I scour off the accumulated grime and confusions of the night and the morning. When I return to the office,

I'm fresh-smelling and stubble-free, but my belly is still complaining of neglect.

Gritch looks up from his newspaper. "You look okay for a tenuously employed hotel dick with a lawsuit hanging over his head."

"We've been sued, too?"

"Oh, you betcha."

"Where's Dan?" I ask.

"I fired him," Rachel says.

Rachel is at the main desk. She seems at home there, more than I ever did. She has her charts arranged, schedules, phone lines.

"When?" I ask.

"This morning. He was an hour and a half late. He had a lame-ass excuse. I fired him."

"I told you," Gritch says. "That's something you should've done a year ago."

"What was his lame-ass excuse?" I ask.

"Something about his wife changing the locks and he couldn't get his shoes."

"The part about her changing the locks is true. She said she'd leave his suitcase on the porch."

"Lame ass," Gritch says. "What was wrong with the shoes he had on yesterday?"

"I wasn't interested in his shoes," Rachel says. "I'm trying to keep the shifts organized."

"You did the right thing, Rachel," I say. "I should have done it a long time ago."

"We make a good team, Joe," she says. "I'll crack the whip, you give a shit."

"What's my role?" Gritch asks.

"Beats me," she says. "If we're still in business, I'm going to hire some people."

"More Presbyterians," Gritch says.

"I think I can find a couple of good people," she says. "Not necessarily Presbyterian."

"Try finding us a nice Unitarian won't think I'm going straight to hell," Gritch says.

"You *are* going straight to hell," Rachel says.

She grabs the phone in mid-ring, speaks low. I check the fridge. She's organized that, as well: juice, water, cheese, apples. I help myself to a few cookies — refined sugar, just for the boost — and also grab an apple for appearance's sake.

"I'm going to take a walk," Rachel says. "Somebody in the parking garage wandering around."

"Want backup?" Gritch says.

"No. He probably can't remember what his rental car looks like. Carry on."

As soon as Rachel leaves, Gritch picks up his ashtray and moves to the desk to sit next to the phone.

"How's the old man?" he asks. "Really."

"He's good. He's stuck in there for a while, but he's in charge. If Theo shows up, lock the door. He doesn't run things, and neither does his little brother." I finish the cookies and start on the apple. "How'd he take it? When she fired him?"

"Dan? He laughed. He said, 'Why should today be any different?' Personally, I think Danny boy is coming apart at the seams."

"I need one of those day-minders," I say. "I still have to drop off some cash to Randall Poy."

"Why bother? Danny boy's not your problem anymore."

"I said I would. I like to follow through."

Gritch shakes his head. "Rachel's right. You've got the 'give a shit' area covered."

"Yeah, well, I've got a few other things to check on, so I might as well add it to my list."

"You hitting the streets again?"

"Leo would like me to get the hotel off the hook if I can."

"How are you supposed to do that?"

"In a perfect world I'd prove that Arnie didn't murder

Buzz, and that would demolish the wrongful death suit our friend Alvin Neagle has filed on behalf of Molly MacKay."

"Neat trick, slugger."

"Wouldn't it be?"

"Axelrode's your best bet," Gritch says.

"He definitely figures in there somewhere. But he's roaming awful free for a murder suspect, don't you think? Driving around, waving a gun, disturbing Buzz's wake. You'd think he'd have been picked up by now."

"He's hard to miss."

"He isn't acting like a fugitive. More like a loose cannon."

The skywalk across Carrall Street was constructed five years ago, shortly after Theo Alexander bought the parking garage and made a deal with his father. It's a convenient set-up for a hotel constructed long before parking was a major consideration. The street below is moving like a river of traffic and airborne city litter. Rachel is coming towards me, heading back to the hotel.

"He found his car," she says.

We pause for a moment above the street, looking down on the traffic.

"That's good," I say.

"You going out again?"

"I need to check a few things for Leo. I've got the cell phone with me if anything comes up."

"You take care of your business, Joe. I've got your back."

"I'm glad you could sign on."

"Hell. This is a vacation. Malcolm wants to install a Jacuzzi. By himself. That should be good for two months of plumbing horrors."

"You've got the job for as long as you want it," I say.

"I know. Let's see how it works out. I don't want to get up Gritch's nose."

"You won't. Gritch is eyes and ears. He's the only person in the world who understands this building, knows where everything is, who everyone is, what scams we can safely overlook, and which ones we come down on. Gritch won't meddle with your system. He may grump from time to time, because he doesn't like change, but he'll be your best source for inside information on the staff and the guests."

"You sound like you're getting ready to quit."

"No. I'm just happy to have someone who knows how to run the regiment while I'm out chasing shadows."

"You'll catch up to them, Joe."

chapter thirty-three

There's a monumental Chinese wedding feast going on in the backroom of the Noodle Palace. I can't see Randall Poy anywhere through the beaded curtain, and it's obvious I wouldn't be welcome to look for him in the crowd of more than a hundred celebrants. I make a mental note to return later and attend to that irritating detail. Then I make a mental note not to forget the first mental note. And as I get back into the car, I remember a separate mental note that got misfiled somewhere. Time to check in with Sergeant Norman Weed.

"It slipped my mind," I tell Weed when I land in his office.

"A murder suspect points a gun at you and it slips your mind?"

"There were other developments grabbing my attention. Leo woke up."

"He did? That's terrific. Is he all right?"

"He'll be getting an artificial hip."

"I could use one of those, and an artificial prostate. So tell me about Axelrode."

"He caused a scene at Buznardo's ash scattering. Tried to get to Molly. I don't know what about. Connie's camerawoman recorded some of it."

"It's Connie now, is it?"

"After that he pulled a gun on me and told me to get out of his face."

"Were you in his face?"

"I asked him about Arnie."

"And?"

"He said Arnie McKellar messed with the wrong people the same way I was. Then he dented my fender and drove off."

"Drove off in what?"

"Me and cars. Let's see. A blue one, big, domestic, Chevy I think, licence W-F-something, four-four-something."

"That'll be useful. What about the gun?"

"Automatic. Not too big."

"I've got to get this information out there," he says. "It might have been more useful three hours ago."

"I said I was sorry."

"Yeah, yeah." He tosses a canvas duffle bag onto his desk. "That's all Buznardo's stuff."

"I get to look?"

"Go for it. She didn't want it."

"His sister?"

"She rooted through it. She was looking for something but didn't say what, and I didn't ask. Whatever it was she didn't find it."

Weed leaves the office to spread the word of Axe's licence plate and personal armament while I sit beside his desk to rummage in Buzz's duffle bag. Not much. A few books, jeans, underwear, T-shirts. Buzz travelled light. There's a leather pouch containing a few guitar picks and tightly rolled strings, a pitch pipe, and a Hohner Marine Band mouth harp in the key of A.

"Not much stuff for a half-billionaire," I say when Weed comes back in.

"Yeah, I know."

"No wallet?"

"Oh, yeah, she took that. It had the car insurance, registration."

"Registration for?"

"Prescott's Mercedes. Neagle said Buzz liked to drive the Mercedes."

"He kept a journal. There's a bunch of notebooks."

"Looks like he was scribbling in them all the time," Weed says. "Mostly ramblings. My guys couldn't find anything useful."

I leaf through the first of the notebooks, the most current one, half of it blank pages. There's a recipe for black bean soup, a drawing of a salmon's jawbone. Weed settles into his chair and looks across his desk at me.

"You've been getting up people's noses," Weed says. "I've had complaints from some very influential assholes."

"And I've been so polite. Did you know the solstice last winter was on December 22 at 3:45 a.m.?"

"They want me to rein you in. They're threatening restraining orders."

"And I wore my good suit and everything. Did you know you can use coffee as an enema?"

"Is that in there?"

"Oh, yeah."

"Cease and desist, they say," Weed tells me. "Makes me think they have things to hide."

"I'm sure they do. There's lots of money involved — a lot more than a suitcase full."

"I told them I'd talk to you."

"And?"

"And I'm talking to you."

"You want me to back off?"

"Shit, no. Shake the tree all you want. Who knows

what will fall out. This isn't an official position, you understand. Officially, I'm advising you to keep your nose out of other people's business. Unofficially, hey, it's a free country, you haven't hurt anyone, you're just making a nuisance of yourself."

"Some pages are cut out of this notebook. Did you notice?"

"I noticed."

"Who's this guy C? He used to visit them in Harrison."

"I don't know. That's all it says — C?"

"Yeah." I read aloud from one of the journals. "C showed up on Thursday. It's becoming a regular thing once a month. They play a game of chess and shoot the shit and have a couple of drinks. It's good for P. They mostly talk about old times, and I'm not part of that. Thursday night C asked me to drive him home instead of calling a cab like he usually does. He asked me how P was doing, health-wise, and I said he was doing better and better all the time. C was happy about that. He admires P."

"Not a clue," Weed says.

I flip through the journals for a few minutes while Weed goes out to the squad room in response to a wave from one of his detectives, the guy with the Elvis hair, who's on the phone. The journals are a mixed bag — song lyrics, recipes, quotes from enlightened luminaries like Black Elk, Kurt Vonnegut, Groucho Marx. Buzz had a roving mind.

Weed comes back into his office. "They just found Alvin Neagle. He washed up by the mouth of the Capilano. A couple of fishermen snagged him."

"How was he killed?"

"Don't know yet. They're still checking the crime scene."

chapter thirty-four

I can see the mouth of the Capilano River as I drive for the second time in the same day across the Lions Gate Bridge. Far below I spot the distinctive orange and yellow vests of cops and Mounties, patrol boats and crime scene tape. The river is shallow where it meets the salt water, and cops are wading upstream and down, hunting for anything useful. I find a parking space in the Park Royal lot and walk the rest of the way. I can't get within a hundred yards of ground zero. There are gawkers and reporters in equal number, all of them straining to see the backs of one another's heads. Weed's arrival, however, is treated with due respect, and a path is made that closes behind him like the Red Sea. None of my many waves to Weed, nor to his partner with the Elvis hair, can buy me a ticket to the main attraction.

"You waving at me or at her, Grundy?"

Larry Gormé squeezes his way through the crowd to get to me.

"Waving at who?"

"Your girlfriend, wee Connie Gagliardi. She's got a front-row seat."

"I can't see her."

"She's out there. She's got a better friend at the cop shop than you have."

"What have you heard, Larry?"

"It's all idle rumour and speculation. All I know for sure is that it's our boy Neagle and that he's deader than either of us."

"What are they doing out there?"

"Having a good time. They hauled him out of the water, so now they have to search the water for a while, I guess, see if he dropped any spare change."

I start angling myself down the bend of the crowd, trying to carve my way closer to the front of the pack. I'm as polite as I can be, and my progress is steady. Being large helps, as well.

"I'm sticking with you," Larry says. "It's like trailing an icebreaker."

I finally spot Connie and her protective videographer, Dee, pushing their way back through the crowd, more or less in our direction. When she spots me, I'm rewarded with a spontaneous grin. She points in the general direction of the ad hoc parking area and the white Channel 20 van.

"I guess this means you won't be pushing it all the way to the front," Larry says.

"You're closer than you were before," I say.

Retreating is somewhat easier than advancing, and it doesn't take me long to make it to the Channel 20 van. Cops and interested spectators are still arriving.

"You leaving?" I ask.

"We don't ever have to date," Connie says. "We can just keep meeting at these life-and-death events."

"I'm not that crazy about life-and-death events."

"Too bad. It's what I feed on. You and I are totally incompatible."

"So it would seem."

"I've got nothing," Dee says from inside the van. "Looks like shit." She appears on the far side of the van, her ever-present Sony on her shoulder, and acknowledges my presence with a polite nod, not hostile, not especially warm. "I'm going to see if I can get up that tower with a long lens and pan down off the bridge. Might get an angle worth ten seconds of air."

"Don't break a leg," Connie says.

"I'll need you for the stand-up in ten minutes," Dee says. "Back by that nice tree."

"I'll be there," Connie says. She turns to me. "I hear your boss woke up."

"He did."

"I'm glad."

"I guess you couldn't see much over there," I say.

"I talked to one of the fishermen who snagged the body. He said he was using light tackle. Seemed proud of himself for landing Neagle without losing his lure. The cops took his lure, anyway. We got a nice shot of the body bag."

"They're stacking up."

"Epic proportions."

"Your ticket to the big time?" I say.

"If I'm out front when it breaks."

In the distance an ambulance bulls its way through the onlookers, heading for the highway. Alvin Neagle is on his way to the morgue. The cops have started to congregate in small knots, exchanging information. Weed is somewhere in the crowd. I can see an Elvis hairdo. Connie looks around and locates Dee, climbing one-handed down from a light standard. Strong and smooth and already looking for her next shot.

"I've got to go," Connie says.

"Any chance of us getting together later? Without cops and corpses?"

"You've got my cell." She winks and hurries off to do

her stand-up report. Within ten steps I've lost sight of her curly head in the crowd.

There doesn't seem to be much point in hanging around. I'm not sure why I came, except that I have no clear plan for unravelling this mare's nest. I'm just following my nose in some faint hope of arriving somewhere. An enterprising catering truck is dispensing weak coffee and overpriced sandwiches near the mall parking lot. Larry Gormé has his back turned while he sweetens his coffee from a small flask. He swirls the java around gently and looks up to see me heading in his direction.

"Shitty morning," he says. "Damp cold goes right through me."

"Yeah, I can feel it, too. Larry, you're the guy with all the files. You ever hear of somebody with the initial C who used to visit Prescott and Jake Buznardo when they stayed in Harrison?"

"C, huh?"

"He must have lived close by. He used to take a cab back and forth. They played chess."

"Oh, sure, Park's old chess buddy, Warren Carleton. He and Prescott were partners when they started out. They made their first million together."

"Know where he lives?"

"Out there somewhere near Harrison Lake. What do you want with him?" He sips his coffee and inhales through his nose, revived and grateful, if only for the moment, that he's still alive. "Tell it to me on the way."

"You feel like a day trip?"

"You'll never find it on your own. It's all cornfields and hazelnut groves out there."

"I've got the hotel car."

"Great!" Larry says. "I hitched a ride."

In no time at all I get us onto a highway that would, should we care to see it to the end, carry us all the way to the Atlantic Ocean. We won't be going that far. Harrison Hot

Springs is a little over a hundred klicks east of Vancouver, and it takes a bit more than an hour to get there at the rate traffic rolls on the Trans-Canada when there aren't any messes. We move along at a good clip.

Larry sips his Irish coffee and stares out the window at the passing blur. "Poor old legal beagle," he says at last. "Came within an eyelash of grabbing a brass ring the size of a hula hoop, and *pow*, moment of victory, it all turns to shit."

"It interests me," I say, "how Hubble and Gowins have managed to keep their skirts clean in all this."

"You don't think those boys do their own dirty work, do you?"

"Maybe not, but who *is* doing their dirty work? Arnie? Neagle? Jeff Axelrode? Kind of low-rent mercenaries for such a high-stakes game, don't you think?"

"They ain't the cream of the crop."

"I'm trying to see it from their end. They seem to be winning the war without doing much. Buzz was their big threat. Now he's out of the way. A hotel security guy with no connection to either establishment is pinned with the robbery, *and* with Buzz's murder, *and* he conveniently 'shoots himself' before he has to answer any questions. The next big threat, Molly MacKay's possible claim on the estate, suffers a major setback when her lawyer — who may have been working both sides of the street — shows up face down in the Capilano River. These guys can't seem to lose."

"'Twas ever thus," Larry says, finishing his coffee to the last drop and then carefully folding the cardboard cup in on itself. "The rich are different. They have insulation."

We drive in silence for ten minutes past motels and service centres, private airports and theme parks.

"Tell me again why we're going to see this guy?" Larry says.

"Don't think I told you the first time. I don't know. He's just another name that popped up, an initial, really, and right now I'm grabbing at straws."

"Seems to me you should be looking for Jeff Axelrode."

"I think Weed has that part covered. He's got a few hundred people on the job. I wouldn't know what to do with Axelrode if I found him."

"When they do find him, we'll be out of town."

"You invited yourself."

"Call it an old news hound's hunch, Grundy. You seem to be all over this thing. Where you go, things happen."

"More like, where I go, things have already happened."

"Close enough," he says. "There's a coffee place in Harrison. I need a pit stop."

"You and me both."

chapter thirty-five

There are huge sand sculptures and castles around the lagoon on Harrison Lake.

"It's the sand," Larry says as we cruise down the Esplanade. "Something about the sand around here. It sticks together or something."

"It'd better," I say. I'm looking at a colossal creation involving Noah's Ark crammed to the gunwales with two of everything. "That thing must be ten feet tall."

"Hey, we're talking world championships. Teams from all over come for the sand. Grab the next right and then left."

We continue out Rockwell Drive along the eastern shore of the lake, past a yacht club and a marina. The bluffs on our right are stacked against a two-lane road of blind corners and sudden dips. A waterfall washes the asphalt, and blocks of rock the size of refrigerators lie at the base of shale slides.

"How far?" I ask.

"Keep going."

"I keep thinking that cliff's going to land on top of me."

"Sort of like life," Larry says. His flask is empty.

When we find Warren Carleton, he reminds me of a walrus. His moustache is snow-white and is obviously the pride of his face. He has the ruddy complexion of a man who spends his days on the water and his nights by a fireplace. Carleton is sweeping leaves off his patio as we come up to the gate. He waves us in to a wide garden of faded flowers and fruit trees hanging on to a few late apples and pears.

"I know you," he says. "Joe Grundy. Hammering Joe Grundy. I used to follow boxing before it got all weird. I saw you more than once. Nice to meet you."

"Thanks," I say. "This is Larry Gormé. He works for the *Emblem*."

"An ink-stained wretch, eh? You look like you could use a drink, Mr. Gormé. How about you, Joe?"

"I'm the designated driver."

"Well, then, we mustn't let you go to waste. Follow me." He parks his broom and barges into his home.

"We don't want to impose," I say through the open glass doors.

"Don't you recognize hospitality when you hear it?" he says from the kitchen. "Besides, I'm lonely as hell this week. My wife is in Vegas for her annual slot machine offensive. I don't approve, but she always seems to come home with more money than she took. Beats me how she does it. I'm having a cold one. What's your poison, Gormé?"

"Beer will be good," Larry says.

"This is about Parker Prescott, I'll bet," Carleton says. "I ran a few reporters out of here some time ago. You may have been one of them, Gormé. Were you up here bothering me last year?"

"Might have been," Larry says.

"Thought so. I've read your stuff." He hands Larry a frosted bottle of Beck's. No glass. "Not bad when you get your facts straight."

"Thanks," Larry says. "If you ran me off last year, how come I'm getting a beer this time?"

"I didn't run you off personally. I ran a mob off. You vultures were getting on my nerves. Besides, not every day I get a visit from a heavyweight contender."

"I was never a contender," I say.

"Never made the top ten," he concedes, "but you were lurking pretty close there for a while."

"The good years," I say. "They didn't last."

"It's a rough game," he says. "Ginger ale, juice, water?"

"I'll have a Canada Dry," I say. "Thanks."

"So," he says, handing me a cold can, "how do you fit into this?"

"I work for the Lord Douglas Hotel where Mr. Buznardo was shot Monday night. I'm looking into the case for the hotel."

"Aha."

"An employee of mine is suspected of having done it. I'm hoping there's another explanation."

"Don't know if I can help you there," he says. He has a deep and satisfying swig from the bottle and wipes his pride and joy. "I hadn't seen Jake Buznardo for almost two years, since right after Parker died."

"I understand you and Mr. Prescott were partners in the beginning."

"Four Star Marine. We made plywood for boats. Finest quality. We couldn't compete, of course, not in the long run. The big outfits were turning out a pretty good product themselves, but we had a few innovations they wanted to get their hands on. We made a good deal for ourselves."

He leads us through a walkway beside the house and onto an expansive deck with a fine view of the lake. The clouds are heaped against the lumpy islands across the water; the sky is in motion.

"We went our separate ways after that," Carleton says. "Park decided he wanted to play the market — he was more of a cowboy than I was. Me, I liked fast foods. I figured people would always be eating on the run — I knew I was — so that's where I went. Franchises, hamburgers, pizzas, tacos. I did okay. Sit down, gentlemen. Let's have a look at the water. That's what it's there for."

"Nice view," I say.

"Yeah, the sky's kind of dramatic today."

"Have you been following the story, Mr. Carleton?" I ask.

"Call me War. That's what I answer to, have since I was a kid. And, yes, I have followed the story. I even called Gormé's paper a couple of times to correct one of their more egregious blunders."

"Which one was that?" Larry asks. "I stepped in it more than once."

"This was the one where you said Park Prescott was visiting spiritualists and witch doctors. Load of garbage."

"I had confirmation."

"You made it sound like Park had gone loony. It wasn't like that."

"How was it?" I ask.

"Not a witch doctor," he says with a look at Larry, "a shaman. Guy named Gene Eugene over near Agazzis. They used to go over there once in a while, listen to the wind or whatever. It was a cleansing ritual."

"How about the spiritualist?" Larry asks. "We talked to her."

"Mazie? She's a sweet old bat. Reads tarot cards and charts the stars. My personal opinion, Park used to visit her for the female companionship. She has a warm and generous nature."

"All this was Buznardo's doing?" I ask.

"Yeah," Carleton says, "after Buzz moved in, Park started getting out a bit. Not the places he used to go. He didn't go to Paris or Hong Kong anymore. He just went to Agazzis to listen to the wind."

"How did they meet?"

"Park and Buzz? The kid brought him a fish. Can you picture it? Kid comes up the beach carrying this salmon, Park told me, comes up to the back door with this nice fish he's caught, and he asks Park if he can build a little fire on the beach to cook it."

Collecting Larry's empty bottle, he clinks it against his own. I waggle my can to indicate I still have a beverage. Carleton then carries the bottles into the house through the open French door, and I follow him through to the kitchen as he continues his story. "Park says, 'There's a barbecue pit on the patio. Knock yourself out.' So the kid cooks the salmon and brings Park a piece, and he eats it. He said to me that it was the first food he'd eaten in a year that tasted like food." He puts the empties into a recycling box and grabs a fresh pair out of the fridge. "Then the kid asks if it's okay if he sleeps on Park's beach before moving on in the morning. Park says, 'Sure, why not?'"

Carleton leans against the sink and turns his head to gaze out at the garden. "That night it rains. Park wakes up at midnight or whatever, and he remembers the kid is sleeping on the beach, so he puts on a hat and goes out to see if the kid's okay, and there he is, Buzz, under a poncho, happy as a clam, watching the rain come down. Park tells him to come up to the house for some coffee. So he does. They sit in the kitchen and drink tea, not coffee, because the kid asked for tea. They sit there until morning, and Park tells Buzz he's on his way out, that he's come here to die, that the doctors have given him only a short time to live. Buzz asks, 'What, you're dying tomorrow?' And Park says, 'They say six months, maybe a year. Buzz cracks up. He thinks it's hilarious."

Delighted with the memory, Carleton laughs, then tells me, "Buzz says, 'Shit, I thought you were dying, and Park says, 'I am dying, goddamn it.' Then Buzz says, 'Bullshit, the sun's coming up, you stupid fucker, what more do you want?'" He wipes a tear from his cheek without embarrassment and flashes me a generous smile.

"Buzz was dying, too," I say.

Carleton stares at me. He's still wearing a damp smile. "I know. He told me. He wanted my advice about how to make sure Molly was looked after. He knew he probably wouldn't live long enough to give it all away. He was going to give it a shot, though. I'll give him that. At the very least it would have exposed the true state of Prescott Holdings' finances."

"What did you tell Buzz?"

"About what?"

"About how to look after Molly."

"I told him to make a will. If he didn't want to deal with lawyers, he should write it out in his own handwriting and have it notarized and his signature witnessed."

"Did he do it?"

"I don't know, son. I didn't see them for a while. Molly was visiting that summer. I think they drove around to some music fairs."

Carleton remembers his mission and abruptly heads back to the deck, talking as he goes. "What a character! He took off one time, disappeared for a month, and when he came back, he had a banjo. Park had mentioned he always wanted to learn how to play the banjo. The kid had gone to Calgary and traded some Haida mask for a banjo. Park said he didn't even know how to tune the damn thing. But the kid said he'd teach him."

He hands Larry a fresh beer, then moves to the railing to look out at the water. "That was it. They played music, took walks, went for drives, camping trips. Fixed up a little sailboat and bopped around the lake. Very quiet life. No stress. Once a month or so I'd drop by, and Park and I would have a few drinks, maybe play a sloppy game of chess, talk about the old days, women we'd known and places we'd been, deals we'd made. He got better for a while, couple of years, anyway, better than when he first got the news. Buzz looked after his diet — holistic, raw food. I don't know much about that stuff. I made my fortune with double cheeseburgers, but it was working. It bought Park a few more years. I started thinking maybe I should try drinking wheat grass myself, but it tastes like swamp water to me."

"It's starting to make sense," I say. "Why he would leave everything to someone like Buzz."

"Oh, sure. But in the end it all came down to what would destroy Wade Hubble."

"He hated him that much?" Larry asks. He's looked half asleep for most of the visit, but he's awake now.

"He hand-picked Hubble," Carleton says. "Thought he would be leaving things in good hands. Finding out he'd been betrayed was a nasty blow, considering the other nasty blows he was dealing with. He wanted to bring Hubble down, expose him. In the end he decided to sic Buzz Buznardo on him."

After a while, we move into the front room of Carleton's house. He gets a fire going in the handsome stone fireplace and serves us bread and cheese and cold cuts. I'm happy to see Larry eat something. Carleton is a good host without making a big deal about it. And he's a good talker, which makes my job a lot easier. He recounts, with great relish, the subtle and nasty war that grew between Parker Prescott and the man he picked to run Prescott Holdings.

"When Park found out he was ill, the prognosis wasn't very good. So he organized things so they could continue after his death. He took Prescott out of any speculative interests, built a portfolio with a steady guaranteed return that could weather market fluctuations. It was a well-considered scheme for a man who was facing the end. But it cut Wade Hubble off at the knees."

"How so?"

"Wade assumed Park was going to die pretty quick. That's what everyone believed. That's what Park himself thought was going to happen. So Wade Hubble sat quietly and waited for Park to disappear. But the tough old fart lived on. And on. And Wade started getting frustrated. There was money to be made, and he wasn't free to make any. He was managing a portfolio that just sat there. At the same time he couldn't get off the bus. You don't walk away from a half-million-dollar salary. There aren't many positions at that level open, and companies that go headhunting new management look for innovators, motivators, people who make things happen, not for people who are just sitting around clipping coupons. And don't forget, from Wade's perspective, there's a fly in the ointment."

"Who's that?"

"Edwin Gowins and the Horizon Foundation. They stand at the pay window every year saying, 'Show me the money.' Hubble has to hand it over. Gowins gets to spend it. And Gowins has his own agenda, of course. He's the man who disburses. He has people doing handsprings to get on his list of worthies."

"I saw his trophy wall," I say. "Very impressive."

"Oh, yeah, old Edwin never met a camera he didn't like."

"Gowins has an old portrait of Mr. Prescott."

"Big gilt frame, right? Gowins hated the frame, wanted to have it replaced. Park heard about it and sent him a note. The portrait stayed."

"So Prescott was in communication with Hubble and Gowins?"

"Only about important things like where his portrait was to be hung, but yeah, he had his finger on the pulse, and once he started getting stronger, after a year or so, he opened up a line of communication. Very quietly. He had a mole inside." He gets up to poke the fire and shift the main log. "A year or so before he died Park got wind that things weren't kosher. He was getting weaker physically, not mentally. He began to see that no matter how carefully he'd arranged things, it wasn't going to stay that way after he was gone. That's when he started getting his affairs in order. Inside six months he legally adopted Buzz as his son.

He had three separate psychiatrists sign off on his mental health, reasoning power, acuity, ability to make informed decisions. He nullified all previous wills and brought in the best estate lawyer on the West Coast to write a new, ironclad one. It was simple, clear, and solid. Buzz got everything — ownership, power, even the right to change the constitutions of both companies.

"Then Park died. Quietly, on the beach, at sunset, sitting in a deck chair looking out at the ducks and the seals. The local doctor had been advised that it was coming. Same with the funeral home and Park's specialist in Vancouver. There was no fuss, no big announcement…"

We sit for a while and watch the fire. The wind sneaks in through the partially closed French windows and makes the flames dance.

"You ever run into a man named Axelrode?" I ask. "Buzz's lawyer hired him to keep tabs on Buzz during the court case."

"I saw him once," Carleton says. "They didn't come up here very much after Park died, but Buzz and his sister were up together a few times. I can't say I warmed to the man."

"Would you happen to know who the mole was inside Prescott Holdings?" Larry asks.

Carleton looks at him, then smiles like a satisfied cat. "He isn't in Prescott. He's inside Horizon."

chapter thirty-six

Larry is subdued, or maybe the four beers have made him sleepy. He's leaning against the passenger window.

"How much farther?" I ask.

"Halfway into Harrison," he says. "You'll see it. It's got a red roof."

"I can't see any roofs. Just trees."

"You'll see it. What are you going to do there?"

"Not a thing. I just want to see the place. You feeling all right?"

"Me? Sure. Just depressed as hell. It's the beer poured on top of Irish coffee. It's a morose combination."

"Want some food?"

"I ate. Crackers. Very absorbent. Saltines."

"Yeah," I say, "that should keep you going."

"Old bastard's got a good set-up, don't you think? Comfortable retirement. Expensive beer. Depresses the hell out of me."

"Envy?"

"Pure and simple. No, not so pure and not so simple. I couldn't have done what he did. Some people have good sense, some people just bang into walls until they find the exit. There it is, on the right, around this bend. Slow down."

The gate is wide open, and a silver Mercedes is parked on the gravel driveway inside.

"Tourists," Larry says. "There should have been security."

I park behind the Mercedes and climb out.

Larry stays put. He waves me forward. "I've seen it."

I'm halfway up the gravel drive when a large man comes out of the back door. It's Bubba. He looks severe for the two seconds it takes for him to recognize me. Then his face relaxes and he gives me a half-smile. "Oh, hey there. Grundy, right? From the hotel?"

"Hi, Bubba," I say, sticking out my hand, "nice to see you again. Saw you at the service for Buzz but didn't get a chance to say hello."

"That asshole ex-cop messed it up. It was nice until he showed. Very spiritual. Molly was happy with the way it went until that prick ruined the moment."

"What did he want?"

"Guy's a psycho. Says she's making a big mistake."

"What's the mistake?"

"I don't know. I tell him to fuck off, he gives me static, I run him off."

"That's all he said?"

"He said I should steer clear of Neagle."

Molly MacKay is standing half behind Bubba. She has one hand on his arm.

"Did he say why?" I ask her.

Molly stares at me for a long moment, unsure whether I'm friend or foe. "I'm suing the hotel, you know."

"Yes, I heard."

"Alvin says we have to cover all the bases."

"You're going to need a new lawyer," I say. "Alvin Neagle is dead, probably murdered sometime this morning."

She grips Bubba's big arm with both hands, and her knees buckle. He has her supported in a heartbeat, moving behind her, hands under her elbows, leaning her against him. They make a likely looking couple. Earth Mother and Mountain Man.

"Oh, Jesus," she says. "Who did it?"

"Don't know yet," I say.

"Probably that Axelrode," Bubba says. "You okay?" he asks her. "You want to sit down?"

She turns and lets Bubba help her inside. I stand for a moment, wondering how much farther I can intrude without getting a two-handed cop shove. I decide I don't have much choice, and follow them inside.

The place has been trashed. Wall to wall, floor to ceiling. Books are scattered everywhere, cushions are torn, drawers are emptied.

"This wasn't vandalism," I say.

"Tell me about it," Bubba says.

"What were they looking for?"

"For the will, Mr. Grundy," Molly says. "They were looking for the will. The one that gives me everything. Buzz wrote it out exactly like the one Prescott wrote for him — word for word by hand. Then he had it witnessed and notarized and sealed. He said I had to carry on what he wanted to do." She is sitting on a broken couch with torn leather cushions, surrounded by wreckage. Bubba brings her a glass of water, and she holds it with both hands, staring at the surface. "I told Buzz I didn't want anything to do with all that money. I told him it would be nice if he left me this place and the car. Those I could use. I told him I didn't want to get involved in all that other complicated stuff. But he did it, anyway."

"What did he do with the will?"

"He had it with him," she says. "With the money."

"Jesus fucking wept!" Larry Gormé is standing in the doorway, looking in on the chaos.

"Who the fuck are you?" Bubba demands.

"He's with me," I say.

"What the hell happened? Didn't you have any security?"

"She has now," Bubba says. "Maybe you guys should take off, eh?"

"Ms. MacKay," I say. "Your suit against the hotel notwithstanding, I'm really on your side. I'm trying to find out what happened to your brother. I think there were a few people involved. One of them probably has your will. I don't think Jeff Axelrode has it, otherwise he'd have tried to make a deal with you. And Alvin Neagle didn't have it, otherwise people wouldn't still be looking for it."

"You don't need it," Bubba says to Molly. "You're his only living relative. You've got a legal claim."

"Only if she didn't shoot him," Larry says.

"You!" Bubba growls. "Get the fuck out of here before I mess you up."

"It's my job to ask annoying questions."

"Do it somewhere else. You're trespassing."

"I'm not his sister," Molly MacKay says.

That quiets things down for a moment.

"I mean, we were brother and sister as much as anybody could be. But I'm not his blood kin." She drinks some water, hands the glass back to Bubba. "Buzz was a foster child. He came to live with us when he was seven. We grew up together. I was a couple of years older than him. We were as close as could be. He was sweet, and gentle, and vulnerable. I looked after him."

"But unless you have the will, you're screwed," Larry says.

"I told you to piss off," Bubba snarls.

"I'm going," Larry says. "I've got a feature to write. Missing wills, dead bodies, romance amid the wreckage."

Bubba starts forward. I'm impressed that Larry stands his ground like a good reporter, willing to take abuse and assault in the interest of a good story.

"That's okay, Bubba," I say. "We'll take off now. I'm sorry we disturbed you."

"It's all right," he says. "It's covered."

I usher Larry back through the house to the backyard. "Nice car," Larry says over his shoulder. "Whose is it now?"

"You want to get him out of here before I hit him?" Bubba asks icily.

"My pleasure," I say.

chapter thirty-seven

I'm back in the car with Larry heading for Vancouver late in the afternoon with the sun in my eyes. Larry's face is flushed. He's scribbling notes in pencil on a folded wad of newsprint. "Drop me near a cab stand," he says. "I've got to get to work."

"You look rejuvenated."

"A *will*, man. A holographic will missing, believed stolen as part of a robbery, maybe the reason for the robbery. A will that's worth half a billion dollars *if* they can find it, *if* it's legit. It's a great story." He scribbles again. "And Molly MacKay has no claim unless they find the damn thing."

"And there's the Neagle development."

"Neagle turning up dead is part of it, definitely, but it isn't mine. The paper will have had somebody else on that one all day. Smartass on the homicide desk. Hoo-boy, this is going to burn his ass." He slaps me on the shoulder. "I knew hanging out with you would be good."

"You going to say anything about Wade Hubble or Gowins?"

"Not much. Nothing libellous, that's for damn sure. Not yet. I'll have to tread carefully on that one. The paper's got two lawyers checking every word I write these days."

"They have to be mixed up in this somehow."

"No doubt. And in the fullness of time, if there is a God, and if I can track down that mole inside Horizon, maybe we can start chipping away at those walls."

We're soon back in the city again. Rush-hour traffic is easing up. My route back to the Lord Douglas takes me close enough to the *Emblem* office that it requires one left turn and two rights to put Larry in front. He collects his scraps of paper and wipes his hand across his face as if he's putting on a face guard, preparing for battle.

"You going to eat something?" I ask as he climbs out.

"Oh, yeah. Pastrami on rye right at my desk. Just like the old days. This one gets the full treatment."

"Where do you get decent pastrami in this town?"

"Gimple's. You should try it."

"Nice place?"

"It's a deli. What do you want?"

"I may have a dinner date tonight."

"Really? Well, I don't think you want to be taking Ms. Gagliardi to a deli on your first big date."

"I guess not."

He stands on the sidewalk in front of his building, gazing up, imagining a front page with his byline. He leans back in. "Take her to the Palm Court. Rolf Kalman will treat you like visiting royalty."

"Yeah, that's exactly what I want — one of Rolf's Hungarian cousins playing Gypsy music in my ear."

"So let her pick something. She probably knows you're clueless."

"I am?"

Gritch gives me a hard time as I attempt to put a reasonable knot in my good tie with the stiff fingers of my right hand. "Been outside the hotel more this week than you were all last year," he says.

"I get out."

"You're a regular man about town."

"I'm broadening my horizons."

Rachel has gone home for the day. A young man named Todd, from Moonlight Security, is managing the shift. Rachel figures to have four permanent staff hired by Monday.

"Did Lloyd get to the hospital?" I ask.

"Oh, yeah, but he took backup — Rolf Kalman with a platter of the kitchen's best, along with Maurice, not to mention Andrew in full uniform. Wouldn't be surprised if he brought along a marching band. The last thing he wanted was to face the old man on his own."

"What about the brothers?"

"Ha! Lenny went. He wasn't part of the putsch. He's the good son this week." Gritch fires up the cigar he's been chewing for the past five minutes. "Gonna run through your entire closet if you're not careful."

"I might buy myself a new shirt."

"Watch out if she starts buying them for you. Once a woman starts buying a man clothes…"

"It's not like that."

"How would you know? You're completely inexperienced in these matters."

"Give it a rest, okay, Wallace."

"Wallace?" Gritch says. "I must've struck a nerve."

"She wants to get posted to Baghdad or Tel Aviv. This has no future whatsoever."

"So relax. You've got no worries."

I stare at myself in the mirror, more or less satisfied with the knot around my throat, when it suddenly hits me. "Damn!"

"What's the matter? It's not a bad knot."

"I just saw how it happened. It's all Arnie's fault."

"How so?"

"He screwed up all their plans. He took the money on the spur of the moment, and when they showed up, the thing they wanted was long gone. That's why Buzz's room was trashed. Somebody was looking for the will."

"And when they didn't find it, they killed him."

"And they, whoever *they* are, are still looking for the will."

Todd knocks on my open door. "Mr. Grundy? There's a call for you in the office. A Mr. Gormé. He says you'll want to talk to him."

"Thanks, Todd. I'll take it right here. Line one?"

"Yes, sir."

"Everything running smoothly?"

"Oh, yes, sir, the hotel is functioning just fine." Todd turns smartly and heads back to the office.

"Geez," Gritch says. "Do I feel redundant? Or merely superfluous?"

"Think of it as being kicked upstairs." I grab the phone and hit line one. "What's up, Larry?"

"It's a picture, Grundy. It's a freaking portfolio. You've got to come and meet this guy."

"Where?"

"At the paper. My desk. I'll leave word downstairs. But don't say a thing to anyone. Swear. This is the big one, baby."

chapter thirty-eight

The young man sitting beside Larry Gormé's desk looks familiar. Fashionably spiked blond hair, butter-soft Italian loafers, alpaca jacket.

"Jeremy?" I say.

Edwin Gowins's executive assistant, guardian of the burled walnut door to the chancel. I still remember how beautifully he snubbed me on my visit to the Crystal Cathedral. Jeremy acknowledges my arrival with a modicum of grace. At least he doesn't sniff. "Mr. Grundy, nice to see you again."

"I wasn't sure you saw me the first time."

"I see just about everything."

Larry Gormé keeps his eyes on the other reporters in the room, like a wolf guarding his dinner. "Look at this gold." He spreads a fan of photographs on his desk — different locations, different lenses, some of them poor quality, but all of them of interest. Wade Hubble and Edwin Gowins, mortal enemies, arm's-length co-managers of Parker

Prescott's fortune, on a yacht, checking into an expensive hotel, side by side at a roulette table. "Thick as thieves," Larry says. "Go ahead," he urges Jeremy. "Tell Joe what you told me."

"They have secret meetings," Jeremy says. "Like Mafia dons. They have code words. They meet on the water, on Gowins's boat, or sometimes in some other city. If Mr. Gowins, say, has to meet a symphony guest conductor in Seattle, Mr. Hubble has to go to Los Angeles for a board meeting for some reason, and they met in Las Vegas."

"See?" Larry picks out a picture. "Vegas. By the pool, sipping tall cold ones and ogling the local talent."

"Who took all these?" I ask.

"I did," Jeremy says. "Some of them. Or I hired someone to take them when I couldn't get away. I had … a special commission. My budget was off the books. I was Mr. Parker Prescott's eyes and ears inside Horizon. He wanted to know if Mr. Gowins and Mr. Hubble were in collusion."

"And they were."

"Oh, yes. They've been skimming money for years. For all the years Mr. Prescott was ill. Perhaps even before then."

"Working as a team."

"They're in it together. For public consumption they loathe and despise each other. Hubble calls Gowins a parasite, Gowins calls Hubble a tightwad."

"Notice that neither one uses the word *gonif*," Larry says.

"You're the one who sent me that picture," I say.

"Yes," Jeremy says. "I tried to give the information to Mr. Buznardo, but he wasn't really interested. He said it would all come out in the wash. I wasn't exactly sure what to do. I was working secretly for Mr. Prescott for three years, putting together a file, bank accounts, transfer payments…"

"Oh, Jesus!" Larry says.

"But I didn't know what to do with it after he died. Legally, it belonged to Mr. Buznardo. Legally, ethically … I don't know. He was Mr. Prescott's heir. The file was part of Mr. Prescott's estate."

"Why not go directly to the police?" I ask.

"I'll be going to the police, Mr. Grundy, very soon. Just as soon as their perfidy is made very, very public."

"You could've made yourself a mint blackmailing Hubble and Gowins with this stuff," Larry says.

Jeremy sniffs. "Mr. Prescott paid me very well for the work I did. He gave me stock in his holding company. I want to do what's best for Mr. Prescott."

"Didn't mean anything, Jeremy," Larry says. "I'm just saying —"

"I know what you're saying. Mr. Gormé. But it's inevitable that the conspiracy will be revealed, and when it is, I'd prefer that I was on the side of goodness."

"And Horizon will probably need a new managing director," Larry says.

"As you say," Jeremy says.

"When can I get a look at the money files?" Larry asks.

"The files are in the possession of Leonard Rosten, an independent forensic accountant. I've told him he should feel free to talk to you."

"Why did you pick me?"

"I got a call from Warren Carleton in Harrison. He said you were the right person to break the story."

"Oh, sweet Jesus on a bicycle," Larry says. "It will be my very great pleasure, in full colour, on the front page."

"I don't suppose there's a picture there with Jeff Axelrode in it?" I ask.

"No, there isn't," Jeremy says.

"Can't have everything," Larry says. "This will do for now."

"Why now, Jeremy?" I ask.

"Because they're at it again. They had to stop for a while during the fight over Mr. Buznardo's legacy. Hubble had to freeze everything."

"That lasted almost two years," Larry says.

"They had a meeting yesterday evening. I couldn't get a picture. They met in the park and kept walking. They were both agitated, triumphant. They think they can open the taps again."

chapter thirty-nine

Larry Gormé says it will be okay for me to give Connie Gagliardi a heads-up about what the front page of the *Emblem* is going to look like in the morning. I manage to get the cell phone to work and give her a rundown on what Larry has. She immediately pushes our dinner back ninety minutes and rushes off to organize Channel 20's handling of the story. She seems excited. I feel honoured that she didn't cancel entirely.

I decide to walk to the restaurant. The rain has stopped, the air is still. Back when I was boxing, I used to wander the streets of whatever city I was in at the time after a fight maybe. There weren't many big victory parties. Morley Kline would attend to business, make sure we were covered, rent a car, whatever we had to do to move on, and then sometimes, not always, I'd go on a walk by myself. In the early years I'd walk and think about what it would be like to fight for the title, what I'd have to do to be ready, who I'd have to face to get that far up the ladder. Later, I stopped thinking about that. I thought about other things. What it might be like to have a regular life. I wasn't sure what that meant, a regular life, but it sounded nice. It seemed then, as it seems now, as remote as a title fight.

The imminent exposure of Hubble and Gowins notwithstanding, I'm still no closer to finding out who shot Jacob "Buzz" Buznardo. I suppose that will come out in the wash, too, as Buzz would have said.

"I wore heels," Connie says. "A major concession."

"They look nice," I say. "You can kick them off under the table."

"I intend to."

Connie picked the restaurant. Il Giardino d'Umberto. Very classy. Scary prices.

"I don't know many places other than the Lobby Café and Connor's Diner next to the Scientology Reading Room."

"You don't get out much," she says.

"There's an understatement."

"Why?"

"Asked myself the same question on the beach this morning, watching Buzz's dust blow away. Seven years, more or less, looking after Leo's house, nice apartment, job security, easygoing boss."

"This last episode must have disrupted your life a lot."

"It's been ... broadening."

She smiles at that.

"I like to know my parameters, my fencelines. In the ring the arena's clearly defined — the contest will take place within these ropes. If a thing happens inside the hotel, to one of the guests, to one of the staff, I attend to it. I have no business poking my nose into things outside the hotel. Corporate malfeasance, financial skullduggery — not my department."

"Definitely mine," she says. "Things like that keep me awake. I hit the ground running. I want to know. I need to know."

Connie orders the wine. I'm not much of a wine drinker, but I can appreciate that it's rich and deep. It tastes of flint and sunshine and the scent of dark curly hair.

"This is good," I say.

"It's a Barbaresco. It goes well with wild boar, don't you think?"

"Wild boar? Is that what I'm eating?"

After dinner we walk for a while. Connie has a pair of Adidas in her leather bag. The high heels, nice ones, have seen only a few minutes' service. We stroll the streets, not looking for a private spot, window shopping, carefully not holding hands.

"Thanks for the call," she says.

"Thank Larry Gormé."

"I already have. He's preparing a speech for his Newspaperman of the Year Award."

"He just might get it."

"Channel 20's going to do all right, too. We've got a big head start. Turn on your television in the morning. I'll wave at you. I'll get Larry to wave at you, too. He'll be my first guest."

"I don't have a television."

She shakes her head. "It's not over for you, is it?"

"I still need to know who shot a hotel guest and who helped a hotel employee to depart the world."

"Not to mention Alvin Neagle."

"Alvin's not part of my job description. If it turns out that the same person who killed Buzz and Arnie killed Alvin Neagle, as well, fine. But it's outside my commission."

"You think Axelrode did it?"

"It's possible. Maybe somebody got to him — Hubble or Gowins. Maybe both told him he was working for pocket change and then gave him a way to pick up a big chunk of dough by getting rid of Buzz."

"Crude tactics for men like that."

"And then there's Grace Ingraham," I say. "The

Heritage Architectural Preservation Society hasn't received a nickel in over two years. Grace is selling off expensive pieces of the collection."

"You honestly think a woman like that would hire someone like Axelrode?"

"She's a big loser in this thing, too. She needs money. And she hated Buzz. She believes he stole Parker Prescott away from her, robbed her of those last precious years they could have had. Buzz took everything from her."

"Is it possible to work three sides of the street?"

"Poor bastard," I say.

"Who?"

"Did anyone think he was sane, or serious, or motivated by simple, genuine goodness?" I stop in front of a travel agency and study a poster of a warm beach far away. "Why is it so hard to believe there's a purely good person walking among us?"

"You'd like to believe he was a saint, wouldn't you?"

"Not really. Just a guy who knew he didn't have long to live and wanted to do something nice before he checked out. But it begs the question — what would a saint do with half a billion dollars? Seriously. I'm asking you."

"She'd give it away."

chapter forty

Olive is onstage with Jimmy Hinds, her bassist, and a wispy guitar player who sometimes comes down on Friday nights. His name is Arlen, he works in a guitar store, and he practises about eight hours a day. His fingers dance like raindrops up and down the neck of his favourite Gretsch guitar. Olive loves the way he plays so much that she's content to cradle his inventions in her rich open chords. Jimmy Hinds is, as are all good bass players, the sure and nurturing heartbeat that keeps it all alive.

Connie and I have a table, the same one we had two nights ago, beside and below the little bandstand, with Olive above us, smiling down because she sees me with a date. And it seems to me that she's giving us a little extra something.

> "In the wee small hours of the morning
> While the whole world is fast asleep
> You lie awake and think about the boy..."

"You finally look comfortable," Connie says.

"Wild boar, eh?"

"Too rich?"

"It was good."

"I have to get some sleep," she says. "Tomorrow will start early."

"Of course it will. I don't want to keep you up."

She smiles sweetly. "I mention that in case you were concerned about how we were going to say good night."

"It's been on my mind."

Her laughter is genuine and in perfect time with Olive's intro to "It Could Happen to You." I look up to see Olive beaming at us. Now I know she's arranging the set to the mood.

A little later we leave Olive's and I walk Connie to her car. It's getting on to midnight. She says she'll need at least four hours' sleep not to look like a frump in front of the camera. I can't see how that would be possible. Without thinking too much about it, I take her elbow as we step off the curb.

"Hey, Grundy, what's this?" Maxine is climbing out of her taxi and heading in our direction.

"Maxine, this is Connie."

"Hi, there,' Maxine says. "This is a first."

"Really?"

"I've never seen Grundy on a date before. He cleans up pretty good, don't you think?"

"Quite presentable," Connie says.

"Connie has to get home. She's on camera early in the morning."

"Your pal Weed was around earlier looking for you," Maxine says.

"He say why?"

"Something about Danny boy's girlfriend."

"What?"

"What's her name? The one from Bangkok he doesn't think anybody knows about?"

"Prana. What about her?"

"Yeah, her," Maxine says. "She got worked over pretty good, Weed says. She's in the hospital. Looks like one of Danny boy's chickens came home to roost. They can't find him, either."

"Oh, Lord!" I say. "I think this is my fault. I was supposed to deliver some money to somebody to keep them off his back. Damn! Can't keep two things in my head at the same time."

"Punchy," Max says.

"Look, Connie, Max can run me over to Chinatown. I'll talk to you in the morning."

"Not a chance," Connie says. "I'll drive you."

"You're hijacking my fare," Max says.

"It'll be a short run, Max," I say. "Not worth your while."

"Where are we going?" Connie asks me as she opens her car door.

"The Noodle Palace," I say.

"Maybe we should have eaten there instead of Umberto's. I hear the noodles are great."

"Next time," I say.

She smiles at that.

When we get to the Noodle Palace, I say, "Drop me off in the lane by the Ferrari. I'll be fine. You head home. I'm sorry things have ended so abruptly, but that seems to be the way it goes."

"I'll wait here," she says. "I want a good-night kiss and I'm willing to stay up another twenty minutes to get one."

"I won't be that long."

"Good."

Entering the Noodle Palace from the alley means negotiating a narrow corridor past a storeroom filled with Oriental smells. I hear noises from the dining room beyond — laughter and food orders being shouted. The main room is crowded with late diners, theatre-goers, and students. The room behind the beaded curtain is empty except for the man I'm looking for. Randall Poy is talking on his cell, happy about something. He glances up as I enter, then looks around quickly. Mikey and Marlon aren't there. He terminates the conversation and stands. "Joe Grundy. It's very late. What do you want?"

"I'm sorry I'm late, Randall. A bunch of things came up."

"I've heard all the excuses in my life. Don't bother."

"All right." I reach into my jacket pocket and take out the envelope with two thousand dollars in it. "This is the two thousand dollars I said I'd give you." I toss it onto the table in front of him. He doesn't look down.

"Okay, fine."

"I don't ever want you sending people into the hotel again. Do I make myself clear?"

"You don't show up, Joe Grundy. What am I supposed to think?"

"I don't know, Randall. But whatever you thought, it was wrong."

"I can't let things like this happen. It's bad for my business."

"Your business include beating up women?"

"I don't beat up women, Grundy. I don't need to do things like that."

"You get one of your goons to do it for you?"

"What woman are you talking about?"

"Dan's girlfriend. One of your people paid her a visit tonight."

"Wasn't me. Why would I bother? She doesn't have any money. Check one of Dan Howard's other creditors."

"I'll be talking to her soon. She'll be able to give me a description."

Randall sneers. "I think they'll send her back to Thailand pretty quick. Anyway, what do you care? Dan Howard doesn't work for you anymore. He told me."

"When did you see Dan?"

Then someone kicks me in the head. From behind. That definitely gets a person's attention. I turn around to look at the guy who's smiling at me. The family resemblance is apparent. Marlon and Mikey have a cousin who goes by the name of Jason. Jason is a few years younger, about four inches shorter, and at least thirty pounds lighter than the smaller of the brothers, which places Jason in the cruiserweight division. Jason has pretty much a full-time job guarding Randall Poy's Ferrari in its private parking area behind the Noodle Palace, but with both Chow brothers currently on the injured reserve list, Jason has apparently been upgraded to muscle. It's a position he's long coveted, and he's prepared himself for this moment. Mikey and Marlon can take the rest of the year off if they want to.

The first thing he does is stick his foot in my face four, five times in a row, straight, snapping kicks, like a good jab with a hell of a reach. While I'm fending those off and trying to figure out a way to deal with this machine, I take a boot across the bad knuckle and it opens up. I'm getting blood on the Burberry. Then he comes at me with fists, straight, hard punches like pistons. I cover up, start to work on some countermeasures, and he steps back and kicks me again. This one catches me on the ear, the next one straight in the chest, and I slam back into the table and send chairs flying. I definitely don't want to fall down with this guy.

He finally leaves himself open for a counterpunch. Unfortunately, I have to use my right hand. It lands nice and solid and his head snaps back, but I feel a cracking pain from my fist to my elbow. If that knuckle wasn't broken before, it probably is now.

In 1991 I fought a man one-handed. He was shorter than I was, built like an anvil, hard to hit. I bounced an awkward right hand off his head in the first round. After that it was jab and dance, jab and clinch. I was lucky. He had short arms. Jason doesn't have short arms.

I'm getting the worst of this round. On any judge's scorecard you'd have to give Jason Chow a big edge for punches thrown and landed. I've only tagged him once, and it cost me the use of my right hand. He knows it, too. He figures he's got me on the run. I see it in his eyes. He's feeling stronger, more confident. He's winning this round and there's no timekeeper. The round will go on until somebody's out.

But he can't put me away. Jason punches hard and sharp, but he can't put me down. He's not big enough, and he doesn't have a knockout punch. It's one of the things you can tell right away. There's no weight to his punches, just speed. I'm going to get hit, that's a given, but he'll have to pay for the privilege. It's time to go to work.

I crowd him back across the room, cutting off the ring, taking his shots on my forearms and shoulders, bobbing my head, getting in closer and closer, inside the circle where he can't use his feet, into a corner where he can't escape. I'm back where I used to earn my money, infighting, head to head and not playing by the rules. My right elbow works just fine at this distance. He tries to spin away, and I get a good left hook into his kidney that makes him sag. When he slumps, his left side is open for a split second, and everything I own is delivered through my right hand to make him go down.

The hand, my hand, is swelling, bleeding, useless, and hurts so bad I can't see straight. I turn around and blink until I can focus on Randall Poy.

"Randall," I say, "if I were a vindictive man, I'd go outside into the lane and customize your Ferrari. Now I want you to take this two thousand dollars that I said I would pay you. I'm sorry it's a bit late, I got called away, but here it is. You'll have to make any further payment arrangements with Dan Howard. He doesn't work for me any longer." I spy Jason trying to rise. "Tell him if he gets up off the floor I'll kill him."

"You think I'm the only one Dan Howard owes money to?" Randall Poy says. "He owes money to the whole world. I'm not the only one looking to collect."

"It's not my business anymore." I grab one of the table napkins as I head for the door, clattering the silverware rolled inside to the floor, and wrap it carefully around my hand. The napkin is red which, under the circumstances, is handy.

"Joe Grundy?"

"What do you want, Randall?"

"Why don't you ask Dan Howard how he paid off Ivan Doncheff yesterday? He gave him ten thousand dollars."

Through the beaded curtain I see fifty faces turned in my direction. "Did he?"

"There are many things you don't know, Joe Grundy."

"Always meant to come here," I tell him, "for the noodles."

Outside, I ask an alarmed Connie, "Could you drive me back to the hotel?"

"Don't be ridiculous. I'm taking you to the hospital."

"I'll go later. I need to get to the hotel. I have to see Gritch about something."

"And then you'll go?"

"Yeah, sure, I'll go. But the doctor can't do much. I don't want a cast on it. It'll immobilize the hand and I won't be able to get the flexibility back. I'll just have to live with it."

"You've got more than a broken hand to fix up."

"The other stuff is cosmetic."

She gives me a critical appraisal. "It's a look, I suppose."

"Don't take me to the front door. I don't want to walk through the lobby looking like this."

"I don't blame you."

She turns the corner onto Carrall Street, the rear face of the Lord Douglas. The Scientology Reading Room is closed for the night, but they have lights on and inspirational slogans illuminated for passersby. Connor's Diner has been closed for many hours.

"There's a fire entrance," I say. "Right here, under the walkway."

"Where will I find you?"

"There should be a place to park out front. The night manager will be on. His name's Raymond. Just ask for Gritch. He'll bring you back to the office."

"And you'll be there?"

"I'll be there. I'm just going through the back way. I don't want to upset the guests."

She drops me off, waits until I get to the fire door. I can't drag my passkey out with my right hand, so I go back to the car. "Would you mind reaching into my pocket and grabbing my keys?"

"Is that what they called it in your day? Anything else you want, as long as I'm in there?"

"That'll do for now," I say. "Thanks."

"Anytime, sailor."

chapter forty-one

It's an open stairwell, like an enclosed fire escape, and you can see a long way up. I have to climb a few flights to get to a door I can open. The mezzanine looks to be my best bet. Three flights from here. I can make it. No trouble. There's a railing on my left side, which is handy because my left hand is more or less intact, though throbbing a bit. Bless Morley Kline. The left jab kept me alive tonight. Hurts like hell, though. Left forearm, too. I'm a mess.

But I'm climbing, dragging myself up by the railing one step at a time. Dogged old warhorse, that's me. One step at a time. Head down, every muscle aching. Had I been looking up I might have seen the mass that crashes onto me like a falling piano and knocks me back down the steel stairs. I feel my broken hand smash itself redundantly against the railing, and a searing pain reaches as high as my skull. My legs are twisted under me, I've done something bad to my left knee, and there's a huge dead weight on my chest. Jeffrey "Axe" Axelrode.

The man weighs a ton. He's been shot, and he's dead, and it's lucky for me he was bouncing off the railings on his downward journey. Had he come straight down he would have killed me.

Crawling out from under Axelrode costs me dearly. I have to use those parts of my right arm that still work, muscling him aside with elbow and shoulder, gaining inches, trying to keep the moans down. Finally, I manage to roll him aside. His body slides down a few more steps and comes to rest on a landing.

I start to climb again. Slower this time. My left knee is swelling. Cruciate ligament, feels like. Torn, probably. That can't be good. I keep going up, past the mezzanine door.

"Don't come any closer, Joe," Dan says, his voice echoing down the stairwell. "I'll shoot you. I swear I will."

"Where are you, Dan? I'm coming up." I keep climbing but can't see him in the gloom. "Stay where you are, okay?"

"I'll do it. I just don't give a shit anymore."

"If you don't care anymore, Dan, why shoot me?"

"Because that's what you have to do!" He sounds drunk. Falsely hearty, even mirthful, on the ragged edge. "Once you start, you can't just walk away from the table. Not while you still have some chips. And I've got chips, baby. I've got fucking chips!"

"They're no good to you anymore, Dan. It's all over. Just think about it for a minute." I pass the fourth-floor fire door, rest for a minute, listening, puffing, keeping my weight off my left leg, touching nothing with my right hand. "Dan, talk to me. Come on, Dan. We've got to work this out."

"Nothing to work out, Joe."

I can see him now. He's two landings above me, sitting on a top step, leaning through the railing, staring down at me. He's holding a gun. I keep climbing.

"I'll shoot you, Joe. I mean it. What have I got to lose?"

Closer now. I'm at five. He's directly above me on six. He doesn't have much of an angle from there.

"We have to talk, Dan. Really, you should talk this out."

"You want to talk, Joe? Sure. Why not? Come on up to my office."

"Where is it?"

"You figure it out. It's your hotel. Personally, I don't think you can make it, boss."

I hear him climbing again, pounding up the stairs at a rate I'll never match. I listen, trying to count floors, listening for the slam of a fire door, hearing nothing but Dan's footfalls echoing, and the faint ringing of metal against metal — his gun against the railing, jacket buttons? — an odd, unsyncopated accompaniment to the fading drumbeat of his ascent.

Come up to my office? What did Gritch say? There are a hundred places in this hotel where he could camp out and no one would ever know he was there. Places, he's happy to point out, of which I'm still ignorant despite seven years in charge of hotel security. Prop rooms from when they used to hold pageants, kitchens that aren't used anymore, cloakrooms, private meeting rooms. The thirteenth floor.

And how did Gritch say you get there? A back stairwell from where? Twelve? No, not twelve, the eleventh floor.

Getting there is an act of will, and it takes a while. I sit, very carefully, on the eleventh-floor landing, outside the fire door, my left leg straight out, the knee so swollen I can see the shape inside my pant leg, my right hand cradled inside my jacket with my ruined tie wrapped around the forearm in a crude sling. If I've dropped my keys back on the stairwell below, I'm going to feel very sorry for myself. But the passkey is where it's supposed to be, and it fits the lock. Then, with a few heaves at the heavy old door, I'm on the eleventh floor.

Floor Eleven is what the hotel's most exclusive and expensive ballroom, formal dining room, and reception space is called. With the attendant private meeting rooms, conference rooms, powder rooms, kitchens and such, it takes up most of the actual eleventh floor, and on nights when there's a major function, it requires a special pass simply to get off the elevator. Tonight it's deserted. There's nothing scheduled here until next week. The kitchens are empty, the ballroom is a vast echoing space, the dining hall is a landscape of bare tables bearing upended chairs.

And the thirteenth floor? According to Gritch, and I wish I'd paid closer attention, the thirteenth floor is some secret back slice of twelve. There's another fire door somewhere, not the main one, but where is it? And then I hear Gritch reminding me that the walls near the elevators are different on this floor.

He's right. I limp out of the ballroom to the reception area, an open space with windows looking down on city lights. The elevator bank is farther along a rich burgundy carpet, past leather chairs and wall sconces, to a wall that shouldn't be there. On the floors below, or the floors above, I could keep heading in this direction and eventually reach the service elevators. The service elevators! They would have to be accessible to the eleventh floor for delivering food and drink, staff and linen.

Back through the ballroom I go, through the dining hall and kitchen, and into the corridor behind the kitchen, where I find the service elevators. That narrows it down. The thirteenth floor is in this quadrant, the northeast corner. The fire door has to be somewhere close by the dining room.

There are discreetly located ladies' and gents', there is a sizable wet bar, unstocked at present, with bar stools and a brass rail in an alcove. I see it in my mind. Images from a more decorous and decadent past. Cigar smoke and cognac, exclusive coteries of privileged men with position and money and an occasional need to indulge in something intemperate, discreetly removing themselves from the ladies and the glad-handing, finding their way to the bar alcove, where an accommodating bartender, privy to the special requirements of his black-tied guests, ushers those with the appropriate password around the end of the bar, through the narrow wine cellar, to … this door.

It opens without a key and leads me to a narrow landing with another short flight of stairs leading up. The railing on my right side is of no help whatsoever. I lean against the wall on my left and slide upward, one leaden step after another.

"I didn't think you were going to make it," Dan says. He's five steps above me by an open door. "Come on up. I've got vodka."

The thirteenth floor. After all the myth and mystery, it turns out to be a cramped, claustrophobic space. A bare hallway with six or eight private rooms, unfurnished, unlighted. Rooms for assignations, high-stakes poker games, sleeping off monumental benders. Dan is in the largest of them. He's appropriated a pair of lamps from downstairs and has run an extension cord from somewhere. His bolt-hole is lit with Tiffany reproductions of grapes and vines. His bed is a cot mattress dragged up from one of the forgotten storerooms. For furniture he has a couple of empty pails upended on the bare floor. I read the stencilled HOUSEKEEPING logo upside down.

Dan's jacket is torn, his shirt is dirty, his eyes are bloodshot. He's running on reserve battery power, movements jerky, voice a rasp. He's angry, and he's very sorry for himself. And he's pointing a gun at my chest.

"Sit down," he orders. "Grab a pail. You look like shit."

I don't mention his appearance, lower myself carefully onto a pail that once held ammonia. I can feel it up my nose. Or maybe the toilets aren't working. "How long have you been up here, Dan?"

"Off and on most of the week. I had to get out from time to time. You know. Phone calls. Like that."

"Trip to the island."

"Ha! We were on the same fucking ferry coming back from Nanaimo. Believe it?"

"How did you get off Gabriola? The Mounties must have been watching the first ferry."

"I was on the last ferry off. I drove right by you when I landed in Nanaimo. You were waiting to get on. Surprised the hell out of me. I thought for a minute you'd seen me. You were right on my ass and didn't know it."

"Why did you stick around in Nanaimo? I didn't get a ferry to the mainland until noon."

"Things to do. Negotiations."

"With?"

"Well, now, that's just it, isn't it? It's the fucking middlemen who kill every fucking thing, isn't it? I have to deal with shitheads like fat Axe Axelrode when it's really the big boys I should be talking to. I told him, too. I told him I wasn't going to sit in some stupid motel room dickering over chump change while he made a sweetheart deal with his superiors. Fuck that. I wanted to talk to Wade Hubble."

"Two hundred and fifty thousand dollars isn't chump change, Dan."

"No? First of all, there wasn't two-fifty, closer to two, after expenses, after burning a couple of wads in Lloyd's fireplace. If I split what's left with Axe, I'm holding a hundred K. And I owe almost that much around town. Can you believe it? I managed to run my tab up close to a hundred K. Fourteen to Randall, ten to Ivan Doncheff, six to the asshole who runs the book for Rolf Kalman out of the staff kitchen. Plus all the vig. That mounts up like you wouldn't believe."

Dan transfers the gun to his left hand and rummages behind himself until he locates a half-empty bottle of Absolut. He puts it between his feet to twist off the cap. The gun doesn't waver. "I was in the hole sixty, sixty-five K." He takes a drink. "Doesn't leave much left over with Prana and Doris on my ass. Not enough."

"Prana's in the hospital."

"I know. I feel shitty about that."

"Who did it?"

"That fat prick at the bottom of the stairs! Fuck him. He still wanted half the money! Can you believe that? Why should I give it to him? He did fuck all. I'm the one who did all the work. I had the whole deal. I knew what I was going to do with it. It was his gun killed the guy. It was his gun Arnie shot himself with. Fuck him. We set up a meet. He told me where, and I told him to screw himself. I was calling the shots, not him. So he went to Prana and tried to beat it out of her where I was. He got what he deserved."

"How did he wind up here?"

"I called Prana from an outside phone. She sounded so small. She said I should watch myself, that the man who beat her would kill me. I told her to get to a hospital. She waited by the phone to warn me."

"You knew where he was?"

"Sure, he was crashing with his dumb-ass brother-in-law in Coquitlam. I had his number. I said, 'Okay, Axe, you win. Come and get it.' Stupid fuck. He got it." He has another drink, keeps his eyes on me, keeps his gun on me. "You want a blast?"

"Sure, why not?"

Dan pushes the bottle towards me with his foot, and I have to lean far forward to grab it with my left hand. I sip carefully, avoiding the split in my bottom lip, then take a deeper pull, grateful for the sudden rush of heat, false strength, and pain relief.

"What the fuck happened to you?" he asks.

"Axelrode landed on top of me. Close to three hundred pounds."

"Yeah. Bet he didn't feel a thing."

I take a last moderate taste, put the bottle on the floor, and push it towards him with my right foot. "How did you track Arnie down?"

"Arnie stole the money, then when he got a chance to sit down and count it, he found out that wasn't the only thing he had. At first he thought it was just some short story bullshit Buzz was writing. It was in ballpoint for fuck's sake — pages torn out of a scribbler. But then he started reading, and the stupid prick realized what he had his hands on. Without even trying he'd grabbed the big prize."

"Then what?"

"He called Neagle and told him he wanted to make a deal. He didn't care who with. Neagle called Axelrode. Axe called me."

"Why would Axe call you?"

He shakes his head. "Figure it out. I told you that first night. I used to work for Axehandle Security. Axe grabbed me in the hallway before you got there. He said I should pick my time and snatch the case, then he and I would split the money. He said the guy wouldn't even care if it was gone. He'd just get more from the bank. He was giving it away, anyway, so why shouldn't he give some to us? I was up to my eyes in shit and a tidal wave was coming. You kidding? I said done deal."

"Axe gave you the gun?"

"Stuck it in my pocket. He said, 'Just in case.' What do I care? I'm already counting the money."

"But when you got there the money was already gone."

"Story of my fucking life." He holds the bottle for a moment, measuring how much is left of vodka, of everything. He has another pull.

"So Arnie had the money and the will he wasn't expecting," I say. "And he wanted to make a deal. And you were supposed to do the negotiations?"

"Arnie said Axe should go to Nanaimo, check into some motel, and he'd call. When Arnie called the room and found out that it was me he was talking to, he relaxed. He asked me to pick him up some food. Lloyd's fridge was empty."

"Why did you kill him?"

"Ah, man, he killed himself. I just helped him point the fucking gun. He was so drunk, and he was crying, the fat fuck. He was weeping like a woman."

"But why? He was no threat."

"Sure he was. He was the loose end. He was going to get caught. And he was the best alibi." Dan stands up. "I've got to piss. Just sit there."

He leaves the room, and I hear him relieving himself into a porcelain bowl across the hall. A tap is turned on, and I hear squeaking brass and gurgling water. The plumbing still works up here. He comes back into the room, his face wet, hair slicked back, bouncing on the balls of his feet, trying to pump a few more ccs of energy into his weary body.

"What about Neagle?" I ask.

"That wasn't me. Swear to Jesus, Joe. Jesus and all his merry men. It was that fat fuck at the bottom of the stairs. He was losing it, going crazy. Didn't trust anybody, figured I was shafting him, that Neagle was shafting him. He was like a runaway freight train. He accused Neagle of making a deal with me to cut him out of the picture."

"Were you?"

"Sure, what the fuck? Who needed him? Neagle was the guy I was doing business with. Why would I kill him? He was the one who suddenly had a client again. If he could've gotten the will, Molly MacKay would've been rolling in it."

"Be hard to get your money up front, wouldn't it?"

"Fuck, think I didn't know that? Having Neagle on the hook just made my position stronger. What I really wanted was to make a deal with Wade Hubble. I knew he could pay cash."

"How much money did you burn up?"

"Shit, that was fun. Only ten thousand or so, but I made it look like more."

"You've got the will?"

"Yeah, I've got it. It's still my ace in the hole, Joe. It's my big chip."

"It's going to be hard to cash in. There's a good chance Wade Hubble and Edwin Gowins are going to be investigated for fraud. They won't be in a position to make any deals with you. And Molly doesn't have any money to pay you up front. You've run out of options, Dan. I think you should start facing it. It's over."

He finishes the vodka to the last drop and looks at the empty with sadness and resentment. "It's that first roll of the dice, Joe. That's the killer. Hoo-boy! Stay away from that one and nothing can go wrong. But roll them one time, one time, you stupid, gutless dipshit, one lousy time, and you're in it up to your eyes."

"What was the first roll?"

"Fuck," Dan says, so wearily it sounds like a whisper. "The first roll? Who can go back that far? Was it the first time I won a hand at poker and said this was the life for me? Was that the reason I doubled my bets all my useless life, looking for one lousy jackpot to get me off the treadmill, one major score to pay them all off, all the debts, all the goons, all the dumb moves I ever made?"

"I'm sorry it got that bad, Dan."

"Yeah. You, Mr. Straight Arrow. Never took a dive for money, did you? Never skimmed a nickel from the hotel, never took a kickback from hookers, or liquor salesmen, or laundry service? Not Joe Grundy. No, sir."

"Tell me what happened with Buzz, Dan."

"Axe said we were going to split the money, but he wanted the legal document. It was in the new briefcase. Along with the money. But fucking Arnie screwed it up before I even got there. I tore the place apart looking for the will, and that fat prick already had it stashed. That was when the guy came back to the room. He had Phil Marsden from room service with him. Phil was waiting at the door. Me, I was in the fucking bedroom. I heard the guy say, 'I'll have to take care of you tomorrow.' And Marsden said, 'No problemo. You got me already.' Then he took off. And the guy came into the bedroom and looked at all the stuff lying around and saw me standing behind the door."

"What did he say to you?"

"Nothing. You know what kind of day I had? At the track? Before I came in that night? Have you any idea what it's like to be up two thousand by three in the afternoon and then cleaned out by five? So broke you have to borrow bus fare to get to the pawnshop?"

"He didn't say anything?"

"He said, 'Take it all.'"

"Why did you shoot him?"

"There wasn't anything *to* take! He was standing there with this stupid smile like he was some kind of fucking higher being and I was this lowlife dipshit. So I thought, *This is what my fucking life has come to. I'm standing in a fucking hotel room in the middle of the fucking night like a complete asshole.* There was no suitcase, there was no money, I was rooting through this guy's dirty underwear, my life was fucked, I owed money to ugly people who were going to kill me any frickin' day, and this prick bastard was smiling at me. So I said, 'Take fucking *what*? There isn't anything, ass-wipe, shit-hole, *to* fucking take.' Nothing. Nothing. Crapped out again. And he said, 'I guess someone got here before you did.' And so I shot the fucker. He didn't have to rub it in."

We hear voices coming up the secret stairs. Gritch's is among them, and Connie's, and Weed's.

"He's got a gun!" I yell out.

"I've got a gun!" Dan shouts at almost the same instant. A warning and a threat in unison.

"You okay, Joe?" Weed asks.

"I'm fine. We're just talking it over. Tell the others to go back downstairs."

"I've got backup coming," Weed says. "Uniforms." His voice is closer now, maybe three doors down the hall. "You've got no place to go, Dan. Why don't you lose the gun and come out? We'll make it as easy as we can."

"How's Prana?" Dan asks.

"She's going to be okay, Dan. She's fine. Nothing broken. You want to talk to her? I can arrange that."

"No thanks," Dan says. "That's all right." And then he sticks the barrel of the gun in his mouth and shoots the back of his head off.

chapter forty-two

We're nicely settled into October now. The Lord Douglas is running smoothly again. Lloyd Gruber managed to hang on to his job, though I get the impression there was an element of grovelling involved. Rachel Golden now pretty much manages JG Security for me. I still pull a few shifts, but mostly I just roam the place and anticipate things. Gritch does his time in the lobby, reading his papers and seeing everything. Larry Gormé is point man for the *Emblem*'s coverage of the Prescott Holdings/Horizon Foundation scandal.

Both Hubble and Gowins may be going to jail if they can't come up with a suitable explanation for the evaporation of a hundred million dollars or more. That trial will drag on for some time. Jeremy, the whistle-blower, didn't automatically become the managing director of the Horizon Foundation — there isn't anything to either manage or direct just now, other than the traffic jams of forensic accountants, tax assessors, duelling lawyers, and court-appointed overseers. Nonetheless, he appears to have gained a level of celebrity as the Crown's star witness in the fraud case and should be able to parlay that into some worthy position in whatever new entity Molly MacKay establishes once she's proven her case. She and Bubba are living in Prescott's cabin at Harrison Lake. I've been invited to the wedding.

The city has seen a succession of vintage days, if you don't mind a steady west wind keeping the skies clear and the surf all worked up. Stanley Park is showing a fine array of autumn colour, and the bright green grass above the beach is littered with red, gold, and yellow leaves, dry enough to dance in the wind.

Norman Quincy Weed, with his eye for complementary colours, has chosen his wardrobe with care this bright morning — purple tie, brown suit, black shoes. If his socks are blue, I won't be surprised.

"Can't we find a better place?" he asks.

"Is there such a thing?"

"Yeah, when the sun shines you forget the two weeks of drizzle that went before. I mean, for sitting down. Last time here I sat on a log. Preparation H didn't do me any good. What's that you're wearing?"

"It's a track suit," I say, feeling defensive. I'm wearing expensive running shoes and I'm carrying a water bottle.

"Very fancy."

"Leo Alexander. I made the mistake of complimenting him on his."

"How's he doing?"

"Fit as a fiddle. We've got a gym set up for him in the penthouse. He's walking a treadmill every day."

We find a bench with a panoramic view of freighters at anchor and gulls wheeling overhead. Weed lowers himself carefully, hiking his creases and giving me a glimpse of his socks. They are dark blue with orange clocks.

"His kids still cruising like sharks?" he asks.

"Not showing their fins if they are. Leo made some business moves too complicated for me to understand, but he pulled an end run somewhere that severely limited their ability to wheel and deal." I hold on to the back of the bench and start some careful stretching, trying not to make too many moaning noises as the joints pop and the muscles protest. "Leo picked up a controlling interest in the vacant lot next door, which means Lenny has to either sell his piece or sit on his thumb waiting to see what the old man wants to do. I think Leo grabbed a piece of the parking garage across Carrall, too. Theo and Lenny had to pull in their horns."

"You know, Grundy, just because you have the fancy running outfit, doesn't mean you have to run in it."

"The way I do it doesn't look much like running." I stand up straight and begin twisting the torso, swinging the arms.

Weed watches me quizzically. "You thinking about making a comeback?"

"Oh, yeah, what the world needs now. I'm just trying to make my knee work again."

"How's the hand?"

"Better than the knee."

"Reading the papers these days?" he asks.

"I'm kind of hooked on *Get Fuzzy*."

"Looks like Molly MacKay's going to win her case."

"Will there be much left?"

"Enough," he says. "Even those two gonifs couldn't steal it all. Has she dropped her suit against the hotel?"

"Weeks ago. According to Leo's lawyers, a case could have been made that Dan was actually working for Axe Axelrode at the time of the murder, and Axelrode was working for Neagle or Hubble or both. It made more sense for Molly's legal team to stay on target and go after the big boys."

"Aw," he says. "I'd have thought she'd drop it out of gratitude."

"Well, maybe, but she has bigger fish to fry."

"Hubble and Gowins are back to blaming each other for the missing dough. Too bad they bought that property in Bermuda together."

"What about Grace Ingraham?" I ask. "She involved?"

"Separate case. The Heritage Architectural Preservation Society tried to go after her for selling off their assets, but they were hers all along. Things she got when she and Prescott were together. She's in the clear."

"That's nice. I felt for her."

"I'm sure she cares. She cleared over two million at the auction house and went to live in Tuscany. Maybe she'll find another lonely rich guy."

"I don't think it was like that," I say. "I think she loved him. I think he broke her heart."

"Throwing her over for a hippie?"

"Because he didn't want to die in her arms."

I've done as much of a warm-up as I can justify. Any more and it'll become the actual workout, and I need to save myself for the jog around the seawall. With any luck I'll make the full seven klicks today.

"Tell Olive I'll be in soon," he says. "To listen to the music this time. If you see me, just nod."

I leave him sitting in the sun in his brown suit and blue socks and purple tie. He adds to the glow of the morning. I start to jog, trying not to pound, straight up and down, arms pumping smoothly. At least that's what I'm striving for. Roadwork was never my favourite thing. Six miles before breakfast, rain or shine, wearing army boots. This is better somehow, a more reasonable hour, no goal save to keep the machine in some kind of shape, and there's the trim little dark-haired woman just ahead, wearing very becoming red shorts and a floppy T-shirt, moving along at a good clip, no-nonsense stride, good runner, takes a hundred yards to reel her in.

"I heard you coming a mile away," Connie says.

"The red shorts had me hypnotized."

"How's the knee?"

"Better than yesterday."

We run in silence for a while, synchronized, with whitecaps to our left and great cedars to our right allowing shafts of rising sunlight to bless the seawall. The air is salted oxygen, as bracing as a love affair.

"This a good pace for you?" she asks.

I let her get a few yards ahead, just so I can watch her move. "Perfect," I say.